Someone to Build Me Up

M.L. Nolan

Book Cover by Courtney Monday
mondaycourtney.com
Instagram @courtney.monday

Contents

1

LET'S RESPECT ZACK'S BODILY AUTONOMY

There's a very handsome man in a high-backed chair in the corner with a sketchbook in his lap. And he keeps sneaking looks at me.

I can't tell if he knows I see him. Usually, I can tell when someone's eyes are on me, and usually, I try not to encourage it. This is a cafe where students hang out, and anyone in here could be in my freshman Shakespeare class or in one of my upper division courses.

I've been coming to Silverskins, a coffee shop two blocks away from campus, ever since I was a student here. It's where I meet friends, where I prepare for classes when I don't need the books in my office.

At a gorgeous campus where half the offices face the mountains and the other half face the ocean, my office is buried in the center of the English building. I'm almost sure it had been a janitor's closet up until recently. There is literally a spigot on the wall.

The man who is looking at me doesn't look like a freshman, though, other than the way he dresses. But even then, he'd look like a freshman from the year 2010. He's got tight black jeans with ripped knees and is wearing a Nine Inch Nails shirt that looks like he bought it back when *The Downward Spiral* first came out. His shoulder bag, also black, is covered in pins—safety pins included. A brain-bucket style helmet sits next to him, although he doesn't look like the type who would have a motorcycle.

And now I'm the one staring. Which, again, I shouldn't be doing. Sure, I've been told I'm a gigantic flirt, but I don't shit where I eat. Looking at this guy, though, is scratching at the door of this old, unfortunate thing I have for emo boys. The kind who would hex my name when I was a high-school water polo player but did very much the opposite when I was a student with them in university lit and philosophy classes. Behind that door, something starving is biding its time.

Not that any of it matters. I'm thirty-five years old and have finally learned a little bit of self-control. Plus, I'm not ready to be in a relationship again anyway.

We make brief eye contact when he gathers his things to leave, which I hope isn't my fault. His eyes are steel-gray, a knife's edge that I know could pare me down to a pile of bones and marrow like a quartered chicken.

I watch him leave, as my best friend, Ellie Berglund, brushes by him. She casts a quick glance over her shoulder as he disappears, then catches the level of my gaze, which was absolutely, 100 percent focused on the gentle curve of his ass. It's much shapelier than a guy with his narrow build should have. Her smart-ass grin tells me she's definitely going to comment. To be fair, I would too.

She wiggles her eyebrows as she plops down across the creaky wooden table from me, schlepping her battered shoulder bag onto the chair next to her. (I'm a little amazed the old chair can handle the blow. I'm pretty sure I've been sitting in it on and off for a decade.) She curls one leg beneath her and folds her hands on the table.

"You really are on the hunt again, aren't you?"

"Oh, go get your coffee," I say and stick my tongue out at her. "I've gotta run soon anyway."

"That's right. Gonna go get in touch with your inner jock." She shakes her head, as if my getting a personal trainer is some kind of deep betrayal, and goes to fetch her usual black coffee.

Ellie is the picture of a hippie academic: vegan, dressed in wrinkly too-large thrift store clothes and loafers that are falling apart. No joke, she was raised in a yurt by a polycule in the mountains right outside the city and never watched TV until she went to college. She's an ethnomusicology grad student, specializing in Swedish fiddle music, and her lack of early exposure to pop culture does nothing to shrink her confidence out in the "real world."

"You know, I hope you aren't doing this because you think you're fat or something," she says. "If someone isn't dating you because you've got a little bit of a paunch—"

"—I don't have a—"

"—then they're not worth your time anyway."

"I do not have a paunch."

She picks up the heavy ceramic mug and blows on her coffee. In the beam of sunlight that shines through the window, the plumes of steam float in all directions. "Anti-fatness is a disease in this country. I'd just hate to see you buying into that bullshit."

I know she's right, but after ten years in a relationship with a woman I thought I was going to marry, dating is super intimidating. Your body and your hobbies, basically everything about you, are just hanging out there for everyone to see and judge. The sad truth is tying my body in knots to even get in the door seems like the path of least resistance over somebody actually accepting me the way I a m.

"Let's just say this is a confidence thing," I say.

"Or is it an I-want-to-ask-out-the-cute-cafe-boy thing?"

"Or, we can say it's a let's-respect-Zack's-bodily-autonomy thing?"

That one gets her. "Fair enough."

We chat for a few minutes about the shady student she caught putting the entire music library's vinyl collection online, until I glance down at my phone. It's ten minutes to two, which gives me an impossibly short time to change into my workout clothes and get to the gym. I leap up, shoving my books and laptop into my computer bag.

T en minutes late, I park in front of the gym, which is in an industrial park two miles away from campus. The name, Calculated Lifts Integrated Training Studio, is written out in big block letters on a sign over the smaller glass door off to the side.

CLITS.

When I first saw the name of the gym online, I thought it was just for women, like an edgier version of Curves.

But now as I park in front of a garage-like space with roll-up doors and horse mats on the ground, I conclude that whoever had named the place just had no idea what they'd done.

Stepping into the gym is completely different than anything I'd gone to in the last several years. The campus fitness center is a heavily air-conditioned building full of cardio and weight machines, squash courts, and an Olympic-sized pool. The only climate control at CLITS appears to be several giant fans in the corners of the room (not running, since there's still some early spring crispness in the air). The only machines are rowers and a couple really miserable-looking exercise bikes with movable handles. There are clusters of barbells that stand on end like spikes at the bottom of a medieval torture pit, black rubber plates in stacks beside them. There are several racks of dumbbells that get steadily fatter at the ends and metal squat racks doubling as pull-up bars lining the entire room. Flags and sponsorship banners hang from the ceiling, including a Progress pride flag, one that says Black Lives Matter, and an advertisement for the nearby sandwich shop, Dom's Subs

.

Off to the side of a wide empty space at the center of the room is a lanky, broad-shouldered woman with her hair pulled into a tight ponytail. She stands over a barbell with the thickest black plates, and then some, clipped to either side of it. When she rubs her hands together, white powder floats in the space around her, like disturbed snow suspended in winter air. Chalk, I recall from my bygone days of strength training, to help her keep her grip on that barbell. That thing has to weigh about 180 pounds.

Depending on what she does with it, that is pretty damn heavy.

As if reading my mind, she bends over into a half-crouch, arms in a wide grip, hands stretching almost the entire length of the bar. Then, in a lightning-quick motion, she snaps it off the floor and over her head, now in a full squat. The man beside her eggs her on, whooping, "Let's go, Bea!" until she stands, the bar still held over her head like a game animal she's just murdered with her crossbow. Delight spreads over her face until she finally lets the bar drop to the floor with a crash that rings through the open air.

She has a big, goofy smile on her face as she interrupts the man's applause to bump knuckles with him. He has a Dodgers cap perched backwards on his head, tufts of blond hair curling out from beneath it. His tank may as well have been one of those late-'90s scarf tops for all it covers up and shows off his enormous chiseled arms and lats.

Good, I think with relief. Their session is running late. I'm not causing too big a problem. The man, who I assume must be Marcus, nods at me from across the room.

"Hi!" he shouts. "What's up?"

"I'm Zack Carter. I'm here for Marcus?" I give him the grin that usually gets me forgiven for being a total doofus.

Instead of saying, "That's me," like I expect him to, the coach points over my shoulder. "I'm Dylan. You can check in with Swizzle Stick over there."

I turn around and spot a desk in the corner, where a figure with a black mop of hair hunches over a sketchbook. When he lifts his head, my eyes widen before I can control myself. It's the man from the coffee shop. He must be the receptionist here. I tamp down a little on the visible shock in my face before sauntering over.

His eyes flick from my head down to my feet and back again, and I automatically pull my shoulders back and suck in my gut. He grabs a clipboard and holds it out to me with long porcelain fingers. He's still dressed in his NIN shirt, but he's taken his rings off and stashed them somewhere. My eyes drift down to the snake bite piercings under his perfectly plush lips, as naturally pink as if he'd applied lip gloss this morning. I know he sees me look, and my ears heat.

Filling out the forms is a quick process, and then I hand them back to him.

"So, is Marcus here, or...?" I look around at the big, mostly empty room. Maybe he's in the bathroom or tucked into one of the corners I can't see from the desk here.

"I am Marcus," he says. Then he stands up, and I notice his ripped jeans are replaced by black joggers and Reeboks. His voice is low as bedrock, dark as his eyebrows, hacked through by the graphite in his gaze. It throws a rock into the pit of my stomach.

"You are?"

Until this moment, his expression had been neutral, but now it hardens to granite. "The last time I checked my ID, yes. Marcus Berens."

"It's just you don't look..."

Sometimes I just really can't stop running my mouth. I wonder if they make pills for that now. Here I am, just digging this hole deeper and deeper. He gives me a blank look, making no gesture to smooth anything over at all. Normally, I'd be able to pick up the slack there, but I can't seem to do anything but stare at him.

And now I notice the way he fills out that shirt. How the sleeves are tight as sausage casing around his arms, how it's stretched taut across his pecs. He might look thin at first glance, but the muscles are there. Oh, are they ever there.

He doesn't pick up my trailed-off sentence, instead leading me closer toward the center of the room, several feet away from Dylan and Bea. It's only when he turns and levels a withering look at me that I realize I'm supposed to be following him.

"I'll show you the facility first," he says.

"This is all stuff I've seen before. Did sports in high school," I say. Then I realize how inane that sounds. Nobody in my phase of life should be using high school as a touchpoint for anything. The judgment in his face reflects that exact thought.

"You'll find that your body responds differently to training than it did when you were a teenager," he says coolly.

"Well, you'd know. You're what, twenty-two?"

"Twenty-eight." His jaw tightens. Clearly, he's not the type who is flattered when someone thinks he looks younger than he is.

"Ah, my apologies. I didn't mean to impugn your abilities." I offer a watered-down smile, then realize maybe I might seem like I'm trying to flex my vocabulary at him. "I mean, I don't want you to think that I'm—"

"I know what impugn means," he snaps.

I bite my lip and catch movement out of the corner of my eye. Dylan is doing a terrible job of pretending he's not eavesdropping. In fact, he might not even be trying to pretend.

"Since you seem to already understand how all this works," Marcus says, weight shifting as he lifts his clipboard and pen, "tell me what you wish to achieve during our sessions."

Obviously, I can't tell him I want to get hot for the dating apps, not even with subtle hints. So, I waffle. "Ah, you know, I'm just getting older and want to start taking better care of myself."

Still looking down, Marcus sighs and clicks his pen. "Could you be less specific?"

"Dude." I can't tell if Dylan's tone is warning or pleading.

Marcus bites his lip, then looks up at me defiantly, flipping his hair out of his face. He's about an inch shorter than me, so when he tips his chin upwards, he looks like he's angling for a fight. This bitchy attitude shouldn't be hot, but I'm always weak for someone who can read the hell out of me.

"How about...I want to get in better shape for my sister's wedding," I say, totally pulling something out of my ass. I can convince myself it's true. It'll accomplish the same thing, right?

His lip curls, only slightly, as if he can smell how full of shit I am. "That'll have to do. Let's test your mobility first," he says.

He sinks to his knees in front of me, setting his clipboard on the floor. He gives me that heavy, judgmental look again before beckoning me to the floor with him.

This is going to be so much harder than I thought it would be.

2

AN APOLOGY LEMON LOAF

The next day, I limp from my second lecture of spring term to Silverskins. I'm not exaggerating—I'm actually limping.

After being fully embarrassed in the first five minutes or so of the training session, things only went downhill. I'd barely been able to do a full squat because my hips are garbage. I'd had to be rescued when I tried to bench press a weight that I remember feeling like nothing the last time I'd done it. Marcus had easily grabbed the bar from where it hovered over my ribs, yanking it back onto the pins with a loud clang. Even two minutes on the rowing machine made me feel like I was going to throw up.

I've never felt more decrepit. I had no idea it was that bad.

As I drag myself out of the way of a student hauling down the side of a concrete hill on his Razor scooter, my phone rings in the front pocket of my bag.

It's my little sister, Katie, the one who is getting married to her longtime girlfriend, Marta, in a little over twelve weeks. Even though I thought I'd be the one getting married first, I'm not jealous. I'm never jealous of Katie. She deserves the world, and we've all done our best to give it to her. That includes Marta, which is why we all like her so much (even though I'm never sure if she likes me back).

"Katie-bara!"

I've called her this ever since we learned about capybaras from a Discovery Channel rainforest documentary as kids. She calls me Quackers because she had too much trouble saying "Zack" when she was little.

"To what do I owe the pleasure?"

"I just wanted to see if you got our wedding invitation?" she says. There's a twinge of anxiety in her voice, the type that's been in there since the day she realized getting married didn't begin and end with getting pretty matching rings with her future wife.

The invitation had been a shimmering tower of red and gold, with Art Deco-style writing. She's leaning into an old, 1920s–30s Hollywood theme. Fortunately, our mom seems to have talked her out of using actual glitter, because I'd bet any amount of money that glitter was in her original scheme.

"I did," I tell her. "Although, I'm in the wedding, so I'm not exactly sure why you needed to send it."

"We didn't want to leave you out!" she says. "Besides, I want you to keep it on your refrigerator door, at least until you can replace it with baby pictures."

The very idea of my little Katie-bara having a baby almost knocks my already wobbly legs out from under me. "Let's just cross that bridge when we come to it, ok?" I laugh. She laughs too; the little beast knows exactly what to say to freak me out. "Everything else ok?"

"Well, we're trying to figure out some details, and mom's getting kind of antsy," she says.

"Don't tell me you're going to do that butterfly release thing."

Our Aunt Linda had put it into our mom's head that the girls could get these little butterflies in boxes and, at the end of the ceremony, release them into the sky. It definitely wasn't the sort of thing Mom would have approved of if she'd been in her right mind, but I am quickly learning that people go kind of nuts around weddings.

"Ew, no. That's barbaric," Katie says. "Plus, we're not doing it outside, and it doesn't fit the theme, like, at all. But now we're still stuck on favors. What do you think of, like, salt and pepper shakers?"

I think about my own salt and pepper setup. Being pretty big into cooking, I've got a gorgeous olive wood salt cellar and a pepper grinder. Come to think of it, I have no idea if people use shakers anymore.

"Who's salt and who's pepper?" I ask.

There's a pause. "I didn't think of it like that," she says. "Might come off kinda racist? Like if she's pepper and I'm salt?"

I shrug. "You'd have to ask Marta. But I know you, and you're a little sassy but not all that salty."

"Oh, yeah? When was the last time you checked?"

A chime sounds behind me, and I step up on the curb to get out of the way of the bicycles streaming into the neighborhood surrounding campus. Most of the students around here ride bikes. You can hardly find a rack to chain one up for as many as there are.

The April sun reflects off the passing wheel guards, as well as the pavement ahead of me, and there's still a nip in the salty air. The students flooding the sidewalk around me are swimming in their hoodies in a way people from anywhere else in the country would laugh at, especially when they saw how most pair them with flip-flops. I've got my half-zip fleece and actual closed-toed shoes, thank you very much. Gotta differentiate myself somehow, although a recent appearance of crow's feet and smile lines seems to be accomplishing that too.

Soon I'm standing in front of Silverskins, trying to wrap up the conversation with my sister.

"Should you be making personal calls at 2 p.m. on a Wednesday?" Katie works at a swanky marketing firm in Culver City. It still bugs her when I make fun of her pantsuits.

"Not really, but nobody's gonna bug me. I don't work with snitches." I can hear the smile in her voice. "Love ya, Quackers."

I tell her I love her too, then disconnect the call, about to shove my phone back into my pocket as I walk through the wide-open double doors into the cafe. It always feels like the ceiling is too low in here, but walking indoors after being under the gorgeous dome of blue sky always makes things feel smaller.

And of course, there's Marcus in the corner again, his sketchbook lying across his lap. I can't tell what kind of shirt he's wearing because, whatever it is, it's covered up by a loose-fitting, black and white striped sweater I would never dream of telling him makes him look like a mime.

Anyway, I'm more focused on the way his elegant fingers grip the pencil in his hand, and the way I am certain I can see the pink tip of his tongue poking out from between his lips.

There's another high-backed chair next to him, a table in between the two, and his cup looks completely empty. He's glaring at the sketchbook more intensely than usual today.

"Hey, Quinn," I greet my favorite barista, who wears a very ostentatious butterfly clip in their hair. I lean in and lower my voice. "That guy over there. Does he ever get snacks?"

I gesture toward the pastry case, which is always refilled in the early afternoon with Danishes, croissants, and cookies for all variety of dietary restrictions. Quinn looks at it judiciously.

"I've only seen him get something once, and it was this iced blueberry lemon cake here."

"Did he like it?"

"Hard to tell, but he ate it in like thirty seconds, so I'm guessing yeah." There's a conspiratorial grin on their face now. "Gonna grab one of those?"

"Two," I say. After all, if it's that good, I might as well give it a shot myself. Snacks aren't really an area where I'm shy. Hence the need for personal training, I guess.

Armed with two slices of iced blueberry lemon cake and a cup of coffee, I maneuver through the jumble of murmuring study groups and individual students barricaded from human contact by earbuds until I reach Marcus. I don't walk quietly, so he looks up at me when I'm a couple feet away, eyes widening with surprise.

"A peace offering," I say to him, setting two small plates on the table, "to apologize for being a gigantic dork yesterday."

Somehow, Marcus can express a lot of emotions with very little movement. It's like he can change the color of his eyes at will, from stormy to calm waters, from iron to sterling silver. They're closer to the latter right now, and I feel all the richer for it. He purses his lips and nods slightly toward the chair next to him.

"I also owe you an apology," he says, once I've taken a seat and let loose an embarrassing little whimper from yesterday's fail-squats.

By most measurements, that's definitely true. When I'd tried and failed to do a full squat, he'd pointed out that my mobility was, and I quote, "abysmal." He'd sniped about the "encyclopedic knowledge of gym equipment" I'd gained in high school when I asked him what some vinyl monstrosity was for (back extensions, apparently—but it looked way too much like Victorian sex furniture). There were a few more biting comments before Dylan had finally come over and whispered something in his ear, smiling a very, "We appreciate your business," smile before walking away.

"I only accept apologies that weren't forced by the management," I tell him. I pick up the loaf and take a bite, and damn, it really is good. I catch Quinn's eye and give them a thumbs-up, and they grin over the head of the customer at the counter.

"Still, I was far too blunt."

"I came in and basically insulted you a bunch before we even got started. Plus, I don't really mind people being blunt with me. I'd rather people not lie to spare my feelings. Never ends well," I say.

It really doesn't. It ends with someone waiting until you're on one knee with a diamond ring to tell you they fell out of love with you years ago. They just felt bad about leaving you because technically you hadn't done anything wrong, well, other than being yourself.

"Eat," I say, gesturing at the table next to us. Gingerly, he picks up the loaf and nibbles on the corner. Then he might as well turn into one of those adorable-yet-deadly little beasts from a sci-fi movie, and the loaf perishes in about thirty seconds. He wipes his lips with the back of a knuckle, like he caught and killed the baked good himself and ate it raw.

I try to force myself to feel less horny about this, but then I start plotting. The loaf is good, yes, but I bet I could make a better version of it. I could bring it to the gym, and then Marcus would make that enraptured face he's making right now because of something I made.

Finally, he comes out of his reverie, looking up at me like he's woken up from an unexpected nap.

"How about this," I say. "We meet each other halfway. I show you some more respect, knowing you might be a little too blunt sometimes, and you try to give me some grace when I put my foot in my mouth or am a little late for a session."

"That is further than most people are willing to meet me," Marcus says, and a smile flickers at the corner of his mouth. I could eat it up.

"Can I ask what you're drawing?" I venture, trying my best not to gawk at the paper in his lap. He catches the way my eyes fall to it, and all but slams the sketchbook.

He looks down, as if alarmed by his own haste. "Oh—um. Just...plans for something," he says.

"Are you a student?" I blurt it out, because I have to know. I'm already a little too invested in him, and finding out he's a student will just make it even more awkward. I know that he's older than most of the other people in this neighborhood, but still.

"Not yet, although I have recently been accepted as an undergraduate for fall quarter," he says. All right, well, gray area, but I can safely say that there's no chance he's in any of my classes.

"Congratulations! First time getting one or...?" I try so very hard not to sound condescending, not make any cracks about how young he looks the way I did yesterday. Fortunately, he nods without looking offended. Thank god. Managed not to step in it this time. "Are you doing exercise science?"

He shakes his head. "Design."

"Really!" Now I'm fascinated. This makes so much more sense for the way he presents himself. "Graphic design or...?"

But he's already slipping the sketchbook back into his bag. "I have to work shortly," he says.

"Oh, yeah, of course," I say, trying to keep my tongue from getting twisted up like a drawstring during a spin cycle. "See you tomorrow. I promise I won't be late this time."

He stands and slings his bag over his shoulder, then bends down, much closer to me than I'd expected. I hold my breath until I realize he's just picking up the empty plates.

"See that you aren't," he says.

Then he straightens up and gives me a look that's so haughty it goes straight to my cock. I'm helpless to do anything other than gawk at his perfect ass again as he drops off the plates and strides into the bright afternoon.

3

DELAYED ONSET MUSCLE SORENESS

When I get to CLITS today, there are several pieces of wood cut to different lengths and widths piled up against the outside wall. Wood dust litters the ground. It's not exactly the sort of thing I'd see at the campus gym, but it's so much more interesting to see this DIY stuff instead of a hive of nothing but plastic and ice-cold air conditioning.

I'm a little early this time, hoping it'll make up for Tuesday, and maybe that it will show Marcus I'm a serious person who is actually worth his time. Worth his time as a client, that is. And worth his time for whatever else he feels like—let's not rule anything out.

I walk into the gym and am completely devastated by what I see.

A man with pearlescent skin and shaggy black hair is doing a pull-up, the muscles of his back moving in symmetrical ripples. His tattoos are vibrant against the paper-whiteness of his skin: a Biblically accurate angel—a creature with multiple eyes and wings ringing its body—hovers over one scapula. What looks like a woodcarving of a demon, all outlined in red and black, disappears into the top of his pants, with a very close approximation of what looks like Blake's Poison Tree wrapping around his side. There's also a half sleeve that I can't quite make out, and a bunch of other colors and patterns I don't have time to identify. I'm honestly good just focusing on the sweat droplets sliding down his spine.

That spine curves as he hoists himself like a gymnast, until he's balanced on both hands, hips level with the bar. He bends over it slightly, and the inside of my head will never be clean again, even if I were to take a power-washer to it.

"Bro! Quit showing off for Bea! She's not even into dudes!" Dylan shouts at him. Bile pools in my stomach, even though I have no right. I don't even know whether Marcus likes men (although if I were a gambling man...).

"Don't be shitty, Dylan," Bea says, strolling up beside the two of us and folding her arms. "Nice muscle-ups, Marcus!"

Marcus dismounts easily and turns around. He's not as furry as I am (I've been told I have a "chest rug"), but his sculpted chest is peppered with black hair that, as my eyes move down, gathers into a black line funneling down the center of his defined abs. There's another tattoo on his left pec with the words "Fix your hearts or die," which I know came from a TV show I haven't seen and can't remember the name of right now. Hell, I can barely re-member my own name, especially now that I notice how, underneath a tattoo of a mushroom cloud, his nipple has a stainless steel bar through it. And yes, the other one matches, because I can't help but check immediately.

At this point, I'm about to swoon like a Southern belle. My pupils must be like saucers. I panic that he'll notice them as he approaches, and like a true man of letters, I stare straight into one of the overhead lamps to shrink them.

Ow. What the hell is wrong with me?

After my eyes have readjusted, I look back down at Mar-cus, who is dabbing himself with a towel. I want to do it for him. Or be the towel. Hell, I'd lick the sweat off him if he asked me to. God, I've got to stop being so thirsty for him, because workout pants aren't built to hide an erection.

"You're early," Marcus says, arching an eyebrow, as if I've blasted past his expectations just by doing the bare minimum.

"Promised I wouldn't be late, didn't I?"

"Considerate."

He's drawing close to me, and my heart hammers. Then he reaches past me to the back of the desk chair, which I'm fully blocking with my body, and snags a black shirt. I release my held breath, eyes dropping to another, clearly unfinished tattoo of a faceless marionette dancing across his abs.

Bea catches me staring and winks, and I have to be blushing a little right now. At least Dylan still seems oblivious.

The printing on the shirt Marcus has just pulled over his head features a big line drawing of William Shakespeare, and it reads Bardfest '22. That's the yearly summer Shakespeare festival held at theaters across the city in several different venues. I've used it as an opportunity for the students I have for summer session to get extra credit. I make a mental note to ask him about it later.

"Ugh, why do I hurt so much more than I did yesterday?" I say after I've changed into my gym clothes, taken several deep breaths, and splashed cold water on my wrists.

"Delayed onset muscle soreness," Marcus says. He pulls a rower off the wall and lays it on the floor, clearly wanting me to sit down on the horrifying contraption for my warmup. I do it, but only because he's hot. "It sets in approximately thirty-six to forty-eight hours after a workout in which one uses muscles that have not been used in a long while."

"Yeah, well, makes it friggin' awful to sit down and stand up," I mutter. Every muscle in my thighs and stomach are screaming at me as I yank the rower's handle and slide back, the machine whooshing with each movement. "Ooooow, and to do this, too."

I think I detect a smile on Marcus's face, but it may just be the way he's tilting his chin. "Many people use it as an excuse not to resume exercise, so you are already several steps ahead of them."

Maybe it's the sudden onset of cardio, but my heart flutters a little at the compliment. If it's even a compliment at all. He has a way of making a compliment sound like a simple fact and vice versa.

"Thanks for saying so." I try not to make it obvious how I'm already out of breath. And fail.

Two minutes of rowing later, I'm trying to keep from admitting that this is already so much easier than Tuesday. The upper body warm-ups remind me that it's not just my leg muscles that are screaming, but somehow they're still easier. Not the kind of progress I'd had in mind, but probably not the worst.

Marcus indicates I should get back on the floor. My quads complain so loudly I feel like Bea and Dylan must be able to hear them across the gym, even as Bea grunts through a series of very heavy-looking lifts.

"Fifteen shoulder taps," Marcus says. I rise into a push-up position, which is one thing I can thankfully still manage, and start alternating a tap on each of my shoulders with the opposite hand.

"Spread your legs wider," he says. "It will provide better balance."

One thing I'm quickly learning about this kind of gym is that practically everything sounds dirty. I went home and looked up the lift I saw Bea doing on Tuesday, where she pulled the barbell straight off the floor and over her head. It's called a snatch. Another one of the moves she did later was called a "jerk." Sure, it makes sense, but come on.

When I'm done spreading my legs, I sit back on my knees.

"Bardfest, huh?" I say through all my huffing and puffing. "I go to that every year. The production of *A Midsummer Night's Dream* last year was phenomenal. Didn't know you'd be into a Shakespeare festival enough to buy a t-shirt."

The corner of Marcus's mouth twitches. "I did not purchase this. Now, stand up. Fifteen air squats."

Purchase. Why does he talk like this? I'm the professor here, and I don't even do that.

"Were you in it, then?"

"In a way," he says.

Now I'm getting somewhere, or at least I think I am. But before I can follow up, he turns to fetch a resistance band from a hook on the wall. That's ok. I can be patient. Sometimes.

"So not an actor," I say when he returns. "Tech crew?"

He purses his lips and shakes his head as he hands me the band, which looks like a calamari ring that definitely should not be eaten by anyone ever.

"Not anymore." He drops into a quarter squat and demonstrates taking slow steps to the side, out, then together, out, together. "Put that band over your knees. Lateral walks from the squat racks to the door and back."

"Aha," I say. I'd say more if I could catch my breath. Who'd have thought that taking a bunch of slow, tiny steps would be so exhausting? "You're making this really difficult, you know."

Marcus picks up that I'm not talking about the exercise. "You do not pay me for conversation."

"I'd like to get to know the guy who's trying to rip my body to shreds. Sue me."

"For many, getting 'shredded' is the goal," he says, and I'm pretty sure I'm falling in love. Terrible habit of mine.

I drop the subject as he helps me set up the rack for bench presses. And then, I'm much too distracted by getting my ass (or I guess my shoulders, arms, and pectoral muscles) kicked to quiz him for a while.

Finally, I get a small reprieve, sitting upright on the bench and trying not to puke.

"You are...a Shakespeare aficionado, then," he says, stilted. Every muscle in my face comes back to life at the word aficionado.

"I teach the freshman Shakespeare course, so maybe just a casual fan rather than an aficionado," I say. "Although

I did play Mercutio in my high school's production of *Romeo and Juliet*."

"I was also in *Romeo and Juliet* in high school." Marcus gives me an unmistakable grin as he slaps a forty-five-pound plate onto one side of the now empty barbell. "Close grip bench press, three sets of twelve. I assume you know what that means, since you are an expert."

Oh, now he's ribbing me. I'd be overjoyed if I weren't dreading the horror I was about to endure. I lie on my back and grip the bar, hands closer together than usual. Doing it in this position, and for so many reps, is a great way to completely destroy my triceps. When I'm done with the first set, I come up gasping.

"Who did you play?" I say to distract myself from my burning arms. "Bet you were Romeo, pretty boy."

Bold, yeah, and if this were the beginning of the workout, there's no way I could've gotten myself to say it. But the chemical changes in my head from everything he's just put me through are working on me like a drug, lowering my inhibitions.

"No," he says, with a smirk. "Tybalt. Your bitter rival."

"Oh, so you *are* trying to kill me."

"That's a long enough rest." The way he advances toward me sends me straight onto my back without a second thought, and thank god all the blood is running into my upper body right now. I make it through the second set with just a little tremble on the last rep.

It takes me a second to sit back up, but looking at him is much nicer than staring at the cobwebby rafters. When I finally manage, Marcus is leaning against the rack, I would almost say languidly. His smile is impish.

"You're evil," I say. "Tell me what you did at that Shakespeare festival. You owe me after all this torture."

"If you do one more set," Marcus says, "I'll answer any question you'd like."

An actual whimper dies in my throat, as I realize this man has the power to make me do basically anything he wants. I make it through the last set with a final unflattering grunt. Then, I look at him expectantly.

"Set design," he says. "*Midsummer Night's Dream.*"

Good god. Talented too. All I can do is shake my head, and pretend my silence is due to exhaustion rather than losing my ability to form a coherent thought. I have so many questions, I don't know if we'll be able to get to all of them in one session. I set my mind on creating more opportunities to ask them all.

4

EQUAL OPPORTUNITY FRUIT ENJOYER

My phone pings in my pocket as Ellie and I walk down the narrow sidewalk toward Silverskins. It's a little awkward to dig out while walking, and I almost trip over a discarded smoothie cup as I read Katie's text message.

We're doing luxeaux then candide and clubbing Weekend of 6/10, ok?

I cringe. Katie has insisted I come along to the bachelorette since I'm in the wedding party, and obviously, I don't want to disappoint her. Normally, it wouldn't be that big of a deal. I'd even offered to cook dinner for everyone before we went out rather than having to spring for a restaurant, then have everyone crash at my place afterward. Everyone from where we grew up comes here for weekend getaways, so it tends to be super pricey.

But then, I found out that Marta insisted Candace still be in the wedding. Candace being my ex, who had lived in that house with me for half our relationship (and who, thankfully, had the decency to let me buy her out of her share rather than fight me for it). But that meant dinner was off the table, so to speak. I've been known to be a little self-sacrificing, but that's too much, even for me.

So it was looking like a luxury spa, then a French restaurant downtown, then whatever terrible dance club that I was certainly way too old and too male to go to. All the while making nice with the person who had broken my heart less than a year ago.

That's the week before graduation.

Yeah but you can spare one night, can't you?

Pleeeeeeease?

I get a photo of my sister, glossy lower lip stuck out with all her might. She's the human embodiment of that big-eyed pleading emoji. Ellie slips in front of me to make room for a young woman in a tie-dye shirt and clashing kaleidoscope leggings. Must be scraping the bottom of the hamper for laundry, and the quarter has barely started.

I'll probably skip out on spa day and meet you at Candide.

Yaaay! Best brother ever!

You and Marta still spending the night?

If that's ok

Swear we'll leave you alone asap in the morning so you can grade papers or write tests or whatever you do

I'd given up on her ever understanding what I do a long time ago, but to be fair, I don't know much about digital marketing, and I refuse to learn.

I heart-react her last text in answer, then slip the phone into my pocket again. Ellie throws me a questioning look.

"Katie. Bachelorette party is the week before graduation."

It's nice to have someone there to groan sympathetically and get incensed in a way that I just can't. Ellie makes a noise like a teenager whose mom is threatening to take the door off its hinges (although, I'm not even sure she had her own room in the yurt).

"I've got a show that night, or I'd go as your emotional support nerd," she says. "You going to be ok with Candy-ass being there?"

Ever since Candace dumped me, Ellie has been calling her nicknames that sound as corny as a conservative pundit dunking on their latest liberal punching bag. Not that I'd tell her that. I appreciate the loyalty.

We walk through the open door of Silverskins, and I scan the cafe. I try not to be disappointed that I don't spot Marcus.

"Yeah, I'll cope."

She gives me a sympathetic pat on the shoulder. We get our coffee and snag a table by the window that's always in high demand. It's got a view of the street and the cyclists that flow like schools of fish riding a current toward campus.

Ellie launches into a story about how the guitar player in her Swedish folk ensemble showed up to rehearsal the night before smelling like aquavit and drew a hairy dick on the whiteboard.

When her flip phone rings, she grabs it immediately at the sight of the lock screen, not bothering to apologize. Her side of the conversation is full of more teenage eye rolling and groans before she half stands and hangs up.

"Jason. He says that there's some kind of demonic sound coming from the turntable in one of the listening rooms. Someone's probably just playing a 78 on a 33 rpm and the tone's all off, but I just know he's going to ruin the 78 and maybe even the stylus if I don't—"

"Get out of here. I've got grading to do."

I wave her away. I have no idea what she's talking about, but I do know how student workers can go from extremely competent to babes in the woods within seconds.

There's a whole stack of essays in my bag from my favorite class, and I'm almost glad to be left alone. Only one person would bring a welcome interruption from reading my upper division students' first essays of the term. I've only read one page when he slides into the tired chair across the table from me.

"You're late!" I feel a little bolder after all the flirting at our last session, and so that means it's time to totally overdo everything.

He blinks a couple of times before he realizes I'm making a joke.

"It seems I owe you an apology, then." There's no smile on his lips, but there's a gleam in his eye, and it makes the hair on the back of my arms stand up. He gestures down at the chair for permission, and I don't hold back my smile as I motion for him to sit.

He reaches into his bag and pulls out his sketchbook and a metal pencil case. Before I can get a look at the whole layer of stickers on the cover, I catch one that says "Queer as in Fuck You." My temperature plunges, like I'm diving into an unheated pool on a hundred degree day. I almost wish I didn't know that I had a chance. It somehow gives my little dorky crush so much more weight.

But holy shitballs, I might actually have a chance.

"What are you working on?" He peers across the table, squinting at the top page of my stack of papers.

"Oh, essays from my favorite class, Movable Feasts: Depictions of Food in Twentieth Century Literature." Ellie had gleefully informed me she'd overheard some undergrads make a lewd joke that involved the course name and my ass, but I decide to put that fun fact aside for now. "This first week I've had them choose a poem that involves food metaphors and analyze it, but we're also going to be looking at short stories and longer works. It was basically my master's thesis, but this is my first year where they finally gave me permission to teach it."

"And how are these first attempts?" He's leaning forward, elbows on the table, looking at me with eyes like pencil strokes on his thick sketch paper.

"Well, I'd only really gotten to that first one you saw, but, um..." I flip through the stack, and ah. "Guess I should have expected this. Looks like I'm in for a lot of fruit and vulva metaphors this weekend."

His lips part slightly a second before the words pass through them. "Is that...objectionable?" It's a serious question, and with any luck, a fishing question.

"Nah, I'm an equal-opportunity fruit enjoyer."

For a second, I think I might shrink to an inch tall and get crushed by my clothes, but then there's a shocking burst of laughter across the table. Marcus has gone from a stone-faced Dracula to a squealing vampire bat colony. I can't help but laugh with surprise as well, and we catch some very cranky looks from the students trying to study at other tables. I couldn't give less of a shit.

When he finally recovers his dignity, Marcus's normal pallor is touched with red high on his cheekbones. I wonder whether it would be better compared to some type of berry or to the riper spots on a peach. I wonder if they would taste as sweet. And now I'm not sure I'm thinking about his face anymore at all. I shake my head, trying to get back into the moment and not let my filthy fantasies run away with me.

"What about you? Working on new designs today?"

He nods, and sits back a little to give me a look at the page, covered in what looks like a chess board and textured curtains. As if reading my mind, he says, "It's still mostly in a brainstorming phase. So far it only looks like an imitation of the Black Lodge."

I cock my head.

"*Twin Peaks*?" he says, looking at me like I've just told him I've never heard of The Beatles. "I would think that as a literary person, you would have some awareness of David Lynch."

"Of course I'm aware. Just never got into it, but I don't have anything against it," I say. A very stupid idea to ask him to come over and watch it with me zips through my head, and I decide I'd better talk about something else before I finally hurtle over this line I've been dancing on. "So here's a question. Why are you working as a trainer when you've got this theater gig going on?"

The smile fades a little from his still-pink face. "It is not steady work, unfortunately, and I have only recently resumed such projects after many years away from it." It looks like there's a story there, one that he might not be ready to share. "Being a trainer gives me more flexible hours than shift work would."

"Makes sense," I say. "Plus you're pretty great at it."

"I almost drove you away with my bad attitude after our first session."

"Key word 'almost,'" I say, and because I'm intent on embarrassing the hell out of myself today, I wink at him.

He doesn't flinch, thankfully. We sit for a minute, regarding one another. Usually, I'm not at a loss for words, but I'm afraid whatever I say next might ruin this comfortable atmosphere that we've breathed into life around us.

"I imagine I should allow you to grade without interrupting you further," he says.

"You can stay and work with me if you'd like," I say, a little too quickly.

His posture relaxes again, and he nods. Then, he opens his pencil case. As he becomes more absorbed by his project, I try not to stare. I try so, so hard to focus on the essays in front of me, but (if you'll forgive the pun), it's a fruitless effort.

5

ATTEMPTED MURDER

I've never been the most moderate guy. Usually that hasn't been such a bad thing, probably thanks to the fact that my parents were pretty great and helped me focus on going wild over things that were generally good for me. Sure, there were a couple years in college where I was kind of a slut and drank an unsafe amount on the weekends, but I reined that in without it becoming a problem.

These days, my overindulgent nature only really shows up as gaining a little extra weight around the middle because I do things like bake everything from each season of *Great British Bake-Off*. Or I find a delicious wine I like at the store and stockpile it like a prepper. Or I read a new book until 3 a.m. the night before a 9 a.m. lecture.

But one big plus of being immoderate is that I've spent the last six weeks going really, really hard at the gym. I see Marcus twice a week, but after the second week, I added another three days to my routine. Mostly it's just cardio and weight machines at the campus gym, but it's getting harder and harder for Marcus to catch me out with something that destroys me.

So today, our session is going really well. I always do better when he's there. Some people would call that "being a people pleaser," but I don't think that always has to be such a bad thing. I never would have made it where I am in my career right now if I hadn't really, really wanted to impress my advisor.

To be clear, I didn't feel about her the way I feel about Marcus. That would have made for several very painful years.

And she certainly never looked at me the way Marcus is looking at me as I finish a set of five deadlifts, letting the heavy barbell thud to the floor. If I'd never done sports before, I might feel weird about someone watching me exercise like they're holding paint chips and trying to decide what color to paint their wall.

"What is it?" I ask him.

"You've put sixty-five pounds on your deadlift since we began," he says. Again, it's a simple fact, but it still feels like a compliment.

"Yeah, well, I used to be a lot stronger. Just needed to get back in the saddle." I barely manage not to stutter, even though I'm not getting any actual praise.

"It will not take long for you to recover your strength at this rate and probably build on it. If you're consistent, which you have been," he says. "You are much stronger than the average person."

We're veering closer to praise now, and I'm not sure my poor, worked-over nervous system can handle it.

"Says the guy who trains people professionally," I say.

Over the past few weeks, he has become much more generous with his smiles. We spend at least one day per week "accidentally" meeting at Silverskins. Mostly we work in near-silence at the same table, but we talk enough that I've grown familiar with his micro-expressions. It's been like reading an old manuscript in a dead language that I'm slowly learning over time. The more I study it, the more easily I see and hear the nuances in the curve of an eyebrow or inflection of a sentence.

"It has taken me a very long time to reach my level of fitness, much longer than it would take other men," he says. "You, however, are a natural athlete."

"Ah." My voice cracks, making my attempt to play it cool a total joke. "I'll be sure not to take it for granted, then."

"I'll be sure not to allow you to."

By the end of the session, he's made good on his promise. The metabolic conditioning part of the workout, where he has me do a lot of lighter movements with only a set amount of time to finish, was clearly attempted murder. When I tell him so, he laughs, strolling away to leave me on my back on the floor, recovering.

I close my eyes, mind blessedly blank as the endorphin rush shoots through every vein. Most of the time, it's hard for me to sit still with my eyes closed long enough to meditate. This is the closest I get, and other than my dumb little crush, these few minutes of bliss have kept me coming back these past weeks.

I'm interrupted by the sound of footsteps on the mat beside me. When I open my eyes, Dylan is standing over me with his arms akimbo. He's got a couple shiny scars on his hairy shins, and I have to sit up so as not to stare straight up at his junk, concealed by what looks like a cross between board shorts and cargos.

"Looked like some hard work you were doing there," he says.

"Seems to do the job," I say, suppressing a groan as I struggle to my feet.

"And you're seeing progress and not just getting tired out, right? That happens more often than you'd think," he says.

"What does?"

"You know...sometimes the programming knocks you out, but long-term it doesn't really..."

Academia has taught me to keep a decent poker face, but I can barely suppress a scowl. Is this guy seriously asking me to talk shit on Marcus's coaching skills? Sure, he'd been a little rude in the beginning, might be the same way to others when I'm not around, but he's been a huge help.

"Have you had complaints about him?" I squint up at Dylan.

"Nah, bro. You're just a professor, so I thought you'd be a straight shooter and tell me what's really up," he says. As if that means anything.

"Nothing straight about me, bro," I say, just because I feel like being a dick right now. I lean over and pick up my water bottle and miniature notebook, where I mark down all my daily totals, and wave it at him. "And I'm making measurable progress, I can say accurately. As a professor."

"Cool, cool. Just checking. Didn't mean anything by it," he says.

He looks less uncomfortable than I'd expected at my coming out to him; lots of guys who are cool with lesbians can turn into enormous homophobes as soon as they find out a dude likes other dudes. Fortunately, I don't have to ask him to hand in the rainbow flag that's currently hanging from the rafters. Not today, anyway.

Before he can say anything else, there's a thud behind me. I turn around to see that Marcus has dragged one of the new plywood boxes out of the corner, Bea following close behind him.

Marcus has been building more and more of them over the past weeks for the Crossfit classes they run here.

"Taking that for a test drive?" Dylan calls.

"Gotta pop its cherry eventually," Bea says.

Without another word, she swings her arms back and leaps up onto the box with both feet. All I can think of is that girl from one of the *Karate Kid* sequels, jumping onto the hood of a car like a tiger pouncing. After Bea hops down, Marcus follows suit. His landing is lighter than hers, stealthier. I want to make a jab about him being the King of Cats, an insult that Mercutio gives Tybalt in *Romeo and*

Juliet, but having Dylan there makes me feel weird about it.

Dylan tests the box as well. His landing is as loud as everything else he does. As he stands on top of the box like the king of the mountain, he turns to me and says, "Get over here and test out Coach Marcus's work."

When I glance over at Marcus, he's frowning. After such a hard workout, I probably shouldn't bite, but I've never been able to back down from a shithead's challenge. In the past, dares have usually worked out for me, and if not, they've been good for a laugh. If you don't want to be a bitter old man before your time, you've got to be able to make fun of yourself.

The way my legs feel, I already know this is a terrible idea. I approach the box and stand in front of it. It looks so much higher than it did from across the room, and I'm supposed to jump on top of it from a complete standstill. Suddenly all my "How hard could it be?" thoughts evaporate.

Bea claps her hands twice and shouts, "All right, let's go, Zack!" She's a nice woman. Not sure why she and Dylan seem to be such good friends.

So, I try it. I swing my arms back, bend my knees...

And the next thing I know, I'm on my back on the floor, five feet away from the box. Sure enough, I immediately start laughing, still humiliated enough to put my hands over my face.

"Sick tuck and roll, bro," Dylan says, joining in the laughter.

When I finally pull my hands away from my face, Marcus is crouched next to me, an embarrassing amount of worry on his face.

"Are you hurt?" he says.

"Just my dignity," I say. "Well...and maybe my leg."

Reflexively, Marcus extends his hand to the big red mark on the side of my calf.

"It's just going to bruise," I say, as his hand runs over it. This isn't sexy. Not sexy at all. He's just showing concern, like a professional is supposed to do. I'm not at all affected by the intensity of his gaze and his hands on my skin.

"Marcus, he's a tough guy. You don't have to paw at him like that," Dylan says.

"Well, Marcus already worked him over so hard, it's kind of his fault," Bea says, elbowing Dylan. I'm starting to think she may have overheard some of our conversation. She throws me a wink, and I try to pretend I didn't see it.

Probably my cue to get out of here.

By the time I've cleaned up, Marcus has wheeled his bicycle into the parking lot and is clipping his helmet on. I stand by my driver's side door, keys in hand.

"You need a ride?"

"No, that's fine. And I apologize for earlier." He looks genuinely remorseful. It makes me want to comfort him, the way you might comfort a dog that lightly snagged its toenail and is now needlessly limping around the house.

I take a few steps closer, lowering my voice. "I'm a big boy, I can make my own decisions, and that wasn't your fault. Don't let them fuck with your head."

His strained expression softens a little, and so does the tightness in my chest.

"How long have you done carpentry?" I ask. I know he has to leave. His helmet is literally on his head, and he's gripping his handlebars. But even after the last few weeks, I still have so many things I want to ask him about.

"I worked in construction for a few years in my early twenties. So you can imagine any teasing I receive here is nothing compared to what I received then," he says.

One more piece of the puzzle clicks into place. "And I think I'm getting a better picture of why you got into lifting. You've just done it all, haven't you?"

A shadow passes over his face. "There are many things I have not done that I would like to do." His eyes flick to mine for a nanosecond, then away again. I would do anything I could to keep his eyes on me. "Unfortunately, I must go. Will I see you next week?"

Fuck it.

"Actually, if you're not doing anything Saturday, my friend Ellie is coming over for lunch. Would love to have you, too," I say. I bite back a nervous laugh at my awkward choice of words.

Something I can't read passes over his face. "I would not want to impose."

"You totally wouldn't be," I say, much too quickly. "As long as you don't mind vegan food..."

"I am not finicky," he says, just as quickly.

Delight zings through my nerve endings. That means when he comes over in the future, I can basically cook anything for him. But I'm getting ahead of myself. Way ahead of myself. Possibly too far for me to ever catch up to myself.

"Great!" I say. "I'll, um, text you my address? Except, I don't have your..."

He takes his phone out of his pocket. It's another flip phone, just like Ellie's. Then we exchange numbers, because he's coming to my house the day after tomorrow. Maybe I hit my head tripping on that box and still haven't woken up. But no, when I look at my phone contacts, his name and number are right there. I watch him cycle away, shamelessly, before I get into my car and crank up the classic rock station, singing at the top of my lungs to Hall & Oates and The Zombies all the way home.

6

LIFE WELL LIVED

Ellie is almost always late to our bi-monthly lunches, but Marcus shows up at noon on the dot. There's a soft knock at my kitchen door, just as my hands are completely coated in bread dough. I'd told him to come through the gate so he could stash his bike on the back porch.

"Come in!" I shout.

And there he is, helmet under his arm, bike likely propped up against the stucco outer wall of the house. He looks like he always does, like a demigod in his graphic tee that's too tight across the chest and shoulders. It's darkened with the barest hint of pit sweat, and how? How can that be so hot?

"Welcome to Casa Carter," I say as he wipes his feet on the rubber mat. His glance falls to my apron, covered in flamingos and piña colada cartoons and looking like it was hit with a flour balloon.

"Wow," he says, sounding genuinely impressed. "You've been busy."

Another plain statement of fact that tricks me into thinking it's a compliment. I need to be sure not to fall into that. That's called "getting the wrong idea."

"More or less," I say, grasping for a subject change. "House-made strawberry lemonade in the fridge. But you're going to have to grab it unless you want it with a good dash of gluten."

Silently, he rounds the kitchen island and opens my fridge. He stands so still for a moment that I wonder if there's been a time glitch. Then he speaks.

"Did you prepare all of this yourself?" I remember that the fridge is packed with covered dishes—leaf-wrapped dolma and baba ganoush and hummus. It's the easiest thing I can make for vegans, and the thing I'm most proud of. I'm sure as hell not experimenting with new recipes the first time Marcus comes to my house.

"Sure did!" I say, trying not to pat myself on the back too hard. "Did most of it last night, because clearly I have a bustling social life."

He snorts. "I can relate." Maybe it's selfish of me, but something inside me relaxes when I hear that. If his social calendar isn't packed, there's a better chance of there being some space for me.

I point him toward the glasses. Candace took the nice ones when we broke up, and I'm still stuck with wine glasses we picked up from tasting rooms and my collection of silly mugs. Maybe I should be embarrassed, but I'm not. Everyone always has too many mugs anyway, so if that's what I have to use until I remember to buy more adult glasses, who cares?

When I glance over at Marcus, he's pouring strawberry lemonade into a mug featuring two crows that says "attempted murder" across the bottom. Then, I can feel his eyes heavy on my back as I heat the cast iron pan to fry the pita bread.

"Can I help?" he asks.

"Right now you should just sit right there and relax. Must be a long bike ride, especially after teaching," I say.

"Not really. The class members are the ones exerting themselves," he says. There's a sound of ceramic against granite as he sets his mug down. "This is an impressive kitchen."

"Thanks! I try to make good use of it." Waving my hand over the cast iron, I feel heat waves rising from it, and I set down the first circle of dough. "Got it renovated this summer. Hired the contractors and stuff back before, uh…" Welp, I started this sentence, might as well finish it, "before I split with my partner. So, I got to do things my way."

Nothing too original here. Black fixtures and cupboards, granite countertops, stainless steel appliances. But it's for cooking, and I was happy to keep it the way I wanted.

"It was going to be pure white with tile and grout and rose-gold fixtures, so dodged a bullet there, I guess," I say.

"That seems like it might showcase messes much more clearly," he says, glossing over the breakup talk, thankfully. Was that a good sign? Or a sign that he didn't care either way? One thing's for sure, I'm not going to turn around and check what face he's making.

Instead, I force a laugh, snatching up the pita with my bare hands and flipping it over. "Exactly what I said."

He's quiet as I keep my back to him, staring at the pita bread like it's the riveting final act of an action movie. I try not to panic. Not every second needs to be filled up with me talking at him. We've spent enough time together in comfortable silence that I shouldn't be so anxious. Plus, I've got to keep an eye on these so they don't burn.

Chair legs slide against the floor, and Marcus says, "May I look at your bookshelf?"

"Course. But those are just the ones I put out to make people think I'm cool. All the tomes that'll put you to sleep are in my office," I say. I have no idea whether he's a book snob—he certainly has been able to keep up with my references when we've talked about my classes, but somehow I'm still self-conscious about him looking at my books.

"You still have DVDs," he says, voice raised since he's crossed the room.

"Oh, yeah. I'm ancient. Don't know if you noticed," I call over my shoulder. I hear him grumble something, but I don't catch what it is.

Finally, I stack the pita bread in a little basket beside the stove, and they're ready to be slathered with pureed chickpea and tahini. When I turn to set them on the kitchen island, I spot him, sitting cross-legged in front of the bottom shelf. He's pulled out all my TASCHEN art books and is leafing through one featuring the works of Hieronymus Bosch.

"Make yourself at home," I say, because I'm too big of a smartass not to. He flinches a little and looks up at me, and I immediately feel guilty.

"I'm sorry if—"

"Hey, I mean it. Look at whatever you like. You could even look at the boring ones in my office too if that's what you want."

The crease in his forehead smooths, and smile lines dent either side of his mouth. "Perhaps when I have finished strip-mining this shelf, I will move on," he says.

"As you wish." I know I'm laying it on a little thick, but who cares? He's definitely flirting with me this time. After I hang up my apron, I make my way over to him and slowly lower myself to the floor until I'm sitting next to him, knees bent, weight back on my hands. He's right, my mobility is pretty bad, so I can't tie myself in a knot like he can.

Unexpectedly, he reaches over and gently grips my calf, just under my knee. I suck in a breath. I don't want him to let go, and I'm afraid that a soft breeze will blow this moment away before I can seize it.

"Your leg has bruised quite badly," he murmurs, not letting go as he examines the angry purple and red mark there from when I bashed it on the box yesterday.

"Pain pays the income of each precious thing."

Fuck, I'm quoting Shakespeare—just because his hand is on me and, again, he is not letting go. I feel like I'm suspended in time as it continues to rest there, and his gaze wanders up from the bruise to my eyes. Maybe it's an optical illusion, but I swear he's leaning toward me.

Before I can do anything about it, the door unlatching drives us both back and away from one another.

"What's up, fuckers," Ellie calls, head whipping around as she searches the kitchen for me. Her eyes land on Marcus and me, still sitting very close together in front of my bookshelf. Her eyebrows wiggle, like I knew they would. "Well, this looks cozy."

"Ellie, this is Marcus," I say, trying to telepathically tell her to cool it.

Marcus rises to his feet without using his hands. Just stands straight up from a cross-legged position like a sexy space alien. He holds a hand out for Ellie to shake, wearing a mask of seriousness that I am just now realizing he's mostly dropped for me. She takes his hand with a sly grin, throwing out some niceties, eyes flicking over to me as I struggle to my feet.

"Should we start taking stuff outside?" She's already making a beeline for my cupboards to gather plates. "I brought two bottles of wine this time, since we've got a new guy. You drink wine, right, Marcus?"

"I would not say no to it," he says. That's a bit of a pleasant surprise too, something else I can share with him.

Marcus accepts the stack of plates I'd hurriedly bought from Target after Candace moved out, as well as silverware and cloth napkins, carrying them outside to the patio table. While he's out of the room, Ellie gives me a manic look, mouthing "Oh my god" at me. I shake my head, thinking that maybe I should have dreaded this a little more. I was just way too busy with my head in the clouds last night, chopping cucumbers for tzatziki and blasting Steely Dan.

One of the best parts about living in this part of the state is that you can leave garden furniture out without worrying about it getting too messed up. I got to keep the big hardwood table with its matching benches, and even though I know it was mostly because they're extremely heavy and probably a bitch to move, I'm grateful. The eclectic collection of bowls and plates laid out on the table actually makes me feel a little Bohemian, a little cooler than I actually am.

Soon we're sitting with Ellie on one side of the table and Marcus sitting on the other side next to me. I'm playing it very cool, even as his thigh occasionally brushes against mine. It's infrequent enough that it could plausibly be an accident, but at this point, I'm not so sure. Unfortunately, he's still fully covered by skinny jeans, but every man must make sacrifices.

Ellie and I chat about the latest drama in her Swedish folk ensemble, and I can see out of the corner of my eye that Marcus is very intent on wolfing down everything on his plate. Every once in a while he makes a soft, pleased noise, and I don't even know whether he knows he's doing it. I wonder if that's the sound he'd make if I kissed him.

I catch his eye and smile at him as he helps himself to more pita.

"You are an excellent cook," he says, almost sounding apologetic. Ok, I'm a dumbass, but that's definitely praise.

"Glad you think so," I say. "Excellent cook and excellent eater, if that wasn't super clear from our sessions."

Marcus sets the pita down and arrests me with his stare. "As your trainer, I must insist that you not say negative things about your own body. It is doing exactly what it is supposed to do to keep you alive, and you—"

He clamps down on whatever he was about to say and bites his lip as if to prevent anything else from coming out.

"I what?"

"I do not want to be inappropriate," he says, turning away from me to awkwardly scoop green olives onto his plate.

If I weren't already eating lunch, this would have made me start salivating.

"Nope. You've gotta tell us now." Ellie backs me up from across the table. Sometimes her audacity comes in handy, when it isn't directed at me (and honestly, sometimes when it is, too). "It should be obvious that you're not sitting with people who like to be appropriate."

He sets the spoon back in its plastic container—one of the only things I bought pre-prepared (because seriously, who makes their own olives?). He takes a long sip of his wine, then leans inward, speaking in a conspiratorial voice.

"Do not tell my fitness compatriots this, but I view a little extra body fat as a sign of a life well lived in many cases." He focuses on me. "Particularly in your case."

Fuck if the compliment doesn't go straight to my dick. If I could look away from him, I might be able to see whatever delighted expression Ellie's got. As it is, I am this close to throwing him over my shoulder and carrying him to the bedroom. Fortunately, I put the kibosh on that caveman urge and grasp for a joke.

"You just don't want me to get ripped because you're afraid you'll lose a client," I say. I hope that the way I'm looking back conveys to him that I'm just messing around. And maybe even that it conveys I would be open to eating him alive (or vice versa) if he ever happened to be interested.

Based on the way he seems to lighten, to tilt his chin at just a slightly higher angle, I think he gets it. Or at least I hope so.

Ellie finally breaks the silence. "Well, it's refreshing to see a trainer that isn't fat-shamey," she says. "If I had a trainer, I'd want him to be like you."

He finally tears himself away from our stalemate. "There is room in my calendar for more clients," he says, the seed of his smile blooming into something full and charming as all hell. I'm hoping I was the one who planted that seed, but I'm happy to see Ellie helped coax it out. I love when my friends get along. Especially when whoever I'm dating gets along with my best friend.

Because I'm starting to think this might not be so impossible after all.

7

Sounds Like an Adventure

Ellie and Marcus, both at the tail ends of their second glasses of wine, are in a surprisingly lively debate over whether the movie featured on Marcus's shirt, *Eraserhead*, is a work of genius or garbage. It should be pretty obvious who is taking which side.

"I just watched it for the first time on a date this summer, and it's boring as shit. I think people just like it because they think it makes them look smarter," Ellie says.

"It sounds as if your vision was skewed by the company you were keeping," Marcus snipes.

Ellie glares at me, and I put a hand to my heart like I'm scandalized. "Keep me out of this! I haven't even seen it."

She scrunches her nose and turns her attention back to Marcus. "You're just a Lynch fan boy who thinks he can do no wrong. I bet you even liked his *Dune*."

Marcus opens his mouth, leaning forward, then shuts it and looks thoughtful. "You are probably right. I am guilty." He takes a sip of his wine, then sets the empty glass back down. "But that movie is not nearly as terrible as people say."

"Ha!" Ellie says.

I have no idea what they're talking about, but I certainly don't mind watching Marcus stepping up to Ellie's challenges. Frankly, it's pretty sexy.

A text alert interrupts my undoubtedly gooey staring, and nobody really notices me checking it. It's Katie.

So, promise you won't be mad at me, but I need to tell you something

My stomach seizes. No good conversation has ever started this way.

Sure, what's up?

I was talking to marta last night
And she told me candace has a new boyfriend

My stomach drops, and I immediately chastise myself for it. After all, I'm clearly pursuing someone. Two glasses of wine down, I'll own that. Why should I be mad that Candace has found someone new?

And he's gonna be at the wedding anyway

Now that raises the hairs on the back of my neck.

Do I know him?

[...]

[...]

Yeah...

Fuck. It's been almost a year already, but a lot of suspicious thoughts are welling up in my head. That this is someone I know makes me feel like there'd been something going on before we broke up. But that's not fair of me either. There's been a plenty-wide time gap since we broke up and now.

Katie.

It's Robbie.

For a moment, everything stops. The music piped out onto the patio. The birdsong. The lively conversation happening around me. My heartbeat.

I know, i'm so sorry

It seems pretty new at least

I just wanted to give you the heads up

I thumbs-up react to the final message, because there's not much else I can bring myself to say. Then, I set my phone face-down on the table and resist the urge to bury my head in my hands. Up until now, I'd prepared myself mentally to handle this wedding alone. The bachelorette party was going to be the first time I saw Candace since we broke up, since she'd moved back down to LA after and gotten a high-level sales job. That was going to be hard enough. But now, she's dating again. And if that isn't bad enough, she's dating my shittiest cousin. The one who pissed in my first car for no other reason than he thought it was funny and spread gay rumors about me when we were in high school, long before I was out as bi.

"Zack? Hon?" Ellie's voice rattles through my skull like a pinball, and I let it shake me out of my trance.

"Hm? Sorry, what were we talking about?"

"Uuuuh...whatever message you just got? You look like someone barfed in your tabbouleh." She reaches toward me with the hand that isn't gripping the stem of her wine glass and taps the blank, dark-stained table top. "Come on. Spill it."

"Candace is dating my cousin." No point being coy about it.

Ellie rears back as though I *had* actually barfed in the tabbouleh. "Since when?"

"Katie says recently."

Marcus shifts next to me. This isn't really something I wanted to talk about in front of him. I already mentioned my ex earlier, and being the kind of person who goes on and on about a breakup is definitely the way to drive off someone new. I know this. But what else am I supposed to do, not tell my best friend?

"This is your former partner?" he asks softly. I can only nod in reply. I do my best to raise my head and give him the courtesy of eye contact and a smile I'm sure doesn't reach above my nose. Sympathy oozes from him, and as I absorb it, it converts into guilt.

Ellie makes a frustrated sound. "I really wish this damn wedding was happening before I went to Sweden. I'd totally go with you," she says.

"I know." Wow, my mouth is so dry that it feels like my voice box is about to crumble. I can't fault Ellie, and I would never expect her to go out of her way like that for me, even if she weren't traveling.

But it sure would be nice to have someone there for me for a change.

"I'm over her, I swear," I say, trying very hard not to look at Marcus as I say it (even though it's mostly for his benefit, an embarrassing sort of plea). The dishcloth that still hides half the pile of pita bread is a good enough audience. "This shouldn't bother me so much; I don't know why it does."

"Maybe because you were together for ten years and it's barely been a year since she stomped on your heart with her fucking kitten heels?"

I snort. "That's an image."

"Which cousin?"

"Robbie," I sigh.

"Ew, the one with all the bad tattoos?" Her attention shoots to Marcus, whose gorgeous raven half sleeve is on full display. "No offense, Marcus. Yours are awesome. This guy just has a bunch of flash sale tattoos all over the place. Like, it looks like a Spirit Halloween nylon suit of them."

Marcus's eyes narrow, as if he sees my terrible cousin in his mind's eye.

For a moment, nobody speaks. Marcus is completely still while Ellie taps the table like she's doing morse code. I'm about to ask her to stop, but then she straightens up and points at me.

"What about a man?"

"What *about* a man?"

"If you were fine with bringing me with you as your date, why couldn't you bring a man?" "Who…"

I cut myself off as I realize what she's doing. I cannot believe the fucking audacity. I don't know if I'm grateful or mortified as she fixes her crosshairs on Marcus. "Marcus, what's June/July looking like for you?"

"I couldn't ask him to—" and I realize that, as rude as she's being, it's probably even worse of me to be talking about him like this when he's sitting right here. I twist toward him on the bench. "Marcus, I can't ask you to—"

"I'll do it," he says before I can finish.

Both Ellie's arms shoot into the air as she whoops like a middle-aged man five beers deep at a football game. "See? See?"

I want to play it cool. I wish I had it in me to tell him it's ok, that I don't need the help. But the fact is, I really do. That need is far outweighing my embarrassment. Maybe I'd been tentatively inching toward making a move with him, but apparently all my strategies have just been blown away like dandelion seeds.

"Really? A-are you sure? You don't have to just say so because you feel sorry for me. I can probably manage if I absolutely have to, but it would be really...it would..."

He nods. "I do not have any mandatory engagements that should keep me from doing so."

Ellie folds her hands under her chin, far too proud of herself. She's just been looking for an opening to pull something like this; I know it. I turn to her, not sure whether I should throw a pita at her head or leap over the table and give her a hug.

Then an unpleasant thought occurs to me. "Are you sure that wouldn't take attention away from Katie and Marta? A lot of people don't know that I'm bi, and I wouldn't want everyone looking at me instead of her."

"If you would rather not come out..." Marcus says, looking puzzled.

"At the lesbian wedding? Fucking come on," she says. "And if it's the attention thing you're worried about, then you two should just establish a relationship paper trail now so people won't be surprised when you get there."

What the hell? Had she planned something like this in advance when she found out I'd invited Marcus over? Is she that diabolical?

"Go out on a few dates. Post some pictures on Instagram. Bring him to the bachelorette dinner. You said you're paying for it, right? Then they shouldn't give you an ounce of shit."

Trying to tamp down on my desperation, I turn back toward Marcus. "Does that...does that sound...?"

I've done so much to try to keep my cool today, and a handful of text messages and my overly excitable best friend have just knocked me over like a house of cards. I'm really at his mercy right now, so much so that I almost wish he'd just change his mind and say no and put me out of my misery.

Instead, his mouth turns up in one of the bigger smiles he's ever given me. "Sounds like an adventure."

When he says it that way, it flips the switch from dread back to want. Something more than desire. Avarice. People can think whatever they want about the way I live my life, the surface-level stability of it, but the way he says "adventure" sends tingles over the backs of my arms. It pulls my dreams from where they've been lying in critical condition for months.

Turns out they're healing, and they're ready to start working for me again.

"Great! Let's get something on the calendar, then," Ellie says, her accusatory hand tapping in my direction once more, pulling me away from the dangerous turn my thoughts had taken.

"What are you, our fake dating concierge?" I chuckle. My head is suddenly feeling very floaty.

"No way. After this, you two are on your own," she says. "I'm just the idea woman."

Well, might as well be brave. Maybe I just need practice. Maybe it'll help me get brave enough to ask him out for real.

"Well, Marcus, how about dinner Friday? What do you think?"

He bites his lip, his piercings poking out just a little further than usual with the stretch. Where did this mannerism come from? Why is it so hot? Why is he trying to kill me?

"I'm afraid I have a prior commitment," he says.

Shit, apparently that was too much to hope. He must have a boyfriend. This is just a favor, after all. I shouldn't have gotten ahead of myself this much.

"But I have an extra ticket, if you would like to accompany me," he says, before I can backpedal. There's that small, sweet smile again, followed quickly by that flip-flopping sensation in my stomach.

Ellie grins. She fills up all our wine glasses with the next bottle of chardonnay without asking permission.

"To the lovebirds!" she says, raising her glass.

The three of us toast. I almost choke on my wine when I catch Marcus's flinty gaze, fixed on me over the rim of his glass.

8

OPEN TO SUGGESTIONS

There's a full week before Marcus and I attend his "prior commitment" together—a week of two training sessions and one afternoon spent quietly working together at Silverskins. Ellie had (very condescendingly, I think) called it "parallel play" a couple weeks ago, but I don't care. It made me happy to be able to sit and work, occasionally looking up to read him a funny quote from one of my books or papers or to peek over at whatever he was drawing. His smiles are getting more frequent, so I don't think he minds either.

And now it's Friday night, and I'm climbing the Mexican tile steps to the black box theater tucked above the ghost of a long-abandoned department store. When I spot Marcus waiting for me, I nearly gasp. He's wearing his customary black, but his jeans are free of rips, and his usual graphic tee is replaced with a black tank with a shimmering nylon overshirt. The only other color he wears is a tiny red jewel dangling from one ear, a delicate droplet over the firm slope of his jaw. It churns up a series of lewd thoughts that I have to push down with all my might.

I can tell when he spots me by the way his eyes widen. I'm not sure whether that's just from him shaking himself from some daydream, or if, magically, he's just as struck by the sight of me as I am of him. Hopefully, the latter. I actually dusted off my iron for this button-up shirt and slacks, and I'm told lavender is a very flattering color for my skin tone.

"Wow. You look great," I say when I reach him. I can't help it. He's fucking beautiful.

"Thank you. You do as well." His eyes drop bashfully for a moment before he lifts his chin, as if he's psyching himself up to do a monologue. We stand for a minute in silence. There are far too many hummingbirds buzzing around my chest for me to be embarrassed about it.

Finally, he waves a pair of tickets, and he leads me off the terrace, through the lobby, and past a refreshments table selling small cups of wine for $5 a pop. The theater itself is black box style, a rectangular stage on the floor level, and seats on three sides that rise, row by row, like more comfortable bleachers. In the center of the room is a series of geometric platforms on casters, and strands of fairy lights are suspended behind them like a glowing beaded curtain.

We sit right in the front row, stage right.

"Wow, I'm usually buried in the middle somewhere," I say.

"Do you want to sit somewhere else?" If it were a month ago, I'd think he was being sarcastic, but now I know he's not. If I asked him to, he'd go exchange the tickets right now. I'd do the same for any of my friends, and it's nice to spend time with someone who'd do the same for me.

God, I'm in trouble.

"So," I ask, "who's your connection here, theater kid?"

This time, his smile is lopsided. "Well, first, me. Second, my friend and former roommate, Jackie, is the stage manager. She helped me get the work."

"Hold on, back up." I hold up one of my fingers, drawing loops in the air like I'm rewinding a cassette tape. "What do you mean, 'first, me?'"

"This," he gestures to the set, sitting dormant in front of us, "is my design."

"Okay, Will Graham," I say. He snorts at my *Hannibal* reference, and I grin. Finally, I've found a pop culture touchstone we actually have in common. "Very good! I like it."

His dusky eyes sparkle like the tiny lights at the back of the stage, with the pure delight of a child that so, so badly wants to describe the plot of his favorite cartoon and is trying not to spoil it.

"Just wait," he says.

So I do. And what I see is dazzling. This being a professional production, the acting is great, the costumes are creative, and the lighting is spot on (sorry—couldn't help it). But Marcus's set is something else.

It's another Shakespeare play, *The Tempest*, a play that is just as magical as *A Midsummer Night's Dream*. With fewer resources and less space than he had at the outdoor theater during that show, Marcus has created something just as reality-bending, and I'm stunned.

The shapes on stage and the lights move to form walls and barriers, grottos and ocean waves and ships. They form the backbone of sight gags. They elevate the images of the actors to the sort of magical levels they deserve, coordinating perfectly with the costumes and lighting.

At intermission, I must be looking at him with heart eyes, because his throat and the arch of his cheekbones flush pink. I feel like I've been shot into space and discovered I don't need oxygen to breathe.

"You're phenomenal," I say.

And instead of denying it, he only smiles at me and says, "Thank you."

"Why are you bothering to go back to school? You should teach classes." His blush deepens. I think I might be obsessed with it, and that I caused it.

"Connections mostly," he says. "Perhaps the opportunity to experiment with film. This is only the second production in which I have been able to take part since I was...since I left my theater program ten years ago."

The pause and correction is not lost on me, but I'm not really into gotchas. If he wants to tell me, he can tell me, but I'm not about to waste my shot here. There had been some talk about this "date" before he went home last Saturday, about this being a chance to see whether we had the chemistry to pull this off realistically. If I prod at him about gaps in his résumé, why would he want to keep spending time with me, even as a ruse?

"Well," I say, "you're definitely going to have a leg up on all those eighteen-year-olds. Probably be first in line for all the internships and job opportunities."

"With any luck, yes," he says. "Hopefully that will make up for the delay."

Questions begetting more questions, but I don't have time to ask them because the lights are going down again.

The second half is just as impressive as the first. All I can get myself to do after the proverbial curtain is shake my head at him. There's no way my feelings aren't totally obvious. Fortunately, he's not running away.

Well, until he does. Almost immediately, he rises to his feet and heads toward the far corner of the room. There's a sinking feeling in my stomach that he's just going to leave without saying anything to me, until he turns around, frowning. I realize he's looking for me, and I follow him. Sheesh, my abandonment issues are showing

The work lights (or at least I think that's what they're called) are back on in the aftermath, the area backstage a series of thin hallways, curtained alcoves, and dressing room doors. People mill around half-dressed in diaphanous fabrics, because, I remember from long ago, that's just what theater people like to do. One of the minor characters is holding the knobby facemask he'd worn under one arm, talking to a stout person, who soon turns toward us.

"Hey there, stranger!" she calls in our direction in a cigarette-husky voice. She has close-cropped black hair and thick square glasses. I can only assume it's the stage manager friend who hooked him up with the job and whose name I've already forgotten.

Fortunately, Marcus bros me out, once his friend has just about squeezed the life out of him. "Jackie, this is my...friend, Zack," he says. His hand closes around my upper arm. As much as it can, anyway. They've gotten thicker with the help of my excellent personal trainer.

"Just a...friend, huh?" She imitates his pause, giving me a very obvious once-over. She winks one heavily black-lined eye at me, and I let out a nervous laugh.

Marcus doesn't answer at all, just wrinkles his nose adorably at her. I'm not sure if that means he thinks she's being ridiculous or if he's just unsure where we are with this whole thing. I'm kind of wondering what test I'm supposed to pass to get to be his fake boyfriend, and if this counts as one of them.

"Well, handsome, insert shovel talk here," she says to me, obviously not buying Marcus's act for a second. "If you hurt my boy, I'll kill you."

I believe her. She looks like the kind of person who knows how to hide a body.

"You have my word," I say, putting a palm to my chest in a solemn oath. I probably sound like I'm joking, but I'm really not.

"You're such a bitch," Marcus says to her, and my mouth drops open.

But she doesn't miss a beat. "You love me, you dick." She reaches up to ruffle his perfectly styled hair. He doesn't move to stop her. She looks back at me. "This one lived with me for probably...what was it?"

"A million years," he says.

"I got to see all the many phases of Marcus," she says. "Still got the scars to prove it." She pushes up one long cotton sleeve to show me an ankh tattoo, with line work so fine it looks like filigree.

"That is the definition of consensual scarring," he says, rolling his eyes and fussing with his ruined hairdo.

"Wait, you did that?" It's impossible for me to keep the delighted surprise out of my voice. "What can't you do?"

"He can't handle positive attention," Jackie says before he can answer.

When I look at him, his head is down, and he's scuffing his boot against the cardboard floor. She's clearly right that he's overwhelmed, but seriously. How the fuck is he so talented?

Before I can stop fixating, Jackie changes the subject. "Are you coming to the cast party?"

"When is it?" he says, glancing at me.

"I don't remember the exact date, but it's after closing night in about five weeks?"

"As long as it doesn't conflict with your sister's party," he says to me.

Okay. Okay, that's a great sign.

"Friend," she scoffs under her breath, but still clearly enough for both of us to hear. "All right, I'll text you as soon as I check the calendar. I've gotta go, but let's catch up before then. I've got lots of questions for you."

You and me both, I want to say. But I keep that to myself.

Soon, Jackie waves us off. It's opening night, and apparently they've got to kick everyone else and take care of some notes. I certainly thought the whole thing was perfect, but I'm only an expert on the text itself—kinda. Not even really an expert in that if you asked the head of my department. More like, just knowledgeable enough to have an edge over people fresh out of high school.

We descend the tile steps together, slowly, since most of the other playgoers have gone. The corridor below is dark, lit by wrought-iron sconces with warm, but sort of ineffective, lightbulbs.

"Give you a ride home?" I offer. "Maybe we can talk about, you know, details. Of this."

Or like maybe how you could actually go out with me for real and make everything easier?

But no. I don't want to ruin the night.

"If you could drop me off at the gym, I left my bike there," he says, completely glossing over the comment about talking about whatever we're doing.

"What! It's late! You're wearing black!"

He smirks. "I have reflective gear, and it's only about a mile and a half from my apartment."

I study him for a long moment, wondering if he's just being polite, if I should insist. The idea of him cycling this late at night makes me nervous, but I have a tendency to mother-hen. Yet another way I might ruin this.

"All right," I say reluctantly, leading him a couple of blocks away to my car.

We forget to talk about our fake dating strategy on the way back to the gym. Mostly it's because I get distracted when "Lovefool" comes on the radio. Maybe it's osmosis from the theater people, or maybe it's just the way I am, but I am forced into an impromptu bout of singing (because with the way my voice is, "bout" is the only correct word for it). I refuse to apologize for it, but from the way Marcus nods along, and the way I see his lips moving during the chorus, I don't think I really need to.

Our gym sessions are pretty focused the following week, and to my disappointment and minor anxiety, Marcus doesn't show up at Silverskins. As I sit at our usual table, trying to focus on preparing my lecture slides rather than his inevitable ghosting, my phone lights up with a text message.

Perhaps we should meet this weekend to discuss our strategy.

I just barely manage not to do a fist pump. It would freak out the undergrads in my class who I am pretending not to see studying at a table in the corner.

What did you have in mind?

I am open to suggestions.

I shouldn't do this. It's silly, and it might make me look like a dickhead show-off, but fuck it. I want to take him somewhere nice. There's plausible deniability, and it might go nowhere. But at least I can enjoy his company and show him a good time.

Can I take you to dinner?

There's that nerve-racking moment, where the little gray dots appear and disappear in the corner several times. And then there's the worst-case scenario, where they stop showing up altogether for over ten seconds. I have to set my phone face-down for the space of a few deep breaths. A flashing reminder of why I hate dating lights up the inside of my head, but I blink it away. This isn't real dating; the nerves shouldn't be this intense.

Yes, I know I'm delusional, but I don't think anyone else in my position could do better than I am. Not with what I'm up against—a desperately attractive man who's just about an inch and a half beyond my reach.

`That would be acceptable, though I know little about what options are available.`

I try to exhale the rush of adrenaline that shoots through me. Hopeless. Both the attempt and me in general.

`I'll figure it out and send you the time and place.`

`Thank you.`

I swallow (gulp), heart-react to his message (fuck, too much?), and set my phone face-down on the mosaic table-top. Already, I know exactly where I want to take him, but I don't want to jump in with it too quickly. Then he'd know I'd been thinking about it for days before this, rather than just casually agreeing to hang out.

I wait until I'm home that evening to send him the name of my favorite restaurant down by the beach, and as soon as I get the thumbs-up, I make a reservation.

9

THE COLOR OF THE SEA

Once again, Marcus has insisted he'll meet me here instead of accepting a ride. I'm not sure why he's been doing that, but, I remind myself, he's not my actual boyfriend. Pressing him about it will make me look weird and controlling. We stand outside the door, which makes the place come off as a little corny—false wooden dock pilings posted up in the front, cloudy glass windows shaped like portholes, a facade in a roughened, nautical blue.

When you walk inside, though, the place has the clean lines and elegant atmosphere of any of the "good" restaurants in town. As soon as Marcus crosses the threshold, he pauses. I don't notice until I see that he isn't next to me anymore. His eyes are wide, as if he's seen an old ghost.

"You all right?" I ask.

He leans close to my ear. "I—I don't think I can afford this place."

"That's not an issue," I assure him, keeping my voice low, because for some reason he seems to want to do things that way. "I'm paying. I wouldn't have asked you here otherwise."

He's a part-time trainer and set designer. I know this isn't in his budget. I'm not that clueless.

"I can't ask you to do that." We're practically chest to chest now, he's talking to me so closely. I wish it weren't for such an anxious reason.

A woman in a crisp, white button-up shirt and a black bowtie approaches, hands clasped behind her back. She addresses me by name, and I ask her to please give us a minute before she can say anything else. She nods and retires to stand behind a nearby barrel and poke at an iPad resting on its stand. I stay close to him, trying to keep my voice low without stage-whispering.

"Look, it's not a hardship for me. I have..." I sigh.

Telling people this is always a little awkward, especially in academic environments, since most people don't have my privilege. I used to tell people that I had a secret money tree, but Candace had told me that just made me sound like an asshole (and she was right, I'll give her that).

"I have a trust fund. It's why I can own a house here on a professor's salary. And I like to do nice things for my friends without them feeling guilty about it."

He rears back from me like I've slapped him, and my chest tightens. I don't know what to say to make this better. It's possibly the worst response anybody has ever had to this news, and I almost expect him to walk out. Instead he takes a visible, steadying breath, and his Adam's apple bobs with a swallow so dry it clicks.

"Could you give me a moment, please? I will come find you." He walks toward the bathrooms without giving me a chance to answer.

The host is very good about not showing whatever judgments she might be having as she leads me to a table by the window. I'm starting to feel really antsy about the whole thing. An imbalance like this is obviously going to be uncomfortable—not only am I one of his clients, there's a huge financial gap. Oh, and I'm seven years older than he is too. Not that I was worried about that until right this second.

I pretend to study the menu, which barely takes up a third of the paper it's on, but I'm not thinking about it at all. It's just so I don't stare in the direction of the bathroom like a puppy with no object permanence. A woman at the next table with a Louis Vuitton bag slung over her chair and evidence of years' worth of facelifts has already given me side-eye twice.

Finally, Marcus reappears and sits in the seat across from me. I set the menu back on the table. The setting sun casts him in warm colors, and to my absolute horror, it shows how red and puffy his eyes are. Somehow I've triggered the shit out of him.

"Are you okay?" I say, hushed. I feel like I'm about to throw up. "We can leave if you want. I'm sorry if—"

He raises a hand to stop me. "You have nothing to apologize for, and I think I owe you an explanation."

"You don't owe me anything," I say. He tilts his head a little, and his face does something I can't interpret. All I know is that it tugs at my heartstrings. If you think about it, heartstrings are just blood vessels, aren't they? The grimness of that fact makes it the perfect description of how I feel.

"All the same," he says.

He looks like he's about to continue, but he clams up as the server sets a pitcher of water on the table and fills up a glass for each of us. When I ask what he wants for dinner, he says that he trusts me to take care of it, and I just say the first things that my eyes land on. I'm sure they'll be fine. I honestly don't care anymore.

When she's gone, I give him my full attention, keeping my hands folded on the tabletop.

He takes a sip of water. "You should first know that when I left my theater program at eighteen, it was under duress. I had grown up in a conservative Catholic household, and my parents were already suspicious of my sexuality because of my involvement in theater. However, they were allowing me to stay with them at no cost during my first year of school, so I didn't make waves. I did not date, I did not stay out late after the conservatory shows where I worked as a tech—it was a requirement for the program I was in—I kept my head down and worked on my art."

His fingers are clenched around the base of his water glass, as condensation slips down and trickles over them. I wish I could hold them instead, to make him feel better about whatever he's about to say to me. He takes another deep breath before speaking again.

"The creative director of the conservatory...he fixated on me within weeks of the first term starting. At first, I believed he was impressed by my work, but now I realize he very likely hadn't seen anything I'd done. How could he have? There had only been minor opportunities to showcase it." He shakes his head, as if noticing he'd gone off track. "I'm sorry, I do not tell this story often."

"That's ok." I force the words through the tightness in my throat.

"I'm sure you can imagine where this is heading," he says. "It started with simple positive attention, which I believed might lead to mentorship. Then small gifts, then...dinners, until finally he had tickets to an out-of-town show that I really wanted to see in San Francisco and. Well, I was still seventeen."

"Shit," I mutter.

I feel doubly shitty for springing this on him. He probably thinks I'm just trying to get into his pants. And fuck, I kind of am, but it's much more than that, and I definitely didn't think it would make him feel victimized. I'm not trying to trick him but—but, I need to keep listening to him right now rather than spiral. I do my best to ignore the gnawing in my gut.

"Somehow, my parents learned of the affair, and they kicked me out. He took me in for a few months, but he soon began to treat me cruelly. Though, I suppose he always had that edge to him and I just hadn't noticed..." he grumbles this last bit, but the disdain seems directed inward, and I *hate* that. "I'd like to say I left him, but the fact is he became bored with me and kicked me out a few days after my eighteenth birthday. After that, I could not afford to continue school. I was functionally homeless, couch-surfing until Jackie finally took me in. Then I floundered, searching for a career with a low startup cost for years until I found something that stuck and that I could hack."

"The construction, the tattooing, and—"

"And eventually I became a trainer and was able to get enough clients to no longer burden my friend," he says.

"She doesn't seem to think of you as a burden," I say. I probably shouldn't have cut in with my opinion like that, but I couldn't stand to watch him blame himself for one more thing. Fortunately, he lets it slide.

"So you see why I may have overreacted a bit to..." He gestures around the room.

"Yeah, no wonder," I say, probably a little too emphatically. "A fucking predator used his money to fuck up your entire life."

His shoulders tense, lips pressing hard together, and I'm afraid he's about to cry again.

"I'm sorry. That was too blunt."

He shakes his head. "No, no, you're right. It's just...still difficult to accept I was victimized, even after more than ten years."

"You didn't deserve any of it," I insist. "And I'm so sorry your family wasn't there for you when you needed them. That's devastating."

Then I give him a choice, setting my hand loosely in the center of the table in what I hope is an invitation rather than a demand. And he seems to take it as such, reaching out to meet me. His fingers are chilly, but even as long as they are, I can still warm them in the palm of my hand.

"Look, I don't want to be your sugar daddy. I want to be your friend," I continue, before he can get too in his head. "If you're not comfortable coming out to places like this and want to pay your own way, no problem. I want to share things that I like with you, but I don't want you to feel obligated to me. You don't need to feel pressured to do anything. In fact, if you decided you didn't want to go through with this whole wedding date thing, I would totally understand, and I wouldn't be upset. And if you wanted to just go back to being my coach and back off of the friendship for any reason, I'd respect that too. I'd be a little sad, but I'd respect it."

He shakes his head. "I do not want to lose your friend-ship. I just—in these instances, I need to be able to decline without fearing retaliation."

"Of course," I say, suddenly doubly glad that I didn't pressure him to accept a ride from me tonight. But the practical fact is all the things I'm asking him to do with me for this wedding are going to cost money. Like, a lot of it. "Would you consider letting me, you know, treat you sometimes?"

"If you are being genuine," he says, "then yes."

"I am," I say, then add foolishly, "I just want to make you happy."

His jaw goes slack, I can't tell whether that's a good thing. Before he can get any words out, the server appears again. I'm not sure whether to be relieved or disappointed that I didn't get to hear what he had to say.

The sense of possibility I've had for the past week, that he might reciprocate my feelings, all but evaporates. I be-lieve that he wants to be my friend, but with all the baggage he has, I can't imagine he wants more than that.

But as dinner goes on, he seems lighter, as if telling me his story had lifted the weight that was keeping him from flying. He splits the wine with me. He laughs—really laughs—at my stupid jokes and roasts me when I confess to my love of 1990s action movies. After dinner he takes an impossibly long time to finish his final glass of wine, and my hopeless mind tries to tell me it's because he wants to be here with me for longer.

By the time we're done, the sun is inches from setting, the sky still pink fading upward into indigo. All light looks good on him, and the gray in his eyes has morphed into the color of the sea. Too soon, I'm signing the check, and we're weaving our way through the restaurant, finally starting to really bustle with the people cool enough to get later reservations on a Saturday night.

I'm about to say goodbye, when he says, "Would you like to go for a walk?"

For a while, we stroll across the hard-packed sand, left bare and wet by the low tide. We're quiet for the first time all evening, allowing the crashing waves and the occasional seagull cry to dominate the soundscape. I watch a couple down the beach from us, their figures barely silhouettes in the dying light as they walk, hand in hand.

"We're losing the light." Marcus's voice yanks me out of my pathetic, wistful thoughts. "Perhaps we should take that photo now."

"What photo?" I say, and for a stupid minute, I'm about to ask him whether he's a photographer on top of everything else.

But he smiles softly at me, and suddenly it hits me. "Oh. You mean...that photo."

He nods, then studies the beach, trying to determine where the best place to stand would be. We settle on having one of the bluffs in the background, staring straight into the remnants of sunlight.

"Ready?" I ask him. He's already sinking into the crook of my shoulder, and I feel like I've died, or it's my birthday, or I've died on my birthday. In the front-facing camera, I see the softness in his face as he poses for our first photo as a pretend couple.

"I'm going to take a few more," I say after the first. As I do, he slowly melts into me, head tilting closer and closer until it's laid against my collarbone. And after I've taken a couple with it there, he turns his face and kisses me on the cheek, bunting his forehead gently against my temple once he's done.

My eyes fall shut, and I let myself imagine, just for a moment, that this is real. I consider turning my head and kissing him, but he's acting. I wouldn't be. It wouldn't be fair to him, and frankly, it wouldn't be fair to my embarrassing, lovelorn self.

Finally, I lower my arm and bring the phone closer between us. His hand is still resting on the small of my back, head still barely leaned on my shoulder. It's making it difficult for me to breathe, but I am a fully grown man, the sort who can control himself when someone he cares about shows vulnerability. I can confidently say that every photo I've taken is a banger, and it's mostly just due to how beautiful he is.

"Okay to post?" I ask. I cannot so much see as feel Marcus nod against my shoulder, giving a soft grunt of assent.

My tongue feels thick and dry, despite the taste of briny sea air filling all the senses that aren't completely overwhelmed by how near Marcus is. He's still resting his head against my shoulder as I tap the post button.

Within thirty seconds of posting, my phone starts pinging with notifications

10

WE ALL KNOW HOW YOU GET

Within minutes, fifty likes rack up under our photo carousel. Every single comment in the growing stack stirs a mixture of joy and apprehension in my gut. Marcus chins my shoulder like a Labrador puppy as he watches the screen, and I get the same level of cute aggression that I would if he actually were one.

"I forgot to tag you," I say, voice foggy to my own ears.

"I do not have a social media account," he says.

Even through my dizziness, I roll my eyes. "Of course you don't, cool kid."

I want to turn my head and see if he is smiling, but I don't trust myself not to kiss him. The feel of his chest against my back and the gentle hand on my hip are almost too much. You could argue it's just the sort of thing one does when getting close for a photo, but tell that to my dick.

We are up to sixty likes now. Seeing other people's happiness for me, laid one on top of another, makes me really wish this wasn't a lie. Seeing their surprise that I found someone new makes me wonder if I should be a little insulted. However, I don't have time to decide before the post is replaced by an incoming call alert from my sister.

"I should take this," I say. Stepping away breaks the tension, sure, but I'm already hungry for the next time he decides to touch me.

"Excuse me, Quackers," Katie says as soon as I answer the phone. "When were you going to tell me, your only beloved Katie-bara, that you have a new boyfriend?"

Whoops. I probably should have texted Katie at the very least before I posted. My family is very supportive, but that means they also tend to be very emotionally invested in my life. Like, to the point of hostility.

"Sorry. Got a little carried away." It isn't even a lie, but I know she won't accept it anyway.

Marcus has walked down the beach, but he is not nearly far away enough to be out of earshot. He kicks at a piece of driftwood with the tip of his Doc Martens, then wanders over to a strand of beached kelp, slowly crunching the air bladders one by one. He looks up at me and smiles, like he's trying to determine whether I'd been watching, like he wants to wave me over to stomp on the kelp with him. It's unbearably sweet.

Katie interrupts my mooning. "Mom is pissed at you too."

"The post has only been up for like three minutes, if that. How could you even know?"

"Because, doofus, I'm with her right now," she says. I hear some indignant shouting in the background, which swiftly grows louder and ends with the sound of a struggle and what I assume are fingertips on the mouthpiece.

"When were you going to tell your mother about your new sweetie?" My mom's voice booms into my ear, echoing off the walls of what is probably the kitchen. Marta, Katie's fiancé, works at the same school where my mother is the principal. The three of them are very close, and they have dinner together at least once a week. Sometimes I get a little sad that I can't be there with them. Sometimes.

"It just happened," I say. Mom huffs, tolerating my answer as much as Katie had.

Marcus isn't even pretending not to listen. He has the close-mouthed, amused expression of someone who's just thought of a joke they refuse to share.

"Well, I am not allowed at the girls' bachelorette party like you are for some reason," she says. Katie pipes up in the background, but Mom cuts her off. "Not that I want to be included in your bacchanalia, thank you very much. But I want to meet your new love...dammit, Zack, I don't even know his name!"

"It's Marcus." A fleeting hope that it's gotten too dark for him to see how flustered I am smashes against the sand like the wave that Marcus is currently fleeing. "It might be a little early for that word."

"Suuuuuuure," Katie yells in the background. She doesn't even know how well she's reading me.

"She's right," my mom says with an audible smile. "We all know how you get."

For a moment, I lose the ability to speak clearly and make an embarrassing sound, made all the more embarrassing by Marcus continuing to grin at me. Suddenly, I've forgotten every word I've ever known because of how his eyes gleam like they're backlit. As he strolls toward me, they become two blades that I'm doing nothing to dodge.

It's a joke in my family, how fast I go completely gaga over someone. Every person I'd dated up until Candace was someone I was constantly on the verge of proposing to; in fact, my mom had to very gently talk me out of proposing to my high-school girlfriend. The fact that it took me almost ten years to ask Candace to marry me was only due to the fact that she never showed the kind of interest I was waiting for. That probably should have been a major clue that we weren't right for each other.

"Plus, he's quite the hottie," my mom adds.

"Mom, he can hear you. He's standing right here."

"Good! Put him on the phone!"

I look over at Marcus in a panic, and a more serious look replaces his amusement. He nods, and I put the phone on speaker. I'll be damned if I make him do this all by himself.

"Hello?" His voice is a little less severe than it had been when we first met, probably because my mom hadn't immediately insulted him the way I had, but still awkwardly professional.

"Is this the new boyfriend?"

"Marcus," I remind her.

"I'm not talking to you, I'm talking to Marcus," she says.

"Yes. I am the new boyfriend, Marcus." The corners of Marcus's eyes crinkle. Damn him, he's letting her win him over already. I probably should be happy about that, but it just makes things feel more complicated.

Also, how have I not noticed before how long his eyelashes are?

"Take good care of our Zack," Mom continues. "He gets so focused on taking care of everyone else, sometimes he forgets."

I wipe the hand that is not holding the phone over my face.

"You have my word," Marcus says, letting his smile be heard through the phone. I'm impressed by how well he's maintaining his cool. Maybe that just proves that his feelings for me aren't anything like the ones I have for him because I'm flustered enough for the both of us.

"Okay, all right. I will grill you about your intentions another time," Mom says. "You two go enjoy the rest of that gorgeous sunset."

That ship has long sailed, but there's still a little bit of a glow in the sky, the phantom of daylight mingling with the newly lit lamps lining the pier. After I hang up, I return my palm to my face and try to cover the embarrassment with a smile.

"Sorry about that. I didn't properly warn you how loud the Carter family is."

Marcus puts his hands in his pocket but doesn't draw any further away from me. "I easily guessed it would be so."

"You dick," I say with a laugh. He laughs too.

On impulse I give him a one-armed hug around the shoulder, the kind one guy friend would give another. He doesn't let me get away with it, lifting his other arm until both circle my neck. As he looks into my face, I see nothing but contentment. My stomach roils with want; I have no idea how long I can cope with him looking at me like that.

By the time we get back to the parking lot, it's fully dark. This time, he gets in the car with me rather than going home in the same way he got here (whatever that was). A fine mist hangs in the air, which makes the stoplights seem like alien space crafts.

"Do you wanna go get some ice cream?" The question just kind of pops out. What I really wanted to do was invite him home for a drink, but it feels too dangerous. I shouldn't do that—not when I am trying to respect all the anxieties he shared with me tonight at dinner.

I just don't want the night to end. Who could blame me?

Marcus is silent for long enough that I look over at him to make sure he isn't completely repulsed at the weird suggestion. There's something about two grown men going out for ice cream that feels a little off. Like when you really hear the words to a song you liked as a kid for the first time and realize it's been about heroin all along.

But Marcus doesn't look creeped out at all. "I wouldn't say no to that," he says.

There's an ice cream shop close to campus, one that is open late and whose youngest clientele are at least eighteen years old. Once we're through the open glass door and presented with two freezer cases worth of perfectly adequate ice cream to choose from, I feel less self-conscious. It helps that we're waiting behind a cluster of four students who reek of weed and look like they'd had to go on a scavenger hunt to find clothes they could wear outside their apartment.

Marcus surprises me by ordering a double chocolate chip cone. The sight inspires a sudden invasive image—me wiping chocolate off his face, him catching my thumb between his cherubic lips and batting those eyelashes at me as he takes it deeper. In the real world, he laves his tongue around the scoop, every lick deliberate and carefully placed. Which is almost worse. I'm torn between wanting to stay out with him until the sun comes up and getting home as soon as possible so I can masturbate until I give myself a friction burn.

Literally the second I order my own ice cream, I've forgotten what I asked for, because all I can think about is his tongue. Somehow, my feet are still carrying me, and the section of brain that hasn't completely succumbed to animal lust is maintaining a conversation with him.

Miraculously, we find a bench nearby that isn't taken already.

"I still can't believe you've never seen *Twin Peaks*," he says. It's criminal how much the moonlight suits him, how gorgeous he looks under it. "I have the DVDs, but I never loan them out."

"Well, I happen to have a shamefully big TV and a ridiculously comfy couch." I couldn't hold the invitation back any longer, but in my defense, there's about an eighty-percent chance he was fishing for one.

"A perfect compromise," he says, smiling as if I'd given him exactly the answer he wanted. And fuck me, I can't help how much I hope. I keep trying to tell myself that I shouldn't, but I can't stop.

"How about you come over for dinner, and we can talk strategy, and then you can introduce me to your all-time favorite show. After all, I should probably know about it if we're going to be boyfriends. Fake boyfriends, I mean. If you want to."

"I want to." He holds eye contact with me for a breathless moment, then looks at his phone. "I've got a class at 8 a.m., so I should probably go."

Fitness people tend to get up before the sun, but theater people don't, at least not in my experience. I file that away to ask him about later—which side of the spectrum he falls on naturally. Unbidden, the thought of him sleep rumpled and grumbling at the sound of his alarm going off flickers in my head. I do my best not to insert myself into the picture.

"Let me give you a ride," I say. My keys jingle as I take them out of my jacket pocket.

Still smiling, he shakes his head. "It's only three blocks, and I enjoy walking."

I want to tell him I enjoy walking, too. I want to walk him home and kiss him against his front door until he's panting. I want to take him to my home and consume all his composure with my mouth, just like he'd done to that damn ice cream cone. But that's not what friends do, is it, even if they are fake boyfriends?

Fake, fake, fake, fake, *fake*.

We linger, and I'm trying to convince myself to move, to step back, give a friendly wave, and get back to my car before I can humiliate myself somehow (by starting to drool, for instance). But then, he takes a step toward me, and suddenly there are two strong arms around my shoulders again. My lips and tongue tingle as if I'd licked a nine-volt battery. I force myself to let go first.

"I'll text you," he says. When he shoots me one more devastatingly sweet look over his shoulder, I take that as my cue to go home. If the MPAA rated my thoughts right now, they'd be banned from all family-friendly platforms. I'm in no condition to be seen by anyone.

When I get home, jerking off barely even takes the edge off. The horrific possibility dawns on me that I'm too far gone for him to be satisfied with anything less than the real thing.

11

GET A ROOM!

Despite my unsatisfied body, I manage to sleep very well. A nice, long walk on the beach will do that for you, I've discovered, no matter how hard you're yearning by the end of the night.

But when I wake up to the dim morning light with a raging erection, all I can do is sleepily imagine Marcus in bed with me. There's a little bit of guilt for touching myself while thinking of someone I know. I make a feeble attempt to replace the image of him with a guy I fucked at a nightclub in Berlin during undergrad (my most inoffensive go-to), but no dice. Even thinking about Tom Holland doesn't work. It's almost like imaginary Marcus is fighting off those other visions with his bare fists to compete for my attention. And who am I to argue with imaginary Marcus?

Really, though, it's just me here, alone, and nobody can see me palming myself under the covers. Behind my eyelids, Marcus turns over, as sleep-warm as I am, full of the same soft contentment he showed me last night. He climbs on top of me and sinks, impossibly unprepared, onto my cock. But this is my fantasy, and the only prep that's necessary is my retrieving a little bit of lube from the drawer next to my bed, then pushing my underwear down my thighs. I take my cock in my hand, cupping my balls gently with the other as I indulgently stroke myself from tip to base and back.

There's no need for me to conjure an image of Marcus with his shirt off. I already know what he looks like. I don't have every tattoo memorized, because I couldn't fully examine his front as I had his back—not while he was watching. But that doesn't matter. I've seen the width of his chest, the thick cut of his arms and abs, the barbell through his nipple that I want to lick and suck until he squirms.

Imagining what it would feel like inside of him, his hands bearing down on my shoulders to hold me down, rips a high-pitched cry from my lungs. Candace had never liked when I made noise; I think it was because she thought it was too feminine, but we never talked about it in depth enough for me to know for sure. I'd just started holding back when I noticed that she was uncomfortable.

But I don't want to think about her right now. One of the few joys of living alone and not having anyone in the room to judge me is I can do any embarrassing thing I want to myself. And it's easy for imaginary Marcus to drop-kick her out of my mind. He demands to have me all to himself.

His metallic eyes cut through me, and I bleed desires I haven't allowed myself to have in years. Suddenly, Marcus isn't riding my cock anymore, the image shifting in an instant as I climb, hand over hand, to my peak. Now he's pushing my knee to my chest in a way that I don't even know if my body can handle yet, and then he's taking me. In real life, my hand tightens around myself, and my movements speed up. In my mind, I can feel him filling me, can feel his hot breath on the side of my neck before he bites, and his thrusts are harder and faster than I could probably handle. In real life, my other hand strays to the furl of my asshole, and at the first tentative press, I come harder than I've come in recent memory.

As I lie there in the aftermath, sweating and panting, my mind floods with new possibilities. It's actually kind of unlike me, but there are so many pleasures that I've denied myself, so many that I've suppressed because they didn't feel like my place to have. Since I knew I could never ask

Candace to top me, at the risk of weirding her out, all that desire had been shoved to a box at the back of my mind.

But as I come back down, I realize that Marcus probably wouldn't want that either. Not with me. That's not who I am to other people. I'm the one who gives. I enjoy giving. I'm good at making people feel good, and that makes me feel good too. Plus, I get to come either way, so it's not too big of a loss.

Anyway, I have to get out of this bed and get real with myself. I need to be able to function this week without obsessively thinking about bending Marcus over one of the plyometric boxes.

But I think I might do a little online sex-toy shopping today. As a treat.

By noon, my filthier thoughts have faded from a roar to faint static. I'm grading essays, and there are other pleasures to consider—like all the delicious literary feasts my students are discussing in their papers. Around the fourth one, my phone buzzes with a text message from Ellie.

So you're going through with it. I didn't know you'd actually ask him out for real though. Good for you.

Get some.

Of course she would see through me like this. She's like a heat-seeking missile for drama.

I didn't ask him out for real. He's just a good actor.

Are you kidding me???? He's kissing you!!!!!

On the cheek.

I don't want her to give me hope. I need her to stop trying to give me hope. I consider turning my phone off, but I'm all out of self-control, and I know I'd just turn it right back on.

Are you seriously going to tell me that look he was giving you isn't real? Because then he deserves a fucking Oscar.

Please hit that.

Except, he's really sweet, so maybe actually date him.

My stomach spins, like it's unspooling. I'd tried so hard to wind myself back up after letting go this morning, and here I am falling apart again. My thumbs linger over the tiny digital keyboard, but they refuse to come up with a clever answer.

The fact that you can't figure out what to say just tells me I'm right. Just make it happen, dude.

Since when are you having a crisis of confidence about this?

Now that's a question I can answer.

Since I had my heart ripped to pieces?

Since the person that I thought I would spend the rest of my life with decided to tell me everything about me is undesirable?

Or maybe when I realized the major power disparity between me and the person you're telling me that I should "Hit."

This time I am the one who is treated to the three dots appearing and disappearing in the corner of my screen.

Look, I get it. But he obviously likes you, trust me. And you deserve

a little happiness after everything that happened to you.

Also fuck Candace for making you feel like that. Fuck her forever.

I almost tell her that there's someone else I'd much rather fuck, but that would just be reloading her cannons for her to shoot me with later. That thought belongs inside my head, and inside my head only, for the foreseeable future.

Speak of the devil, a text from Marcus pops up as I'm still looking at my phone.

Thank you for dinner last night. And for comforting my anxieties. I am looking forward to our grand caper.

Two threads twist in my chest; one is that stubborn hope I can't seem to shake off. One is an ache that comes from the vulnerability he's shown me, the fact that he trusts me not to take advantage of him. I absolutely refuse to betray that trust. No matter what happens, even if I'm driving this whole escapade, Marcus is the one holding the map. I'll do whatever he thinks is best.

I take a deep breath and type out an answer.

Me too.

Thank you for trusting me. All I want is for you to feel comfortable.

I couldn't live with myself if I made another person I cared about feel trapped.

Thank god for context, because I manage to keep my thoughts pretty tame when I get to the gym on Tuesday. Being forced to work out until I'm totally incoherent is a great way to keep the blood flowing everywhere but where it would be awkward. On the other hand, Dylan and Bea keep looking over at Marcus and me, so I'm still a little bit self-conscious.

Eventually, we reach the end of the session—the part where my soul leaves my body, and I have no thoughts other than leaving sweat angels on the floor. That's when the two of them decide to come over.

"Congratulations." Bea winks at me, not for the first time. It makes me wonder if that's a thing that actually works for her on women, but then, who knows how successful Bea's love life is. "Can't say I'm super surprised you two got together," she says. "Whew—all that chemistry!"

"I super didn't notice." Dylan's voice is abnormally high.

"Course you didn't," she says.

Any chemicals that might scream "urgency" have already been used up. Plus, it's not as if us being together is a secret. Beside me, still on his feet, Marcus's jaw is tight. Weirdly, he's not nearly as relaxed about this as he was about talking to my mom. Or maybe it's not that weird. He does work here, after all, and Dylan does have a tendency to needle at him.

"I forgot you follow me on Instagram." There's finally enough breath in my lungs to talk, but I'm trying to keep my promise to myself to let Marcus lead the way. I don't want to say the wrong thing to the people he works with. If he wants to tell them it's fake, he's welcome to.

Instead he nods awkwardly and says, "Thank you."

"Wait, holy shit," Dylan says, looking as surprised as if he's just found out scallions and green onions were the same thing. "Bro, you're, like, really gay?"

"I am," he says, squaring his shoulders and lifting his chin. "Is that a problem?"

Now I am getting a little nervous. I try to get up as fast as I can without looking like I'm ready for a fight. Marcus isn't weak by any means, but putting him next to Dylan is like putting a ballet dancer next to a super-yoked swimmer. If Marcus's "guns" are shotgun barrels, Dylan's are bazookas.

But Dylan swiftly shakes his head. "Nah, man, I'm just sorry for the times I've been rude to you now."

Marcus's posture, already challenging, doesn't change. However, Bea rounds on Dylan. "Excuse the fuck out of me? Were you saying homophobic shit behind my back?"

Dylan takes not one, but two, steps back from her. "No, no, no, I just was kind of a dick in general, and like, I don't want to be a dick to the gays."

I can't help it. I burst out laughing, doubled over with my hands on my knees. There's an abrupt cackle next to me, and Marcus covers his mouth, too.

"That–that's great, Dill." Bea forces the words out in between wheezes. "We can go to the allyship bakery and get you a cookie after this."

"My cheat day's not 'til tomorrow," he says as they wander away, and Bea grabs a foam roller off the wire shelf against the wall. I don't think he's being ironic.

When I turn back to Marcus, he's wiping his mouth with his hand, as if he's trying to physically pull the tension out of his jaw. The thought pops up in my head that I wish I could take care of that for him, so I guess that window of appropriate thought has closed.

"You okay?"

He nods. "I did not expect to have that conversation today."

I cringe inwardly, because it's obviously my fault that he's been outed to whoever happens to look at my Instagram. "Sorry," I say.

He flinches like I've thrust a picture I want him to see too close to his face. "Why are you sorry? It was my choice to do this with you, and I have no regrets."

There's this weird prickling feeling that I get at the back of my throat, like I want to gag or cry or just smile bigger than my face can actually handle. There's one thing that I do know, and that's that I can't speak in response to that. Fortunately, he doesn't seem to expect me to. I think I smile at him before heading back over to where I've ditched my gym bag.

"When am I invited over?" he says, taking me completely by surprise.

I almost say 'whenever you want', but I stop myself before I can sound too desperate. "Thursday night? When you're all done here?"

"I suppose I'll see you Thursday, then," he says with a nod. His eyes dart over to where Bea and Dylan still stand, and he cocks his head like he's asking me a silent question.

I'm sure the look he's giving me right now is supposed to mean something, but I'm not sure what.

Until he kisses me, that is.

It's chaste and quick. Too quick for me to register before he has pulled back. But it's still a kiss, and still noticeable enough for Bea to yell, "Get a room!"

I try not to look shocked. I try not to break character. But I also try not to think about how I'd respond if this were real—because if it were, I'd never let him get away with a kiss that light. But for now, I'll take whatever he's willing to give and enjoy it while I still can.

12

FAMILY RULES

It's one of those days. The kind that, for the past few months, had been blissfully few and far between. But in the past few weeks, they've been showing up as frequently as they did just a few months after Candace left.

It's the sort of day where I wake up hyper-aware of how empty my bed is, and the fact that there's nobody to say goodbye to as I head out the door for work. For the first time in months, I totally forget to make a half-pot of coffee instead of a full one.

On days like this, not even blasting my emergency playlist helps (I know things are bad when not even Wham! cheers me up). On days like this, my loneliness absorbs extra sound, and it sucks out extra energy along with it.

It's obviously because of this wedding that I'm feeling worse and worse. It's because I'm going to see her again.

And it's because I'm going to see her with one of the worst people I know. At a wedding. For my younger sister.

Things aren't much better when I get home from the gym, even though I've already seen Marcus once today, and he's coming over for dinner. Somehow it makes me feel worse. All I can think about is how it's just an illusion, no more real than the last few years of my relationship with Candace had been.

But when I hear the clicking latch and squeaking hinges of my back gate, I react like a golden retriever whose owner has just pulled into the driveway. If my ears could perk up, or if I had a tail to wag, that's exactly what would be happening. The only thing that saves my dignity is that I manage not to run to the door before he can get to it.

He gives me a breathless hello. As he unclips his helmet, I'm treated to the sight of his hair, usually impeccably styled, matted and askew in a way that not even the gym can evoke. All I can think about is getting a fistful of it, so I force myself to talk over my own thoughts.

"So, if you've been here once, you operate by family rules and make yourself comfortable. Grab yourself a drink, decimate my bookshelf again, whatever you want." I turn around to check the meat thermometer, just for the sake of taking a break from being seen.

"In that case, I'll just be a moment," he says, heading for the hall bathroom.

After he gets back, his hair is completely tamed again. I let myself entertain the thought that he'd done that for me. That he cares how he looks for me. And then I absolutely have to stop thinking about it before I make an ass of myself.

He's wearing one of those white Daniel Johnston t-shirts with a little cartoon alien on it. Like the rest of his shirts, it's threadbare, tight around the shoulders and chest, and riding up over his black studded belt. As he comes around the kitchen island and leans his hip against it, I catch a strip of snowy bare skin.

"You're really cooking for me?" He sounds genuinely surprised, as if I hadn't already told him that I would.

"No, you can't have any. Gonna eat it in front of you," I say. He pouts adorably, and if he were my real boyfriend, I'd lean in and kiss it off his lips. "Don't be ridiculous. You're my guest. Plus, it's just roast chicken. Easy."

"I cannot recall the last time someone cooked for only me," he says, and my heart is in a straitjacket.

"Criminal. Well, that's one of the perks of being friends with me. Just ask Ellie." I don't know why I threw that in. Maybe because I'm afraid to make him feel too singled out, like I think he's special. It's really stupid of me, because he is special, and he clearly needs to be reminded more often.

I'm not sure I've ever seen someone devour a chicken so thoroughly. I almost wish I'd cooked something with marrow in it so I could watch him crack one of the bones open and suck it out. And if that's the most pervy thought I have all night, I'll be doing ok. (It won't be. I know myself well enough to know it won't be.)

"We should probably get all the boring details all out on the table," I say. Really, I'm not sure why it's taken so long to get here. It's probably because I've just been enjoying his company so much for the past week, I'd lost sight of the real reason we're spending time together.

Marcus straightens and interlaces his fingers, as if he's sat down at a roulette table. Then, he raises a single eyebrow at me. Maybe he doesn't know how sexy he looks when he does that, but I bet he does. Bastard.

I push through the distraction. "First, there's a bachelorette party next week. I don't know if you're going to be free, but if you are..."

"I can be. Where will it be?"

"The rest of the wedding party is coming up here from, like, Sherman Oaks and Santa Monica or wherever else, and we're probably going to do the club-hopping thing downtown." I spare a cringing wish that I won't run into any of my students. "We might be the only guys, and I think Candace will be there, so…"

"So, I'm especially needed?"

"Yeah," I nod, relieved he understands.

"May I…" he begins, then clamps his mouth shut.

"You can ask me whatever you want." I know Marcus would never ask me a question just to be hurtful. Sometimes he can be a bitch, and I adore that about him, but he doesn't do it when he's concerned about me, apparently.

"What happened between the two of you?"

The only reason I know that I'm jiggling my leg is because I see ripples in my wine glass. I suck in a breath through my nose to steady myself.

"Kind of a boring story," I say. It really is. That's part of what makes it so awful. "We got together after college. Met through some friends whose names I don't remember. The first several years were really fun, and we were good partners to each other basically the whole time. But after a while we started to drift apart, and I think I started to sort of annoy her, but I never could figure out what I'd done wrong."

She'd stopped laughing at my jokes. She'd started working very long hours, and no, she wasn't cheating on me, unless she was KGB-levels of sneaky. The extra work was mostly done at home, and if I ever surprised her at work, I'd always find her hunched over her laptop.

"We didn't really fight. She'd get irritated with me, but she was usually really civil. It was just..." Lonely. Desperately lonely. "I thought she might be annoyed that I hadn't proposed after ten years together, even though she'd never brought it up that entire time. Proposing to her was kind of a Hail Mary, and that was when she finally admitted that she wasn't in love with me anymore."

There's another soft pout on Marcus's lips, mostly due to how he's balanced his chin on one upturned palm. A moment passes, in which he's probably waiting for me to say something else. Then he sits up, lips tipping into a cheerless smile.

"Plans seldom unfold the way we think they will," he says.

I wince. "I'm sorry for whining. What happened to me totally doesn't compare with what happened to you."

"Then don't compare them. Heartbreak is heartbreak. It is irrelevant whose pain is worse."

For a split second, I think I might be able to breathe, but then I realize this conversation is going to get even more awkward. There's a gnawing in my stomach that should not be there after the meal we just ate.

"So as long as we're having uncomfortable conversations, maybe we should talk about money. All the wedding stuff is pretty pricey, and you're doing me a huge favor, so I don't want you to have to take on a bunch of...but also I don't want you to feel like..."

"Like a male escort?" he asks.

My cheeks are suddenly very hot. Now, we're dancing far too close to his trauma. "Exactly."

"I'd prefer not to be thought of that way," he says.

"I don't—"

"I know you don't." He puts a hand up to stop me from the long string of excuses I was about to make for myself. "However, I am not sure I can...if it's going to be a formal event, and out of town..."

"Right," I say. "How about this: I take care of transportation, rent you a suit"—I try not to linger on the mental image of him in a tailored suit—"and your, um, hotel."

Cool, that's an even worse place to linger. However, the ball is in his court, so I have to sit with it. He actually gulps, and my eyes fix on the bob of his Adam's apple like the hopeless case that I am. The only thing I can do to stop myself from gawking is close my eyes, then redirect my gaze to my empty plate. The silverware is jiggling the slightest bit, and I dig my fingers into my leg to keep it still.

"I can get us two beds, or I can even see if we can get you an adjoining room or something. If you're not comfortable sharing," I say.

"But that would likely not support our ruse."

Our ruse. My head snaps up, but his eyes are now fixed on the decimated chicken carcass in the center of the table.

"I am not opposed to sharing a bed when necessary. We are adults."

My mouth waters, the way it does when I bake cookies, and that sweet smell permeates every corner of the house. "Ok. That makes things easier," I say.

Does it though? Or does it make everything a lot more difficult?

"So, ready to talk logistics?" I ask.

I'm a little surprised when he stands up and retrieves his backpack, then I remember he just has a flip phone. I've totally forgotten what it's like not to have access to a million calendars and reminder and to-do list apps to keep my life together. It's miraculous that I got through college without them. Instead it was all Post-it notes and planners full of my own handwriting that I couldn't read half the time.

Marcus pulls an honest-to-god Mead notebook out of his backpack. It's covered in stickers, the free kind they hand out at indie bookstores and microbreweries, and the bits that show between them have been mauled by colored pens. The familiar sense of curiosity I have about him flares up again. I am desperate to know what happens in his head, because these little flourishes tell me it's got to be so much more than I can imagine.

I slowly give him each date, along with the address of the venue off the Pacific Coast Highway where the wedding will be. He fills it all in like a timeline, refusing to let me jump around the way I might normally. Every stroke of his pen is deliberate, just as confident as his drawings.

By the end of our conversation, he's written out every milestone in the next three weeks. I try not to think about how it's a detailed map that leads straight to the end of our time together.

Then he's on his feet, zipping the notebook away and picking up both of our plates to take to the sink.

"You don't have to do that," I say.

"You said we're operating by family rules," he says a little petulantly. "That means you let me help."

The words lodge in my heart like he's used it as a dartboard. I swallow back the gigantic cotton ball that's suddenly taken up residence in my throat.

"Save the bones, I make broth out of them," I say, voice frustratingly rough. The appreciative look he gives me is emboldening. "I make some mean soups when the weather's right, even though it doesn't really get wintry here ever."

"Broth is useful during any season, I'd imagine," he says.

"That's right, all you fitness people are freaks for bone broth." Fitness influencers are notorious for taking normal food that people have eaten for ages and turning it into something gimmicky. "It's criminal how expensive they've made that stuff."

Marcus nods. "I'm inclined to agree. If I had the...time..."—he says time as if he's deliberately settled on the wrong word for some reason—"I would follow your lead. As it is, I'm restricted to bouillon cubes."

"In that case, I'm bringing you a jar on Tuesday," I say. "But don't tell Dylan. He can't have any." He sets the bones from our plates on the platter with the rest of the carcass, then sets his sights on the mess I've made of the stove as I was cooking the rice pilaf. I know, I know, clean as you go. Not my forte.

The confident way he moves through the kitchen, how he easily finds the storage containers and scolds me for using plastic instead of glass, makes it so I can't bring myself to shoo him away. Maybe it's because someone demanding to help me is like the satisfaction of walking out of a dingy lecture hall and getting a face full of sea air.

But maybe I just like having him close by. I'm not ashamed to admit that to myself, although it's starting to make me heartsick. You never really think about how kindness can hurt when you don't get enough of it. It's a bit like the gym, actually, that sore feeling of muscle microtears. But then they mend themselves, and you're stronger for it. Maybe Marcus is doing the same thing to my heart as he did to my muscles.

Or else it's just my body anticipating how much it'll hurt after the wedding, when this is all over.

13

SAD-SACK ZACK NIGHT

It's impressive how two men can sprawl enough to completely monopolize a four-seater couch. Ellie would be horrified if she were here. Thankfully, she's not, although for the amount of action between Marcus and me, she might as well be. I am being a total saint tonight. It's kind of annoying, actually. Case in point: I have made green tea for us to drink rather than opening another bottle of wine.

The recessed lighting is dimmed, and Marcus's normally angular features have softened around the edges. I don't know whether it's my imagination or if he's just that relaxed. Either way, it would be better to have something on the screen to distract me from what I'd rather be doing with him.

Marcus digs in his backpack, then pops back up with a quiet, yet delighted, "aha!" and brandishes a nylon zip-up case. It's shiny black, although some of the piping is frayed into dull charcoal.

"Oh my god, you've transported us to 1999." I put a hand to my cheek in pseudo-shock.

"1990 actually," he says. Clearly, he appreciates the opportunity to be the most correct person in the room, and I am not going to stand in his way. "That is, if you're still open to me forcing my tastes on you."

I switch on the TV and adjust the settings before I can tell him he can force whatever he wants on me. Or tell him it isn't possible for him to force something on me, because I'll take whatever he wants to give.

He weaves around an armchair to kneel in front of the entertainment center. There are more dials and mini-screens than there are at the International Space Station, and I'm about to give him directions when he spots the DVD player and sets the disk in the drawer. It makes me wonder whether there will be anything I have to explain to him before he figures it out on his own. He always seems to be a couple steps ahead of me.

The whole show famously revolves around the dead girl trope, where everyone is a suspect in the murder of the blonde homecoming queen. I'd expected that, but mostly, I'd expected a kind of campy '90s show. What I get is a surprisingly heart-wrenching pilot episode featuring a lot of very fresh grief. Technically, being an English professor should mean tropes like this shouldn't get to me. But books don't quite feel the same as movies and TV, not to me, anyway. When I read, I can mostly control what images my mind conjures up. Not so here.

By the time the first ten minutes have passed, I can feel a little hitch in my throat that I struggle to breathe around. I've always had a hard time seeing fictional women hurt and killed like this, and hearing people crying, no matter how fake it is. It kind of makes it difficult to watch, well, anything.

Sheesh, if that doesn't say something about our culture, I'm not sure what does.

Any other night, I'd be able to stick it out—maybe sit through long enough to get to all the fun kitschy stuff I'd expected. However, after feeling like the loneliest garbage can in the tri-county area all day, I don't seem to have the fortitude.

"Are you all right?" I jump at the sudden sound of Marcus's voice, realizing how lost in my own head I'd been.

"Um—" I try to talk, but if I say anything else, my voice might shake. As far as I'm concerned, that would put tonight firmly in the 'disaster' category.

"You don't have to keep watching it if it's upsetting you." He only studies me for another second before he picks up the remote control from where it sits between us and hits stop. The menu comes up, an eerie landscape of fog and conifers. "Zack?"

I blink a couple of times and take a long breath through my nose. "Fuck, I'm sorry. I guess I'm a little sensitive today. Sometimes seeing stuff like that brings up some bad memories."

Marcus's face pales, and I quickly reroute.

"Shit. No. Nobody got murdered. Sorry," I say. "It's just...ah, you know? I don't need to get into all that."

His lips press together, then part as the tension in his mouth moves up to crease his forehead. "If you want to, I can listen."

"Yeah, well, this was supposed to be fun, and it's turning into Sad-Sack-Zack night." I'm trying to laugh this off, but it's just not working. "But I'll tell you about it another time?"

"I thought we were supposed to be getting to know each other better." He tilts his chin in a gentle challenge, and I can't back down from it.

"All right, all right. You win."

I'm just going to have to try really, really hard to keep it together, but I remind myself that everything is okay; she's safe and healthy and happy, and so am I. Mostly.

"When we were kids, Katie and I ended up being pretty close," I say, "but there was that phase where she was just my pain-in-the-ass little sister. I was nine and she was five and always wanted to hang around me."

As I speak, it occurs to me that Marcus is younger than my little sister. I'm still not sure how I feel about that.

"So there was a day where I got sick of her following me around. Me and the kids across the street—who were my age—were playing soccer. And I finally yelled at her to leave us alone, and she started crying, then she started running home."

"Oh." Marcus, a step ahead of me as usual, knows where this is headed.

I nod. "Yeah. Straight into traffic."

There's a lot that I don't remember about that day. A lot that I've worked on not remembering too vividly. My parents had put me in therapy to help me process what had happened and gave me plenty of assurance that they didn't blame me. But I remember running to my mom while everyone around me panicked, and how she ran right past me and—badass that she has always been—jumped right into action. I also remember the way Katie looked on the ground and, later, in her hospital bed.

"Christ." His body is turned toward me, feet now tucked underneath him as he listens so attentively that you'd think I was going to assign homework on it.

"She was in the hospital for a long time, and it was really, really hard to see her like that," I say. "So sometimes stuff like that just gets to me. Not all the time, just sometimes."

"Understandably," he murmurs.

"Anyway, I kind of overcompensated after she got better. Once I didn't feel too guilty to visit her, you know. Got really protective, spent loads of time with her, punched some bullies—just the boys, obviously. But let's be honest, I probably would have done that anyway."

God, he has got to stop smiling at me like that. I scramble for a way to lighten the mood, but all I can think to do is lean forward to retrieve my mug of tea. There are only dregs at the bottom of the mug, but I drink it anyway. It tastes exactly like Sad-Sack-Zack night feels.

"It's probably why I let her get away with so much, too."

"Like keeping your ex in her wedding party?"

I nearly choke on spent tea leaves. "Well, yeah, but I'm pretty sure Marta demanded that. She and Candace got really close over the years. And it's not like Candace did anything heinous. Just..."

"Just pretended to love you for years to avoid 'making it awkward,'" he says, oozing disdain.

Maybe a few months ago that would have made me defensive, but it feels kind of nice to have one more person on my team. Ellie does a lot of heavy lifting in that area. Talking about the breakup around my family was delicate. It wasn't often that I got to talk to my mom on her own, and I worried that anything I said to Katie might find its way through Marta and back to Candace.

Marcus cares about me, at least in this way. And it's in a way that I need more people to care about me. Whatever else happens, I'm happy to have this.

But also, I'm pretty sure I'm falling in love. "You salty bitch."

"I think you like that about me."

Whatever I was about to say dies in my throat and transforms into a wheezing laugh. It takes me a moment to recover myself, though I'm still grasping for something to say, something to do that will keep me from just staring at him like he's this evening's show. It hits me that the whole pretense for our getting together tonight is gone, and we've probably reached the end of our time together unless I can quickly come up with some other reason for him to stay.

But naturally, before I can, he does it for me.

"Perhaps we should have a palate cleanser. Something you prefer," he says.

It suddenly registers that he's not going to run away from me, not tonight. Apparently, he really does like me and doesn't just tolerate me. It's hard not to second-guess that feeling after everything that happened with Candace, but nobody's looked at me this way in a very, very long time.

Be that as it may, I made a promise to myself I'd be a safe person for him. If he feels more than friendship for me, he'll have to make the first move.

"Oh, the true test of your mettle—the infinite streaming scroll." I reach over to where he'd set the remote control on the coffee table.

He snorts, bouncing down from his perch and resuming a comfortable sprawl. "I'll take your word for it."

"What does that mean?"

"I only watch physical DVDs," he says, as if it's not the weirdest thing he's said all night.

"How? How am I the academic, yet you're the pretentious one?"

He blinks as if a fly has landed on the tip of his nose, grimacing with exaggerated horror. "Pretentious? Me? A spurious accusation!"

"Spurious—"

"And how am I the trainer, and yet you're the meathead jock?"

Nope, no follow-up. Too overwhelmed by seeing him come charging out of his shell just so he can own the fuck out of me.

"Why, Professor Carter, are you at a loss for words?" His tone and posture are puffed up, imperious, and it's so sexy I am about to tackle him. With enormous effort, I dig my teeth into my bottom lip and wedge myself into the back and arm of the couch. Marcus gloats as if he's beaten me at Monopoly, eyes on me long enough that the grin slowly relaxes into something more thoughtful.

"I should apologize, actually. For Tuesday."

For a second, I try to remember whether I'd fallen over a box again or pinched my finger while re-racking the bar. Nothing's coming to mind. Marcus looks puzzled at my slow uptake.

"For kissing you? Without your permission?"

Oh, as if that would ever bother me. The only complaint I have is that he hasn't done it since, but if he's so concerned that he's offended me, that is probably too much to hope for.

"I just thought it'd make things more realistic and I thought you'd caught my signals..." he tilts his head a little, trying to clue me in on a secret language. I'm all for learning to read him, but apparently, I'm not there yet.

"Nope," I say. "I don't know if you've noticed, but I'm oblivious as hell. It's incredible I even got a high school diploma, much less a doctorate."

He snorts. "I figured it might help make our act more convincing..."

"It's totally fine. Inspired, in fact."

Just like he said. It's 'our act,' not something real. And yes, I knew that's what it was right after it happened. As much as I've thought about it, trying to isolate a memory of the way it felt outside the overwhelming surprise, I haven't fooled myself into thinking it mattered. To him.

"However, I thought we might need something more potent for the outing next weekend, if we're to make an impression."

My stomach flops like a sea lion hurling itself out of the water in its enclosure. He can't mean what I think he means—a full-on display in front of my ex as an act of revenge. Dear god, I fucking love him.

"Damn, Marcus. I'd thought you'd just be there for moral support, but you're out for blood, aren't you?"

There's a sudden flash of apprehension on Marcus's face, like he's walked into the wrong lecture hall. I have to say something before he backtracks.

"Sounds great. I'm in. What did you have in mind?"

That does the trick. He moves closer, and I shift so he can draw up to my side. My pulse is hammering so hard and fast that I'm afraid he can see it through the thin skin of my throat. Then his face, the razor-sharp eyes, the plush, pouting lips, are inches away.

"Something like this..."

He leans closer, stopping short so he can reel me in that final ten percent, so he knows that I want it. The game is fucking impeccable, and so is this kiss—hotter, more luxurious than the one he'd given me Tuesday. His lips are even softer than they look, hiding a wicked tongue that traces the inside of my upper lip and turns every nerve in my spinal column to flashing neon.

He pulls back a few inches, face glowing with the pride of a conqueror. "Acceptable?"

I might be letting him drive here, doing my best to make him feel safe, but here's the thing. Well, two things, actually. One, he made the first move. Two, I am extremely competitive.

So I wrestle the eye contact away until I'm sure that I'm the one holding his gaze captive. "I don't know," I say. "I think I need more data."

I don't risk him moving away any further. Lifting my hand to the side of his face, I pull him right back in. I'm less artful than he was, forceful and a little sloppy. But that's who I am. It's the horse he hitched his wagon to, if for only this short span of time. He doesn't back away a single inch. In the end, I do, leaving him out of breath, clumps of dark hair falling over wild eyes.

"Yeah, that'll do it. We'll fool them all," I say with forced casualness.

Then I wait. It's his go. It's his turn to show me that this wasn't just a flex, that it was more than an escalation in a fun little game he thinks we're playing.

He doesn't take it. He sits back, studies my face, and gives me an appreciative smile. So, at least he didn't hate it. But the longer he looks at me, the more it seems like that this was just what he said it was—part of a spiteful little conspiracy. I'm happy to be in it with him, even if I'm a little let down.

There's unfortunately no more kissing, but he does take my arm, set it around his own shoulders, and make himself comfortable against my side. I've never been more confused, but I give him a squeeze as I look for something extremely unromantic to put on the TV.

14

CURTAIN UP!

Candide was a good choice for Katie and Marta's party, and I pulled for it hard while the girls were planning. It's the sort of place where I could call someone and plan the menu in advance. Maybe that makes me sound like landed gentry, but I really couldn't care less. It cuts the chaos, and the decibel level, in half. So, on top of Katie's voice—which could drown out a drill sergeant—people won't be talking over each other to give complicated orders. Everything's just out on the table already, so to speak.

And that brings me to the biggest perk: the fact that this back room is completely isolated. My sister and her friends can shout all they want.

I'm sitting in the seat closest to the corridor, here right on time for our reservation and about fifteen minutes before I expect anyone to show up. Other than Marcus, that is, who appears from behind the privacy curtain wearing the same outfit he wore to the theater. I'm not complaining in the slightest; in fact, I'm very gratified to see the return of that gorgeous, form-fitting top. The sunset, glowing through the bank of windows behind me, paints his bone-white skin in warm pastels and makes his garnet earring sparkle.

I stand when he approaches and pull out a chair for him beside me. Instead of sitting down right away, he presses a kiss to the corner of my mouth. I'm stunned motionless, and as he takes his seat, Marcus looks like he knows he's just answered every question right on one of my quizzes.

"Nobody was here to see that," I say, not a single drop of reproach in my voice.

He looks at me haughtily. "I'm endeavoring to get into character, thank you very much."

"Oh, is it so difficult?"

I sit too as his eyes sweep over the long banquet-style table and land on my place setting. Then he shakes his head, smirking.

"What?"

"Nothing. Only that you are embodying the stereotype of what Jackie calls 'a bisexual disaster.'" He gestures to the cluster of glasses sitting in front of me. There's a glass of pinot noir, a glass of soda water, and a negroni, all with a sip or two taken out of them. Well, the pinot might have more than a couple sips.

Sue me, I'm nervous.

"Hey, I'm not driving tonight, and I intend to have a good time," I say. I leave out the part about how anxious I am, because I'm pretty sure he knows already. I was pretty weird in our training sessions this past week, but thankfully, he'd gone easy on me.

"Make more affectionately biphobic jokes in front of Marta if you want her to like you."

"Noted," he says, looking curiously at my cocktail. "What is that?"

"A negroni—gin, campari, sweet vermouth. Would you like one?"

He hesitates in a similar way he had when we'd gone out for dinner. There must be some lingering uncertainty about the whole money thing. That's no good.

"Look, get anything you want tonight, all right? I want you to. This is supposed to be fun. You can spend my money and then slap me across the face and leave if you want, and I won't regret a thing," I say. Maybe a little hyperbolic, but at this point I'd do just about anything to convince him that I'm not out to manipulate him.

"Is that something that interests you?"

Is it me, or did his voice get a little huskier?

I'm about to fall out of my chair when Dana, our server, shows up. Marcus deftly orders "one of these," gesturing to my drink, as I sweat horrifically.

"Oh, and just so you know, Candace is the one—"

"I know what Candace looks like," he cuts me off.

For a moment, my insides somersault as I try to remember whether there were still pictures of her around the house. That would definitely send the wrong message. But I'm pretty sure I didn't do that. There probably are some left up on my Instagram, though, because taking them down would also have felt kind of pathetic. We were together for almost a decade; it's not like me taking her pictures off my timeline would change that.

"Wait a minute, I thought you didn't have social media," I say.

There's mischief in his eyes when he says, "I do not. However, Jackie does."

An image of him blooms in my mind. In it, he's craning his neck over his best friend's shoulder as they cyberstalk my ex together. I'm kind of flattered and also dying to know what was said about me. And about her. And about, well, probably a lot of other people in my life.

"So you probably know what everyone else in my family looks like, too," I say. He shrugs. "Even my Aunt Linda?"

"Yes. She has some...strong opinions about alternative medicine," he says.

"I wouldn't recommend sitting next to her," I say, and he chuckles. I grasp for a subject change, "Hopefully, I wasn't the only source of entertainment at the cast party."

"It was not the cast party. I was there to go over the sketches I've been working on for their next production," he says. His eyes flick down to his hands and stay there, leaving me with a perfect view of his eyelashes again. "The cast party is next weekend, if you would like to come with me."

It warms me up inside to hear that he wants me there, more than any negroni ever could. "Of course!" I say. "I think I can probably hold my own with that crew."

Marcus's smile widens, turning me to putty. "I am eager to see you try."

No clever retort comes to mind before Dana reappears and sets his drink in front of him. He looks at it suspiciously before taking a sip. His face scrunches slightly.

"Uh-oh, you hate it," I say, reaching for it, ready to call Dana back to get something different.

He gently shoves me away with the hand that isn't holding a drink. "I do not hate it. I just need to adjust to the flavor." He keeps his hand on my chest as he takes another sip. Then he makes a big show of sighing, eyes rolling up to the ceiling in exaggerated ecstasy.

"Smartass," I mutter.

The hand on my chest drifts up to grip my shoulder. He sets the drink down, then cups my chin with his newly free hand. It's a little cool, a little wet with condensation, and before I realize what's about to happen, his mouth is on mine again.

It's quick, but it's just enough to filter through every cell in my body until each one is overfull, expanding with the heat that comes just from the touch of his lips and his tongue teasing at mine.

"Careful," I say as he draws back, eyes twinkling. I'm amazed at how steady my breathing is. "You keep doing that, and I'm going to think you actually enjoy kissing me."

"Is that not permitted?" His eyes are still on my lips, his voice striking a frequency that feels like it's coming from the center of my own chest. Then his glance shifts to over my shoulder. He wiggles his eyebrows as he, heartbreakingly, sits back. "They're here."

Ah. So the curtain's up.

I turn in my seat, and sure enough, the literal burlap curtain has been pushed aside, and women are streaming into the room from the hallway. My sister and sister-in-law-to-be lead the way in a ballet-pink dress and cream linen pant suit respectively. Katie gives me a mock-scandalized look, and I know everyone must have seen Marcus kiss me. That's probably why he'd done it in the first place.

There's a desolate pang at the pit of my stomach that I really don't have time for, but it's soothed a little by a citrusy perfume that's been a part of my life since I was sixteen years old.

"Quackers!" Katie shrieks as she throws her arms around my waist and squeezes. Then she rears back and baps me in the pec. There's enough muscle there by now that I barely feel it. "That's for me having to find out about your boyfriend on Instagram."

"Wow! You've been saving up that one," I say, rubbing my not-at-all-sore chest indulgently. Her smile looks recently whitened, skin pink and glowy from whatever treatment they'd all gotten at spa earlier.

"She really has been. Hasn't shut up about it all day," Marta says. Her dark hair is pulled back, so none of it gets in my face as she leans in and kisses me on the cheek.

Sassy bitches that they are, they're both wearing cross-body sashes that read "One V for Eternity." I chuckle. Mom must have hated that. As if reading my mind, Katie looks down and rubs the satin between her thumb and forefinger.

"Yeah, Mom says that she'd 'switch out our wedding cake for crab cakes' if I didn't get one photo without the writing."

I start to reach for my pocket. "Do you want me to just—"

"Nah!" she waves as if shooing away an invisible bee. "I'll just doctor the footage later."

"You rebel, you," I say. But she's already turned her attention to Marcus, who's standing nearby, face almost jarringly relaxed.

She hunches a little, extending her hands like she's asking a toddler for permission to pick him up. "Do you hug?"

"I'll hug you," Marcus says. The slight smile actually looks genuine, and, welp, that ache in my stomach is back with a vengeance as she springs into his open arms. There's actually a lump in my throat. God, what have I done?

The ambient volume in the room rises, as Marta puts her hand out to give Marcus's a strong shake. For all that she seemed to have been fucking with me when she invited Candace, she's not giving off any hostility toward either of us.

That's because this isn't about me. I keep trying to remind myself of that. It's Marta's right to include her close friends in her special day. And I'm a mature adult. And to be fair, I never let myself show her how devastated I was by Candace leaving me. And—

An arm slips around my waist; fingers digging into my side pull me out of the gyre I'm circling. Marcus's thigh, up to the hip bone, is flush against mine, like he's ready to help me walk if he needs to. It's not a moment too soon, because there she is now, standing at Marta's side.

Candace's mouth is schooled into a tight smile. There are a few more fine lines at the corners of her eyes than there were the last time I saw her, and a lot less meat on her bones. LA people probably think that makes her look better, but it makes me think maybe this all has been harder on her than I thought it might be.

But not harder than it's been on me. That much I'm sure of.

"How are you, Zack?" Her eyes volley from me to Marcus and back. She looks like she wants to lean in to hug me, but Marcus has inched forward, as if he's ready to step in between us if she tries. It makes it so what I say next isn't a lie.

"Pretty good, actually. This is Marcus." Marcus is stone-still. I nudge him with my hip in a silent message not to lay it on so thick. Not that it's not an enormous turn-on, because it really, really is.

"Hello." His voice is like ice, a thousand degrees cooler than it was the day we met.

Her bottom lip disappears between her teeth, the mask of politeness she'd put on slipping enough for me to see her discomfort. It should feel vindicating, but it honestly just makes me a little sick.

Then, Marta sets a hand on her shoulder. "Come on, Candy. Wine." She nods toward the center of the table, then back at me. "Thanks for all this again, Zack."

Candace lets Marta herd her away from Marcus and me. Katie all but skips after them, wiggling her fingers at the two of us. Marcus's arm loosens around my waist; then he's got his hand on the center of my back and is coaxing me into my chair.

He leans toward me until I can feel his breath hot against the hinge of my jaw. "Are you all right?" he murmurs.

And because that interaction drained all my self-control, I hear myself saying, "I'd be better if you kissed me again."

And I'll be damned if he doesn't smile and do exactly that.

15

A LITTLE YOUNG

The sky is a dark blue-violet when we leave the restaurant. I'm not sure how much I've had to drink—at least one cocktail and a few glasses of wine. But since my tolerance is pretty high, there's no telling whether this fuzzy feeling in my head is because of the drink or because every time Marcus touches me, I vibrate a little faster.

And he's been touching me a lot. His hands strayed to my knee every time he caught me glancing nervously over my shoulder. He twined our fingers together between courses. He leaned his head on his hand and ran his thumb over my knuckles as he listened to my dumb little stories and cooking tricks.

Now, we trail after the rest of the party. Usually, being so close to the Pacific Ocean, there's a nip in the air. Tonight, I'd almost call the air sultry. Or that might just be the look Marcus shoots me, sidelong, when he thinks I'm not looking.

"I'll probably have to skip our training sessions this week with finals," I say, trying to keep from looking as disappointed as I feel. It's scary how much his permission actually matters to me, but the surprise has worn away. He's got me to the point where I'll basically do anything for him, and he has to know it.

"Considering this will be the first week you're missing since you began, I'll allow it." His arm tightens around me in a quick but reassuring squeeze.

One of the women walking in front of us makes a frustrated noise. She's wearing don't-fuck-with-me hoop earrings and fuck-me heels, although she is limping enough that they're definitely fuck-my-life heels by now. I'd worn a pair of shoes like that as a gag for some school spirit event once and could barely walk by lunchtime.

"Katieeee, do you even know where we're go-iiiiiing?" She shouts loud enough to be heard where Katie and Marta are walking arm in arm.

By now, I don't ask Marta and Katie questions like that when we go out. For all their differences in temperament, they're an intimidating team. Right now, I assume we're on our way to a club, but for all I know they could be dragging us to the beach to murder us in pickup volley-ball or to one of the fake Irish bars to spank everyone in pub trivia.

"Don't ask questions, bitch," Marta calls back over her shoulder. "That's my wife!"

"Not yeeeeeet!" Katie wobbles a little bit as she turns to Marta for a peck on the lips. I'm not sure how much she had to drink at Candide, but I'm guessing it'll be a lot by the end of the night.

I love my sister, but she's a beanpole, and the term "white girl wasted" may have been invented just for her.

Finally, we end up in front of a club with a neon sign that reads 'Snappers' featuring a bloated game fish, its cherry-red mouth opening and shutting.

"You can't be serious! Isn't this a gay club?" The woman in the hoop earrings sounds like she's been in the desert without water for weeks rather than walking away from one of the best meals of her life (yes, I am confident enough in my own taste to say that).

"Um, hello!" Katie gestures between herself and Marta with one hand and hangs off her shoulder with the other. Marta puts two steadying hands on her waist, and I really am loving the fact that it's now someone else's responsibility to care for her when she's drunk. What could be more romantic?

"Yeah, but like, for men," the woman says.

"The website says it's inclusive. As long as the straights don't act like assholes," Marta says.

"Besides, we have two whole men here!" Katie says, raising a hand to point at Marcus and me as she sways. Then, she throws a fist in the air as if she's leading us into battle. "Let's fucking go!"

It's not quite as bad inside as what you'd expect from a place called Snappers. They're not playing gay porn on the screens that line the walls—just music videos from the '90s and early '00s. Around here, with all the tourism, the wine tastings, and the WASP weddings, it wouldn't be a super smart move for a downtown bar to be that niche.

The bar looks like the hull of a ship, complete with portholes underneath the counter and nets rigged to the ceiling. For our homebase (a.k.a. the purse babysitting station), we settle on a booth underneath a 3D painting of a burly pirate almost completely encased in tentacles aside from his absurdly large, hairy chest.

"I'm buying you a drink. Negroni?" Marcus releases me as I sit. The tabletop and benches quickly fill with tufted clutches and designer shoulder bags.

I nod. "Take my card," I say, reaching into my back pocket and drawing out my wallet.

He bats my hand away as if I'm trying to show him a millipede. "Unacceptable. I'm buying you a drink." There's a surprising amount of intensity in his face, and my mind flashes back to our talk about his boundaries and issues with feeling like he owes someone a debt.

I put my wallet back in my pocket. "Anything you say, sir." I say it as loudly and theatrically as possible, and the smolder I get in return makes me glad I'm sitting down.

As Marcus follows the ladies to the bar, someone with an uncannily familiar face slides into the booth across from me. I caught sight of them earlier in my periphery, but I had been so involved in talking to Marcus that I'd never given them my focus. Too late, I realize they can totally tell I'm staring at them, but they're generous enough to offer me a smile in return.

"I get the feeling we're about to be on purse-watching duty," they say. It's the voice, familiar, if slightly more nasal, that finally tips me off.

"Maddie? Is that..."

"It's Mads now. They/he," they offer, helpfully.

"Holy shit, you look amazing! Congratulations!"

"Thanks!" Mads is grinning now. Our families were neighbors growing up, and apparently still, and the two of us had been one another's dates to a lot of events. People had insinuated for years that the two of us should eventually get together, but there'd never really been a spark for either of us. Part of the reason why seems pretty obvious right now. Hard to really spark with someone when you're not comfortable in your own skin.

We chat for a while as I wait for Marcus to get back from the bar. Apparently, Mads had moved back in with their parents for a while to recover from top surgery, and my mom had invited them over regularly to hang out at the Carter house. Which means they'd helped with a lot of the wedding planning stuff I'd been too far away to do. For that, they deserve my endless gratitude.

Soon, Marcus is back, in his wake a short, plump woman with a heart-shaped face framed with black curls. She slides in next to Mads, and even in the dark, I can tell they're blushing.

"Here you go," the woman says, sliding a martini glass with two olives in front of them.

"How did you know what I wanted?" They glance sidelong at her. In all our years of friendship, I've never seen them this flustered. It's kind of adorable.

Then Marcus slides a negroni in front of me, and I'm the one blushing. "Marcus, this is Mads and…"

"Jessie," the woman with the curly hair says, reaching across the table to shake our hands.

"This is my boyfriend, Marcus." I marvel at how easy it is to say. I don't trip over my words at all, but adrenaline washes through every membrane, flash-freezing me. Maybe if I just say it enough times, the words will simply become a fact that nobody can argue—not even me.

"Marcus, Mads and I were…"

"Monarchs of the prom," Mads says helpfully.

Marcus smirks. "Of course you were the prom king."

He looks at me the same way he does when he adds an extra five pounds to the barbell, just to be a prick. I meet the unspoken challenge in his eyes, leaning forward and kissing him on the tip of his nose. While this has been excruciating in a lot of ways, in this way, the way that we interact with one another, it's been surprisingly easy. This time, I feel confident enough to take his hand and squeeze.

Katie is suddenly at the end of the table, sucking down something electric blue through a paper straw. A gummy shark lurks at the bottom of her swiftly emptying glass.

"Marcus, you dance, right?" she asks.

He nods, glancing at me out of the corner of his eye. "I do."

"Well come on, then!" She dives across the empty booth, grabs him by the wrist, and yanks. "Zack, you've gotta give him up!"

"Oh!" His eyes are wide when he turns back to me. "Will you be all right?"

I nod, letting go of his hand. It's better that he make nice with them on his own terms. Plus, Mads and Jessie are sitting here too. I should be fine.

"Hell, yeah! And don't eat my shark, Quackers, it's my special day!" Katie shouts over her shoulder as she hauls Marcus onto the dance floor.

We got here early as far as clubs go, but the place soon starts to fill up enough for the volume to climb, and it's getting more difficult to hear one another. Since the girls took it by storm, the energy on the dance floor has gone from zero to ninety, and the DJ has clearly taken notice.

Laser lights and disco balls are now in full effect, and each new song has a faster tempo or heavier bass, as if to say "it's ass-shaking time."

The younger men, the ones who should probably be studying for their finals right now, have flooded onto the dance floor. I can no longer see Marcus or Katie in the knot of people on the dance floor. I assume they're on the opposite side of the bridal party circle, or if I know Katie, in the middle of it.

Right on cue, I see Katie's head and torso pop up over the rest of the crowd, a look of shocked delight on her face. The circle expands around her, and I spot Marcus with his hands on her waist, lightly setting her down again.

"Jesus Christ," Mads says.

"You're telling me," I say. Some of the younger guys, clustered together, openly ogle my fake boyfriend in the same way I probably am right now.

"Sorry, dude, but she's probably going to recruit him for the wedding party dance now that she knows he can throw her around," Mads says.

"Ooooh, do you think he can do that one lift from *Dirty Dancing*?" Jessie says, eyes still locked on the dance floor. But I'm a little stuck on what Mads just said, dread suffusing me all the way to my bone marrow.

"Shit, I forgot all about the dance," I say.

There's definitely a video flagged in my inbox right now with an entire dance I'm supposed to learn for the reception. I don't mind dancing, but I cringe at the thought of group choreography. At first, I expected Marta to nix it, before I forgot she's a frickin' PE teacher and it was probably her idea in the first place.

Mads laughs at the angst that must be dripping from me and puddling on the table. I pull the soggy paper straw out of Katie's drink and fake throwing it at them. They flinch, blocking their faces as they laugh harder, as a song I haven't heard since senior prom starts thudding from the speakers.

"Seems a little early in the night for the 'Cha-Cha Slide,' doesn't it?" I say.

I have half a mind to ask Mads to go dance it with me for old time's sake, but then I see the way Jessie is looking at them, tugging lightly at a pinstriped sleeve that's rolled up to the elbow.

Maybe we can save a dance for the wedding, I think. I'm the one who should stay on purse duty, and I'm not about to cock-block an old friend. Mads shoots me a nervous grin as the two of them slide out of the booth to join the dance.

And then I'm alone at the table, left with a spice cabinet's worth of complicated feelings. Seven herbs of nostalgia. A ten ounce tin of yearning. And still that vial of grief-infused anxiety, a single drop of which contaminates the whole batch. I take my phone out of my pocket, hoping to dissociate a little bit from this whole thing, maybe run down the clock on the rest of the night before I can go home, crawl into bed, and remind myself that none of this is real.

When I sense someone slide onto the bench across from me, I first think it's Mads again, then maybe Marcus, or maybe even one of the younger guys who I'll have to very politely decline.

Instead, when I look up, I come face to face with Candace.

"May I help you?" I mean it to be glib, but it comes out frustratingly neutral, and Candace doesn't flinch.

"Just thought I'd take a break. It's been a long day, and I'm tired." She doesn't look tired with her arms folded on the table. She's looking at me the way she used to do when she had gossip she couldn't wait to tell me or was about to spray someone down with unsolicited life advice.

Briefly, I imagine that maybe if I sit still enough, she won't say anything more. Like she's the *Jurassic Park* T-rex who won't register me if I don't move. No such luck.

"How long have you and Marcus been dating?"

Sheesh, right to the point. She didn't even commit to the "I'm just tired" bit for ten seconds. "About a month," I say.

I can't remember if that's where we landed on the back-story, but I'll just have to update him with whatever comes out of my mouth later. It might not even matter how well the stories match.

Ultimately, Marcus is just here for moral support. Except right now, he's not here, and Candace is taking full advantage of that.

"You know," she says, lips tilting with irony, "I never figured you for the kind of guy to sleep with his students."

I blink dry eyes as all sound drains from the room. Then my ears start to ring. "I'm sorry, what?"

For all the time Candace and I were together, I can't remember ever getting truly angry with her. Frustrated, sure. Annoyed, of course. Hurt, most definitely. But right now, I feel like if I open my mouth, whatever comes out will burn this club down. Hell, maybe this entire block.

But she's still looking at me, clearly expecting an answer.

"He's not one of my students. And he's twenty-eight," I finally force through tight vocal cords.

She cocks her head in surprise, and she seems a little relieved, too. Briefly, I flash back to when I accused Marcus of being twenty-two. I guess it's not the most ridiculous thing a person could think, even though it's a huge dig on my character.

And of course, instead of apologizing, she doubles down.

"Still, don't you think that's a little young? I mean, god, Zack, he's younger than Katie," she says.

"Who is a grown-ass woman about to get married." I gesture toward the dance floor where the 'Cha-Cha Slide' is still in full swing. "Just because you're too young for a serious relationship doesn't make you the norm, Candace."

She rears back like I'd hit her. Jesus, she looks haggard. Maybe I should feel vindicated to see that, but instead it just makes me depressed on top of fucking furious.

"I just didn't expect the break-up would throw you into a mid-life crisis...thing." She gestures incoherently, like someone who conned her way into doing ASL at a press conference.

"Oh, you didn't expect my life would be completely thrown off by my ten-year relationship ending without any warning?"

"Without warning? Were you paying any attention at—"

I cut her off. Yeah, it's rude, but I hadn't made a habit of it in the past. Maybe I should have.

"You've also got a hell of a lot of nerve to talk to me about dating someone too young when you're dating a literal manchild."

"Is there any other kind? At least Robbie—"

The rest of her sentence could have been anything, but I don't notice because there's a strong grip on my upper arm. My head snaps toward where Marcus is leaning into the booth, one hand on me, and the other flat on the table top.

"I would say I hate to interrupt, but I would be lying," he says.

Candace freezes under the arctic blast of his glare. She doesn't reanimate until Marcus has coaxed me out of the booth, but if she tries to say anything else, I don't notice. I'm too focused on him and how firmly he holds my hand as he leads me toward the center of the club.

16

DANCE WITH ME

A wave of our fellow partygoers sweep off the crowded dance floor, mostly with their shoes in their hands. We wade into the center of the mass of bodies like we're fighting against a current. It's a big-enough crowd, held captive by a thumping bass that demands our heartbeats match its rhythm, for us to get lost in it.

Suddenly, Marcus swings me around to face him, slings his arms over my shoulders, and puts his lips to my ear. My eyes shut on reflex, so I can focus on nothing but his words and their warmth against my neck.

"I'm sorry. I should not have left you alone," he says.

"What are you talking about? That was amazing."

He huffs, as if I'm letting him off the hook too easily. "I had a single task, and I failed."

"Knock it off," I say. "You're here as my date. That's the only 'task' we agreed on. And you're going above and beyond."

He draws back, but only enough that we can clearly see one another. "That isn't a problem, is it?"

Every tight knot of hurt inside me comes undone as I force myself to shake my head. No sound could possibly escape my lips right now; I'm too enraptured by the look of him.

His eyes are black tunnels carved through solid rock, his mouth slack and pink, and—I know for a fact—delectable. Both glisten with naked desire, now so undeniably real that it seizes something deep in my chest and draws me toward him, an immovable object trapping me in its gravity.

"I neglected to ask you if you'd like to dance with me."

The soft hint of remorse in his words is nothing like it had been when he gave me that extremely unnecessary apology. I'm getting the feeling that he isn't actually sorry for anything. And he shouldn't be. Everything that's happening right now is so much more than I'd let myself want.

"Well, I would definitely like to dance with you," I say. "For a start."

He raises a single eyebrow; he's so fucking sexy I want to suck him off right here in the middle of the dance floor. But now his hand is on my back, and we're dancing. I think we're dancing, anyway. We're moving at least, and his mouth is scant inches from mine, nose brushing feather-light against my cheekbone. He's so, so close I'm afraid I'll breathe too hard and blow the sand off this moment to reveal it's only a dream.

I'm not sure how long it goes on. Enough that one song blends into another, then another; that his hands are on my shoulders, then my back, then my hips; that he's eventually pressed up against me so hard that I can feel his erection grinding against mine.

When I lift my chin, it's apparently the opening Marcus was waiting for. His hot, demanding mouth smothers me, one of his hands tightening in my hair as he holds me in place and takes and takes. It's just like my fantasies, but way more intense than my weak imagination could conjure. He's obliterated the boundaries of how badly I thought I could crave someone, just like he's pushed me beyond so many other physical limits.

His other arm is the only thing keeping me upright as my knees turn to rubber.

All our kisses so far have been chaste, sweet, performative. But now he licks into my mouth like he'd devour me whole if he could. Over the music, I can't hear my own whimper, or his greedy, answering hum, but both shiver through me like electromagnetic pulses, knocking out everything I use to measure my place in space and time. And all the while, I'm getting so fucking hard my dick could cut glass.

Finally, he pulls away—or pulls me away from him, rather, by a handful of my hair. It stings, but in a way that feels so good that I shamelessly rut against his thigh.

"Please, Marcus." I don't know what I'm asking for, but from the way the corner of his mouth twitches, the way his hand tightens around my wrist, he does.

Then he's dragging me to the back of the club to the bathroom, which isn't so much a bathroom as an open hallway with a line of fancy toilet stalls on one side and a line of sinks on the other. I don't feel my feet touch the floor until I nearly trip on a step. He shoves me into a stall and locks the frosted glass door behind us.

My thinking has recovered just enough that I push him up against the wall before he can do it to me. He's been so dominant up until now, I'm surprised he allows it, but then I'm out of control again as he deftly undoes my belt and fly. When I try to do the same for him, he slaps my hand away with a grunt. It hurts my ravenous little heart that I have no room to step back and admire the cock that he's pulling out of those skin-tight jeans, but I peek down just in time to see him take both of us in hand. He's bigger than I expected, I can tell from the feel of his shaft against mine and the way he can barely keep hold of us both.

"Where do you keep that th—"

His other hand is in my hair again and he's smashing our mouths together so hard it's a wonder neither of us loses a tooth. I brace my arm against the wall next to his head, whining as he releases us long enough to draw the flat of his tongue over his palm. A string of saliva breaks at the tip of his finger, and I moan with anticipation. My mouth would be too dry for me to do the same, I'm so ruined already.

When his hand starts to slide over us both, I almost come on the spot. I can't even bite back my sob before he pulls me down and drinks my cries as they pour out of me.

They're still so mortifyingly loud that they send the only blood that isn't in my straining cock up into my cheeks.

"Fuck, Marcus," I whine against his lips.

"Shh...you're all right. I'm here, baby," he whispers. If I were in my right mind, I'd be surprised that he went for "baby," but right now I can only shiver and thrust up into his grip. I'm caught. He could start reciting all my lifting totals and I'd probably just start weeping with pleasure.

But then he keeps talking, clearly determined to test that theory.

"If there were more room in here, I'd put you on your knees. I think you'd like that," he says.

"Hnngh—fuck. Yes. Yes," I pant.

His mouth is everywhere he can reach; he nips at my throat between every word, hand yanking at my shirt until the top button pops off and pings against the glass before disappearing forever.

"Yes? Would you let me fuck your mouth? It looks like it was made for sucking cock. Drives me out of my mind." He bites down on my collarbone. It hurts, and it's going to leave a nightmarish bruise, and if he stops doing it, I may die. "And you love when I pull your hair, don't you?"

"Please. God, please."

I can hear him smirking into the cradle of my shoulder. "Inaccurate, but you're free to call me that any time you'd like."

"Oh, fuuuuuck you," I groan, but my body betrays me with another involuntary jerk of my hips.

He's laughing again, in between vicious bites that are going to send me to Ralph's for cheap concealer tomorrow. And I can't just let him get away with it with no consequences.

My hand slips under that wicked nylon shirt, its movement answered with an interested hum from Marcus. As it moves up his torso, I relish the sensation of his soft body hair and skin I wish I could lick the sweat off of. He sucks in air through his nose, but before he can say another devastating word, I roll one of his nipple piercings between my fingers. His head jerks back, and he's the one whining now, the one rolling his hips against mine.

"Uh-oh...I found your spot." It's not an impressive taunt, but it's the best I can do with all my nerves lit up, the flood of pleasure and pain drowning every thought other than, 'Is this really happening?'

The noise he makes is high and needy, and it sends me grasping for something clever to say. But he interrupts me with an urgent, "Zack, I'm going to come."

There's no need for me to say the same. Instead, I lean in to cup his chin and capture his mouth again as his hand speeds up around us, slick with a mixture of his spit and our mingled precum. I'm trembling on the verge of my release when he tenses and groans into my mouth as he comes. And I thought simultaneous orgasms were a myth, but tonight, at least, I'm proven wrong.

The moments afterward are all dampened lyrics, the jolt of the doors to either side of us slamming, muffled voices and all the very unsexy other sounds you'd expect to hear in a club bathroom. But I still only exist right here, in this tiny enclosed space, still propping myself up on the wall as Marcus leans over to snag some toilet paper off the roll and clean us up. He puts me away, buttons me up, then pulls me against him with both hands. I allow my weight to settle. He seems happy to take it.

"Thank you," I sigh into his shoulder. A little embarrassment at how helpless I sound itches in the back of my throat, but it's really the most honest thing I can say. Also, "I really wanted that."

He hums. "Thank you," he echoes, then kisses my cheek so tenderly it slices me to bits. "Are you ready to rejoin the party?"

I am. At least after one more kiss. –

When we finally stumble out of the stall, I immediately hear Mads call my name.

"Zack, we're a woman down." With a smirk, they look from me, as I wobble like a piece of overcooked linguine, then to Marcus, who looks as smug as I've ever seen him. Then they nod to an open stall at the far end of the row.

I follow their gaze to where Katie's legs are jutting out from the mouth of the doorway. If these stalls weren't made for blow jobs, they're even less friendly to puking, which seems like poor planning on Snappers' part.

Marta is crouched in the doorway with her hands full of blonde hair, and Candace is standing at the bottom of the steps, forehead wrinkled with concern. Her eyes widen when she sees Marcus and me approaching.

"Need a hand?" I ask Marta, ignoring Candace's questioning glare.

Marta comes up on her knees and gently pulls my sister upright. "You good, pendejita?" I hold back a snort at the affection in her voice as she calls my sister a dumbass.

"I'm okay, I'm okay." Katie makes a pathetic effort to look back over her shoulder at Marta. "You're so nice to me. I wanna marry you."

"Aaaw, babe," Marta says, like she's talking to a puppy who has tripped over its own paws for the tenth time. "Did you forget why we're here?"

Katie grins, eyes bloodshot under the dim lights. "Oh, yeah!" she squeals and lurches toward Marta, who pulls back.

"Ah! Nope! I love you but no kisses until you brush your teeth, okay?"

Glancing up at me, Marta relinquishes one of Katie's arms, and we pull her up off the floor and down the steps. The hem of her dress is a little wet, her makeup is running, and she's sweating, but otherwise she looks as delighted as a toddler after an hour in the sandbox.

"Can you walk, Katie-bara?" I say, biting back a laugh. I glance up at Marcus, who is obviously suppressing laughter too.

"Lemme see," she says. She takes a single step and almost takes down all three of us. The way she can almost knock over both me and her soccer coach fiancée is a statement to her power. "Nope."

"All right, all right," I say. I crane my neck to meet Marta's eyes. "Do you mind?"

"Please," she says, releasing Katie.

"All right—one, two..." I scoop her up into a bridal carry, and I assume the others are following me as I make my way out of the club.

"You're not my wife!" Katie shouts at me over the aggressive bass and autotune warbling of early '00's hip hop.

"Oh don't worry, you'll get her back in a sec." We break out of the sweaty air and into the sea-scented night air. Finally clear of the doorway, I gently put her down. "Where are your shoes?"

"Got 'em," Candace says. Sure enough, she's holding a pair of strappy heels in her hand. Marcus stands behind her holding Katie's tiny purse, which is only big enough to hold an ID and a tube of lipstick. The rest of her stuff is already back at my house, where they dropped it off this morning. Nodding toward Katie, I hold eye contact with Candace. "Will you take her for a minute?"

Candace nods and switches places with me to take my sister's elbow. The rest of the party is trickling out through the front door as I walk back over to Marcus. The buzz from earlier isn't gone. Invisible tendrils of energy reach toward him from the center of my chest, and I would love nothing more than to let them pull me toward him, let me haul him against me like a tractor beam.

So, I take a chance. "Come home with me?"

Thankfully, he doesn't freeze the way I was afraid he would. His face is still soft, lit with amusement, and I'd like to think a little bit of affection too. Affection for me.

But he still gently lets me down. "You seem to have your hands full," he says, handing me Katie's bag.

I can't help but try again. "I'll make brunch tomor-row..."

Marcus cocks his head. "You have a lot of work to do, remember?"

"You're right." Normally I'd be impulsive, tell him I don't care and beg him to come over anyway, but doing this tonight was about as impulsive as I can afford with finals next week. There's simply no time. "But...but you would?"

He squints at me, the way a very content cat would, and all but purrs, "Yes. And I would prefer to have you alone."

I swear under my breath. It's about a millimeter away from being a whimper, but that would be far more embarrassing in the open air, with my sister and ex standing a few feet away.

"Let me get you a Lyft home? I insist. Since I know all you've got is that flip-phone thingy." I open the app on my phone and hand it to him.

He stands deliciously close to me as we wait for our cars to arrive. When his ride pulls up to the curb, he kisses me goodbye as if there aren't dozens of people watching us.

I run a hand through my hair, realizing how much sweat is drying on my forehead and how badly I need to shower. But my confusion about him is creeping closer to hope, to comfort. Whatever's going on, it's nice to feel desirable for the first time in years.

I try not to think too far past that.

17

YOUR BEST SELF

It's mid-morning the day after the party, and I'm alone in my kitchen. There hasn't been any stirring from the guest room where Katie and Marta are sleeping, so I'm left alone to corral breakfast ingredients. No matter how much grading I have to do, I'm not going to not make brunch for my sister and her fiancé when we're all hungover.

My hangover is folded into hazy daydreams about how Marcus treated me last night, seasoned with disappointment that I hadn't woken up to him in my bed this morning.

It isn't just about the dirty things he whispered to me while he stroked my cock, or how his kisses put breath back into my lungs (although, that is a lot of it). It's also how he kept a protective hand on me for most of the night, how he distracted me when he noticed my mood dropping, how he'd defended me from Candace when he didn't even know what our fight was about. I don't really know what I'd imagined he would be like as a boyfriend before, but this is so much better.

Except, of course, the part where he isn't actually my boyfriend. Remembering that makes the bacon sizzle a little bit more quietly in the pan, and the sunlight through the living room window isn't quite as bright as it was a minute ago.

It had felt so real, but then, I assume Cinderella's night at the ball had felt the same way.

But at that moment, my phone lights up on the counter, and I recall how Cinderella didn't have the prince's number.

Thank you for last night. I had a very good time.

Jesus, I haven't felt like this just from getting a text message in years. Dizzily, I try to come up with a response. "I want you to shove your cock down my throat, but no worries if not lol" isn't very smooth.

I got that impression. ;-) Thanks for coming.

I press send before I realize the door I've left open, and Marcus doesn't waste time walking through it.

I should say the same to you.

If I were close to a wall instead of standing over a pan of bacon, I'd knock my head against it. Instead I send a face-palm emoji.

Sorry, I'm not very good at this

I doubt that very much.

[…]

[…]

As the dots appear, disappear, and appear again, I regret my choice to cook breakfast in sweats this morning instead of jeans. I'm not sure I'm going to be able to keep texting Marcus without getting a boner, and Katie and Marta could come out of that guest room at any moment.

Am I correct that you're canceling your sessions this week?

God, finals being this week is such bad timing for as badly as I want to see him. Then again, if I trained this week, I'd probably drop a barbell on my own head due to horny brain fog. You'd think by now I'd be better at compartmentalizing, but I don't know if I could look at his hands now without remembering how they felt wrapped around my cock.

Yeah, unfortunately. Too much to do to wrap up the quarter.

My thumbs hover over the tiny keyboard as I think about what to say next. Fuck it.

`I'd invite you over tonight if I didn't.`

A door creaks open, and I slip my phone back in my pocket, trying to ignore the way my blood is rushing like I've just thrown myself over the edge of a cliff. Marta and Katie shuffle into the room; Marta wears a black velour tracksuit that, if she had chest hair, would make her look like a mobster, and Katie is in flannel pajamas. Her eyes look like they're unable to open beyond slits, as if letting more light in will melt her face like one of the guys from *Raiders of the Lost Ark*.

"Ready for breakfast, Katie-bara? Or do I need to make you dry toast so you don't barf?" I remove each strip of bacon with tongs and put them on a rack to drain the excess grease.

"Got it all out last night." Katie plops onto one of the barstools at the kitchen island. "Wouldn't leave without my French toast, Quackers. Just...headache now."

I snort and try not to dip my hand into my pocket to see whether Marcus has answered me. Whatever his message says is either going to embarrass me or I'm going to em-barrass myself with the way I react to it. Marta picks up the carafe on the counter and fills up the two mugs that I'd set out with coffee.

"I like Marcus. Looks like he makes you happy," Marta says. Her gaze sweeps over the table, and before I can ask if she needs anything, she's on her feet and crossing to the fridge.

"And what *else* do you have to say, Marta?" Katie uses the prodding teacher voice she inherited from our mom. My curiosity is definitely piqued.

Marta lingers behind the open fridge door, as if she needs a moment to collect herself, before reemerging with a carton of cream. When I glance over at Katie, her face is solemn in a way that probably has nothing to do with her hangover.

"Candace told me what she said to you, and I wanna apologize. It was really bitchy, and you don't deserve that."

"Wow. I mean, you don't have to apologize for her behavior, but thanks," I say. A childish part of me insists that, yes, she should apologize actually. She's the one who invited Candace in the first place. "When Katie told me Candace was still in the wedding, I thought maybe I'd done something to make you mad."

Marta sighs as she returns to her stool. She focuses very hard on pouring just the right amount of cream into her Donald Duck mug before looking up at me again.

"It wasn't that. I just thought, we're all adults, and she's my friend, and you weren't acting like you hated her or anything. Like, maybe by now it was water under the bridge, or maybe you even—"

She cuts herself short, then brings the mug to her lips and takes a sip. I wait, a thought worming its way into my head that I can't help but voice.

"Marta, you weren't trying to get us back together, were you?"

"No," Marta says, much too quickly.

Katie makes a warning noise in the back of her throat, like a cat right before it hisses. "Ok, ok. It was...a thought," she mutters into her coffee.

"Marta, what the hell?"

Somehow that's even worse than her just doing it to be an asshole. I can't stand to look at her right now, so I turn my back to check the French toast. When I flip it over, it's just a little too dark.

"Well, that was before she started dating Robbie! That's got me questioning everything I thought I knew about her."

"He's so awful, Quackers." Katie's voice is muffled, as if she's holding her pounding head in her hands.

"He's a piece of shit," Marta says. "He showed up with her like…I guess it was about a month ago? Anyway, once I got over being really confused that they were together, he just would not shut the fuck up."

"And he's really mean to her!" Katie says. Something vindictive bumps the temperature of my blood up a degree or two, and I do everything I can to keep from turning around to face them. "He started in on all this bullshit making fun of her for being on her period?"

My vindication cools a bit. Candace always had a lot of problems in that department and was really sensitive about it. It was no skin off my teeth to just be nicer to her during that time. In fact, I'd bake what we called "blood ritual cookies" every month. Not to pat myself on the back too much, but this is a hell of a downgrade for her.

Marta picks up the story. "Someone shut him down—"

"Me."

"Katie shut him down, but he kept making little snide comments for the rest of the day about it. Real tired shit, too," Marta says, "like he started calling Katie a feminazi and then being like 'Jk! Jk!'"

"And he kept misgendering Mads."

"Yeah, well, I don't know why you're surprised. You knew him growing up," I say. Then, emboldened, I turn around to stare at both of them in turn. "I'm not sure why you thought it was a good idea to invite him in the first place."

"Because if I didn't, Aunt Linda would get all weird with Mom again and it would be a whole thing," Katie groans.

Valid, I've got to admit. Mom comes from a family of five kids, and her relationship with her older sister, Linda, is always teetering on the verge of a feud. There are the big political differences, there's this weird, one-sided sense of competition with her kids and us (which she has fully and completely lost), and then there's the fact that Linda takes anything outside her agenda as a slight. She's probably still fuming that Katie didn't want to do that stupid butterfly release thing and will bring it up at Thanksgiving dinner five years from now.

"Look, I guess Candace hurt you more than I thought," Marta says, "but she can't possibly deserve to be with someone that shitty. Right?"

"So why is she? It's not like she doesn't have a choice," I say before I can stop myself.

"She's all messed up," Katie says. "Just...kinda lost?"

"That's not my problem anymore." I grumble and turn back to the stove. The French toast is burnt on one side. I dump them out into the garbage by the sink, then slap two replacement slices into the pan.

"Sorry," Marta sighs. "I'm just trying to be a good friend."

Well, you're being a shitty sister, I think. In real life, I shrug, hoping that we can just drop the subject. As a treat, I allow myself to look at my phone again. My mood slightly ticks up when I see Marcus has responded to me.

Do you wish for me to enable you or encourage you to be your best self?

It occurs to me that I could use that kind of encouragement right now, but maybe not for the reasons he's thinking.

Tough choice. I'm gonna force myself to say the second one.

The dots start appearing and disappearing again, and the way my chest warms is a warning sign to hide the phone in my pocket again. I ignore it.

Then no, I will not come over tonight.

You'll do exactly what you said you'd do and finish your school year

with integrity. You will have to wait until next weekend to see me, but I'll make it worth the wait.

Jesus Christ. I'm starting to realize I must have some kind of kink that's just been waiting to launch itself at my throat for…months? Years? The way I feel when he gets like this makes me wonder how well I truly know myself. I'm right on the edge of swooning, but instead I swallow hard and reply.

Ummmmm, yeah. Think I'm good with that plan.

Excellent. Although I cannot promise I won't send you distracting text messages in the meantime.

This really is going to end my life. I'm sure of it.

So, the bad news is I'm going to have to stand facing this stove for another minute or so until I can calm down a little bit. But the good news is I'm significantly less angry. When I do turn around with a heaping plate of French toast, I steer everyone into a subject change. The rest of our conversation is pleasant, then Katie and Marta drag themselves to their car and head home.

Then it's just me, several stacks of final papers, and a brain that refuses to focus on anything other than what

Marcus might have in store for me next time we see one another.

18

FBWB

Wednesday evening, I'm home before the sun has gone down, preparing food for a potluck I'm throwing for the Moveable Feasts class. It was the students' idea, and they've got most of the dishes covered, inspired by their own final projects. Obviously, I can't *not* participate, so I'm trying my hand at a "succulent hash" mentioned in *The Great Gatsby*, which had been a source of a weird amount of controversy. I swear, English majors can fight about anything.

They're great kids, and most of them are graduating this weekend. It makes me a little achy to see them go, but there's plenty to distract me from my wistfulness. Which reminds me...I dry my hands on a threadbare dish towel and pick up my phone to text Marcus.

So I lied. I do need to see you before the party Sunday.

It's a little bit of intentional baiting, but if he's allowed to tease, then so am I, dammit.

Oh?

You've got to try on your suit to see if it fits.

Do I need to go to a tailor?

He probably doesn't even need to try on the suit at all. It was carefully chosen off the rack and adjusted (yes, by my tailor) to fit his measurements. Even if it's a little off, he's not part of the wedding party, so in an emergency, we could find him something else on the way south. At the core of everything, though, I just can't wait that long to see him.

Nah

Just wanna make sure I don't need to take you shopping next week.

I cringe at how paternalistic that sounds, putting my phone back on the counter. I pick up my potato peeler and a half-bald russet from my colander and try to pretend it doesn't matter. The water mixes with the starch and dirt from the skins coating the stainless steel in a gluey film.

After one more potato, I decide I can't stand the silence and wipe my hands again. Then, I change the subject completely to something that's way too much to hope for.

So when you come over next time, what do you want me to cook for you?

I would consider myself a failure if you have the energy to cook when I'm through with you.

Potato and peeler thud into the colander. I'm already halfway to my bedroom and unbuckling my belt when I text him back.

Go on...

I would if I didn't have a client. You will simply have to think about what you'd like me to do. But if you bring it to the gym tomorrow night after 9 p.m., I'll try it on.

You got it.

With a bone-deep sigh, I flop back on the bed and unzip my pants. For now, my imagination will have to fill in the blanks.

The next evening I pull up in front of CLITS just as the moon peeks over the mountains. Our suits are freshly retrieved from the tailor downtown and hanging from a hook in the backseat. The gym bay doors have been rolled down and there are no other cars out front, but light glows from the glass entrance door. The deadbolt clunks against the frame when I try to open it. Almost immediately, I spot Marcus jogging over, keys jangling in his hand.

Between Saturday night and now, he seems to have taken on more dimension—every line and color of his skin and hair on his head are so much more pronounced. It's like going from standard to high definition. The energy radiating from him as he greets me teases me into thinking he might feel the same way.

However, kissing him in the doorway doesn't seem right. It would be taking too much for granted, skipping to the kind of familiarity that I haven't earned yet. Maybe if we were a real couple, but not just for...whatever this is. I'm going to say FBWB—fake boyfriends with benefits.

The gym smells of cleaner, and I spot a mop bucket leaned against the far wall and a basket full of cleaning supplies nestled between two of the dumbbell caddies.

"Did you lose the toss or something?" I joke. The glint in his eye cools into a vague reflection of how he looked at me when we first met. Shit.

"As I took out as little in student loans as possible, it seemed like a simple way to supplement my income."

"Oh. Yeah, obviously. Sorry."

Some people need to actually work for a living. Good going, Carter. Graciously, he shrugs it off and gestures to the plastic garment bag I've got in a headlock over my forearm. I unzip it and pull out a glossy black suit and a deep red dress shirt. It was as close as I could think to get to his everyday look without making him look like he was headed to a funeral.

He's silent as he takes it from me and looks it over with the piercing gaze of someone with actual taste. My stomach constricts as I try desperately to read his expression.

"Is it ok? If you don't like it we can go back on Monday. I just thought—"

"Shush. It's just fine," he says. I keep my mouth clamped shut as he peers into the still-open bag. "Is that one yours?"

"Oh! Yeah. I tried it on at the shop, though," I say. To go with Katie and Marta's "Old Hollywood" theme, it's a tuxedo with satin lapels. It fits well enough, and I was assured it didn't make me look like a scruffy maître d, but it's still not what I'd choose for myself.

"I want to see you in it," Marcus demands and as he turns, he gestures to one of the bathrooms and gives me no time to argue as shuts himself inside the other one.

Welp. Guess all I can do is what he says.

I take a look at myself in the mirror as I button up the top two buttons of the crisp, paper-white shirt. The fluorescent lights set off the film of sweat on my forehead and the five o' clock shadow that makes me look sloppy instead of sexy. Part of why I didn't want to train this week is just because finals and graduation wear me down to a nub of a human being.

My chin dips as I fix my cuffs. The pants are just going to have to be a little too long since I didn't bring my shoes with me. I pull on the jacket and straighten it as I hear the door to the bathroom beside me click open. One more look, a hand combed through my too-greasy hair, and I try to ignore the fluttering in my chest as I step back out into the gym.

The sight of Marcus sucks the air out of my lungs. The suit combined with his thick, unruly hair and piercings makes him look like a fucking rock star. Somehow, even with those edgy little embellishments, I feel outclassed, even a little schlubby.

But judging from the way his eyes crawl over my body, he doesn't agree. He takes a couple steps toward me, smoothing his fingertips over my shirtfront. It makes my chest ache, like my heart is straining toward him through my breastbone.

"Well, hello." The sentence ends in a gasp as he pulls me toward him by my lapels and lunges for my mouth. He kisses me with teeth, like he's starving, as his hands slip under the jacket and around my waist.

"Was this your plan all along? To pounce right after I got here?" I say as soon as he lets me breathe.

He gives me that look that turns me into a puddle, like I'm the most adorable dope on the West Coast. "You were the one who insisted on seeing me. Move."

He spins me around and shoves me out of sight of the front door. Before I know what's happening, I'm pushed up against the plaster and Marcus is going to his knees on the horse mats in front of me.

"You're going to get your suit dirty." Honestly, I don't really give a single fuck about the suit, but I feel like someone should.

He rolls his eyes, which I totally deserve, and hauls himself to his feet, disappearing around the corner then returning with a clean towel.

"I just mopped," he mutters defensively as he lays the towel on the floor in front of me then sinks to his knees again. Then, much more importantly, he unbuttons my pants and yanks them halfway down my thighs.

"Even worse. They'll get—" I was going to say wet, but I'm silenced by the drag of his tongue over the bottom of my shaft. "Oh, fuck, Marcus. I thought that this was going to be the other way around."

He pulls back, wrapping a fist around the base of my cock as he looks smugly up at me, probably remembering how quickly he'd demolished me with his dirty talk the other night.

"If you dare fuck my face, I'll send you home." Never has such an honest threat been so fucking arousing.

"O-of course not." I shiver as his tongue swirls around the head and his smooth yet callused hands gently push back my foreskin. "You seem to have it covered."

And that's the last coherent thought I have before he takes all of me into his mouth and down his throat. There's no risk of me thrusting into his mouth; he keeps one hand wrapped around me while the other pins my bare ass to the wall. It's overwhelming, how ravenous he is, how he barely pauses for breath as he works me over with his lips and tongue and—Jesus H. Christ—his throat.

Looking down at him will end this too fast, but I can't help it. How can I miss out on seeing the most gorgeous man who has ever touched me with his candy-red lips around my dick? He meets my eyes, irises sharp, platinum rings around blown pupils. The way he sucks a yelp out of me leaves no room for doubt that he's still in charge.

His hand is no longer wrapped around me, and the sound of his zipper barely registers beneath the wet sucking of his mouth on my skin. Then his eyes are closed again as he grips the bare skin over my hip bone, and I wish it were hard enough to bruise.

The sight of him is stunningly hedonistic, like he's letting a truffle melt on his tongue. Like he's never tasted anything better. Like he wants nothing more than to devour me whole.

"I'm not gonna last," I warn, which he takes as a challenge.

He urges me forward with a muffled groan that I would never, ever tell him sounds desperately needy. Gently as I can manage with this knot of urgency vibrating in my gut, I curl my fingers into the hair above his temple. The groan becomes a whine, and that's when I start to unravel.

Selfishly, I hope he swallows as I start to come, and does he fucking ever. He swallows so hard and for so long that I start to worry I'll need to push him away before he finally pulls off. My eyes fall shut as I devote all my energy to keeping myself on my feet. Oh, and breathing, which is somehow harder for me right now than it had been for Marcus when he had my cock down his throat.

When I open my eyes again, he's standing in front of me, cheeks flushed with starbursts of pink. His eyes glisten, a little wet at the corners from his efforts. He cleans off his hands and the corners of his mouth with the towel, then drops it on the floor to try to put me back together.

"Did you already..." I sound drunk. Maybe I am.

"I took care of myself. And before you ask, no, I didn't ruin the suit."

I gasp theatrically and put an offended hand to my chest. "But you've robbed me!"

He huffs out a laugh and leans forward to gently kiss my cheek. "I've been teaching since noon, had my own workout, *and* cleaned. I've spared you."

"I don't know..." I try to disguise the thought with my goofiest tone of voice. I don't know whether he'll be horrified by the fact that I'm not at all repulsed by the idea. Thankfully, he kisses me before I can dig myself a deeper grave.

He pulls back, the endorphin high unmistakable in the curve of his lips and his half-closed eyes. "I'll see you Sunday, then?"

"Course," I say. "After I help you finish cleaning up this place."

He only looks like he's going to argue for a moment, squinting at me like he's trying to spot sights of a trap in my expression. But I take that moment to slip past him and change out of my tux. If this is how I get to buy more time with him, I don't mind a bit.

19

JUST A BOX STEP

It's around noon on Sunday, and I'm heading back to the main English department office with a stack of extra diploma jackets. My graduation robe is unzipped over my clothes, but I'm still sticky with June heat as I spot Ellie coming toward me from the other end of the corridor. She's got a battered fiddle case in one hand and the lines and furrows of a wrung-out washcloth all over her face.

"I thought you got all your concerts out of the way during dead week." I gesture toward her case with my free arm.

"Got roped into a global studies graduation ceremony at 9 a.m., and I swear to god I'm two inches away from puking up last night's pinot," she grumbles.

I laugh and take a long step away from her, as if to protect myself. It serves her right. She'd teased the hell out of me after nudging the story of Katie's bachelorette out of me, and I hadn't been able to confirm my relationship status.

"When are you headed to Oopsie-doopsie?"

"Uppsala, you ugly American. And I leave tomorrow morning."

"Need a ride?"

She freezes, like a dog who's been caught nosing through the garbage. "If you don't mind getting up at the ass-crack of dawn on your first day of break..."

"Obviously not for my best pal."

"Not gonna be dragging you out of your boyfriend's bed, am I?"

I sigh. "I'm still not sure whether that's..."

"Uuuuugh, sorry. I'm too hungover for romantic angst. How about 5:30 tomorrow? Meet you out front of my apartment?"

Damn, that is early for the first day of vacation. But I love Ellie, so I nod. Then we both make our way home—her to finish packing for six weeks in Sweden, me to put on something that doesn't make me look like a total square for the party this evening.

Jackie's house is in town rather than out by the university, a bungalow with a stucco arch and a squat palm tree out front. Smoke from browning meat on a charcoal grill hangs in the air, and music crackles through cheap speakers. Relief bubbles in my stomach, that I can eat something without cooking or paying out the ass. Or else those are butterflies from the thought of seeing Marcus for the first time since our gym encounter.

It's Jackie who opens the door, still wearing all black, but with shockingly bright green lipstick. She shouts my name in her raspy voice and elbows Marcus back from the doorway so she can hug me first. She smells like baby powder with a trace of cigarette smoke. I don't know if she's testing me, or if my stock has gone up with her, but I'm definitely not too good for a hug.

Marcus is the second one to hug me and plants a lingering kiss on my cheek. I return it, wings beating at my stomach lining as I fight the urge to turn my head toward his mouth. When he draws back, his eyes are wolfish. He grabs me by the elbow, and I trail after him through the green-linoleum hallway and cramped galley kitchen to the backyard.

From the top of the shallow concrete steps, the yard is a colorful sea of people dotted with the occasional patch of black. Even offstage, the actors are screaming for attention with every thread.

"I don't know these people very well," Marcus admits.

I want to tell him it doesn't matter, that he's the only one I care about seeing today. Instead the brain-drain takes over my mouth

"But you lived here," I say.

"Yes, but they didn't." Marcus gives me his patented 'you dumbass' look that only makes me grin. He scans the crowd, "I had two other roommates in addition to Jackie. Mercedes and Amber."

He raises his chin toward two women standing side by side in the feeble shade of a sycamore. One is shorter and looks overheated in 1950s greaser getup. The other is a blonde with a neck like an egret's and the posture of a ballet dancer. Both of them look dubiously at a guy I recognize as the actor who played Prospero. He's got gluey residue where his false beard used to be, and he seems to not have done enough monologuing during the show and is trying to make up for it now.

Jackie pipes up behind us. "Your room is still open at least through the summer. Unless they raise our rent again." She smacks Marcus's shoulder with the back of her knuckles. "Have you even offered your man a drink yet?"

"He just got here," Marcus says in a whine I've never heard before. It hits me that I'm getting to see him with his family before he truly sees me with mine, the whirlwind of a bachelorette party notwithstanding.

I wonder why he hasn't told Jackie what's really going on. Ease? Authenticity? (*Wishful thinking?* the more optimistic side of my brain offers.)

All thoughts leave my head as he tugs at my wrist again and leads me over to a fold-out table. The spread is a couple steps up from a college party—they have brie and Italian cold cuts instead of Costco party platters and hot dogs. The beer is from the regional, mid-size brewery instead of piss-light lager. Marcus won't let me open the bottle myself, instead popping the cap off for me and handing over a sweating bottle before retrieving his own.

Even with my social battery at about two percent, I'm able to sustain a series of polite conversations. Well, about as polite as you can expect from a yard full of the-ater nerds—each person's volume is dialed up at least a couple clicks from what would be considered normal, but I'm the last person who should complain about that. The music is a chaotic blend of pop and musical theater tunes that, every few minutes, send handfuls of people bouncing toward the yellowed-patch grass to dance and sing along.

It only takes a beer and a half before I'm drooping like one of the thousands of fresh graduation leis must be by now.

"Are you all right?" Marcus's hand is soft on my shoulder, his face drawn tight.

"Yeah, sorry, just starting to crash a little bit. Been a long week."

"Do you need to go home?" His tone is casual, but I can tell he doesn't want me to leave yet.

"Not yet," I assure him. Becoming even more of a zombie will be absolutely worth it for the way his face lights up.

We amble over to rescue Mercedes and Amber from Prospero, and I can see how they both formed the load-bearing wall that balanced Jackie's brashness and Marcus's reticence. Amber is, in fact, a soloist in the city ballet company, and Mercedes moonlights as a trumpet player in a local rockabilly band. (I don't admit to having seen them at a couple wine-tasting events over the past couple of years—it'd draw too harsh of a line between us.)

As the four of us talk, Marcus draws closer and closer to me, until he's standing with his chest to my back, head hooked over my shoulder and arms around my waist. He doesn't flinch as I lean against him. I'm almost sure that if

I fell asleep on my feet, he could, and would gladly, hold me up.

The sun sinks behind a line of eucalyptus trees at the end of the block and the sky turns from violet to indigo to a deep navy blue. Cigarette butts glow like fireflies and a chill nips at my nose and ears. The music is still going strong, but the crowd is thinning. We've migrated to sitting on the beige brick wall that holds back a mound of ice plant.

But then, the brash horns of a familiar pop song sail through the yard, and I freeze in horror. Anxiety drips from my tired adrenal glands. The quiet feeling of "there's something you've forgotten" that I've had all day finally is staring me right in the face.

"Fuck," I mutter.

Three heads snap toward me. Mercedes, in the thick of a story about a drunk guy who tried to steal her trumpet at her last gig, stops mid-sentence.

"You okay? Not a Bruno Mars guy?"

"No, no, sorry, it's...my sister's getting married and I haven't learned the stupid reception dance yet." Jackie, Mercedes, and Amber groan in sympathy. Marcus snickers right next to my ear.

"Shut up, or I'll make you do it instead." My scowl is almost genuine. Almost.

"I'm not the one with the tux." His lips graze my ear, drawing out a vivid memory of what he'd done to me the other night while I wore said tux. I bite down hard on the inside of my cheek and try to keep it together.

"Amber can help," Mercedes volunteers.

"I could. Do you have video?" Amber cranes her neck toward the phone sitting on the wall beside me.

"You don't have to..." But she's already hovering over my shoulder on the side where Marcus isn't sitting. Feeling kind of like a shitty brother-in-law, I open my email to find what Marta sent us all two months ago.

"Oh, this'll be good," Jackie says. "Is it just the song, or is it like, a bunch of shitty songs smooshed together?"

"No, it's just the one, I think."

Within minutes, I've brought up the private YouTube link and am trying not to sneer at the tiny Marta on my screen. Her hair is tied in a messy bun, and she's teaching the moves like she's talking to her PE class. Amber's eyes are glued to the screen, limbs twitching minutely as if the information is being downloaded into her body. Finally, the video finishes, and Amber nods and pushes to her feet.

"Okay, up."

I obey immediately. She must teach from time to time, because she's definitely got the "your-attention-please!" voice down.

"You too, Marcus. Be a supportive boyfriend." Jackie comes up to one side of me, shaking out her arms and legs. With a sigh, Marcus oozes over to stand at my other shoulder. At least I won't be making an ass of myself alone. Across the patio, a few stragglers shoot us curious looks.

"Don't worry, it's very easy. You have rhythm, I hope?"

"He does," Marcus says.

Jackie snorts and echoes, "He does," in a goofy voice. He squints at her in a toothless threat. Amber, fully absorbed in the lesson, ignores them both. Thankfully, she ignores my blush, too.

"So, then, start with your legs hip-width apart like this...and clicking your fingers like this..."

"Oh my god, finger snapping!" Mercedes hoots with laughter.

"You play rockabilly. You have no right to call anyone else embarrassing." Marcus's look would make me dive under the nearest piece of furniture, but she seems unfazed.

I'm trying not to be stunned at the fact that Amber learned the entire dance from watching the video once, but then, she is a professional. I'm just doing what she says, and what Jackie and Marcus are easily doing on either side of me, as if they learn a dorky choreographed dance every Sunday night.

But Amber is right. It's not that hard. It's mostly little hip pops, dramatic poses, fanning ourselves, and enough snapping that I'm probably going to bruise my fingers. Then, the instrumental bit comes in, and I'm totall y baffled.

"Wait, wait, wait, slow down, what is that?" I wave my hands for a timeout after Amber rushes through a flurry of footwork.

"It's only box step." She's done an excellent job not looking at me like I'm a rube this whole time, but apparently halfway through 'Uptown Funk,' the gloves come off.

"It looks more like a circle than a box."

"Some boxes are circles," Mercedes shouts over the lip of a whiskey glass she retrieved in order to escape the impromptu dance lesson. Amber glares at her.

"Hat boxes are circles!" Jackie says, and Amber's glare shifts to her before focusing back on me.

She goes through every microstep, one-by-one, then makes the three of us do them again and again. Jackie and

Marcus, naturally, get it the first time, but they're doomed to pay for my shortcomings with me. Coach Marta would be humbled by how hard Amber is putting us through our paces. For a moment, I can't help but picture her in some echoey studio shouting at a room full of frightened Russian teenagers in tights.

Miraculously, we reach the end, and all that's left is what Marta calls "freestyling"—whatever that means. And it's at that point that the group across the patio can't hold back anymore. As soon as Amber starts the song over for us to run through, they break into a much more complicated routine. I assume they did it together for a show or something. Because that definitely couldn't be improv, right?

"Hey, fuck you guys!" Jackie shouts. She grabs me by the shoulders and whirls me around to face away from them. By now, I'm laughing too hard to remember much of anything. She and Marcus drag me giggling and stumbling through the three minutes and however many seconds the song lasts until I'm finally flat on my back in the dead grass.

Marcus kneels beside me with a smirk. "Had enough?"

I cover my face with both hands and can only get out an incoherent whimper. The music moves on to something a little less energetic, but the party now seems to have gotten a second wind. It's going to have to sail on without me, or

I'm going to wake up right here on this lawn tomorrow morning.

When I open my eyes again, Amber is standing over me with her arms akimbo.

"You are not so bad. Just a *little* more practice," she says, clearly ready to fight anyone who criticizes me. My success apparently belongs to her now.

Finally, with Marcus's help, I struggle to my feet. And there, in front of his best friends, he presses a knee-melting kiss to my lips. It almost sends me right back down into the grass.

"I'll get you some water." He squeezes my bicep before jogging back toward the house.

"Sure you don't want another beer?" Jackie pats me on the back a couple times as he goes. "You're a good sport."

"Being shameless helps," I groan. It's only a half-truth, because I'm definitely ready to crawl under one of the juniper bushes so nobody can look at me ever again.

Mercedes and Amber have wandered over to pick at the leftover food, so now it's just me and Jackie. She looks over her shoulder toward the house, then back at me, her smile flattening a little.

"Hey, do me a favor?"

I nod and send up a silent prayer that I'm not about to get an actual shovel talk.

"Could you make sure he's got his designs all ready for the kickoff production meeting Thursday? I don't think he's going to fuck up or anything, but he's kind of got a history of self-sabotaging when he's in a relationship, you know?"

"Yeah, of course."

The heat that's built up inside me cools in an instant. I had no idea Marcus was presenting his stage designs this week. Guilt rolls through me, with a twinge of hurt that he hadn't told me about something that was such a big deal.

There's no trace of skepticism in her face, and I hope that means she can't tell I didn't know.

"You're definitely not like the others, but he's been with a lot of really shitty guys. And he gets kind of lost in people when he's in love, so..."

"I know the feeling," I say. And then the weight of what she's said finally crashes into me. "Wait, did he tell you he's—"

"No, but come on, you just have to fucking look at him." She rolls her eyes. "He's obviously got it bad for you."

I draw in a deep breath, senses filling with smoke and singed earth. It barely steadies me, because I'm so thrown off balance. It's impossible to deny that she's probably right. But that realization is a little overshadowed by how I've just selfishly been going about my life without much of a thought about what he needs.

His silhouette is dark against the glow of the screen door, prismatic light passing through the water glass he holds. My chest constricts at how brightly he beams at me as he hands it over and slips his arm around my waist.

He's just moved out on his own for the first time in a ridiculously expensive town. He's going back to school after ten years, after getting his life wrecked right out the gate. He's had his heart smashed over and over again by men who didn't appreciate him. And all I've done is made him a pawn in some petty game with my ex.

If I love him—and fuck, I really think I might—I've got some serious thinking to do.

20

Twenty-Four Hours!

I swear as I fumble the key card to Marcus and my hotel room, and it sails from my sweaty hands to the emerald green industrial carpet. Before I can recover, Marcus has already dipped down and retrieved it.

"Are you all right?"

"Just a little wired from driving, I guess."

He gives me a skeptical look as he hands back the card. The traffic was some of the lightest I'd ever experienced driving to LA on a Friday, even with how early we left.

There'd also been a lot of singing along to terrible '90s pop music. I hadn't shown any signs of being uptight until the lobby doors whooshed open.

The light over the door handle blinks green, and I push my way inside, Marcus on my heels. Katie and Marta have picked a perfectly nice hotel for the wedding. Not super fancy, but fancy enough to have a courtyard with a fountain for the ceremony and rooms that smell fresh instead of musty.

I'd been too chicken to ask Marcus to spend Thursday night with me, mostly because I had an irrational fear that something would go wrong and ruin the weekend before it began. Besides, I'd reasoned, he'd had a busy week. With his presentation, and the fact that he'd crammed all his Friday clients into the earlier days of the week, I'd figured it wasn't the best night for us to take that step.

But now we're here, in a hotel room with a single king-sized bed. And I'm staring at it and blushing like a virgin.

When I finally shake myself out of it and look at Marcus, his gaze falls from my face to his backpack. We unpack in silence, and I take a minute to lock myself in the bathroom with its newly polished chrome and unexpectedly flattering lighting. Honestly, I'll take any flattering I can get right now.

I emerge, and Marcus brushes a little closer to me than he needs to as he takes his turn. I unzip the garment bag and carefully hang up our suits next to two fluffy white hotel bathrobes, trying not to think of all the ways I might make a fool of myself later. In front of him, yes, but also in front of all of my family and a lot of my friends.

Before I can turn back around, strong arms are clasped around my waist, and breath warms the back of my neck.

"How long do we have?" His voice is husky, irresistible, although I'm sure going to try. If I give in now, it's going to be impossible to leave the room.

"Not long enough." I take a slow breath to steady my trembling nerves. Still, my hands find the soft hair of his forearms and wrists, stroking them as I allow my head to fall back against his shoulder.

"That's a shame." His lips are soft against the vertebrae at the base of my neck; his hands roam over my body like it belongs to him. I want it to, so badly.

I'm not sure whether I'm relieved or disappointed when we're interrupted by a sharp knock.

"Is everybody decent?" The voice is muffled by the door, but that doesn't make it any harder to recognize.

Marcus releases me and takes a step back, and I smile weakly at him as I call, "Yup, just a sec."

When I open the door, my mom is standing there, dressed down in jeans and sneakers, shoulder-length blonde hair half done-up in a clip. Beside her, looking up at me with wide, eager eyes, is my eight-year-old cousin, Sam. His unbuttoned black overshirt is a little too long for him, even though he already comes up to my mom's shoulder.

"Someone couldn't wait to see you," Mom says.

I consider Sam more like a nephew than a cousin, partially because of the age difference and partially because he treats me like an uncle. (Maybe I actually will be an uncle soon, it occurs to me, and the realization rushes over me like a bucket of ice water.)

"Are you too cool for a hug?" I hold my arms out; he gives me a chastising grimace before launching himself at me with so much force that I'm glad I've been working out. It's like the time Marcus threw the twenty-pound medicine ball at my chest without warning. And also there's something pointy in his hands that legitimately might have just bruised my solar plexus.

"Oof, I'll take that as a no," I say. "Did you just stab me?"

"Nooo." He shakes his head violently. Then he holds up the culprit, a glossy plastic Rubik's Cube. He flips it up to show me nine white squares completely making up one side of it. "I solved this whole side already!"

"Oh my gosh, you're way smarter than me," I say (he is).

"There's a guy on YouTube," Sam says magnanimously. "He teaches all the algorithms. Mom says after I finish with this one she'll get me a four-by-four."

"Wow."

"Zack, I think you're forgetting something?" Mom says.

Suddenly, I'm aware of Marcus standing with perfect posture at my flank, and I lean to the side so he can shake my mom's hand. When he holds his hand out for Sam to shake, Sam looks up at me with a "Who's this guy?" expression.

"Sam, this is my boyfriend, Marcus," I say. Then, sotto voce, to Marcus, "He's not really a hand-shaker."

Marcus withdraws his hand and gives Sam a solemn nod instead.

"Lovely to finally meet you, Marcus. The girls had nothing but good things to say," Mom says. "You two can change for dinner later, but I've been told we're needed immediately in the ballroom for 'secret dance' practice."

"Mom, you're in the secret dance, too?"

"You bet your bottom!"

Sam wrinkles his nose.

"I know, she's really embarrassing, isn't she, bud?" The corner of his mouth twitches. Then, he looks back down at the cube in his fidgety fingers, and I know he's trying desperately not to change the subject to what really matters to him right now.

"Can you keep a secret, Sam?"

He makes a dismissive sound. "I already know about the dance. Mom was practicing in the room."

Choking back a laugh, I try to picture Mom's younger sister, Laura, with her master's of divinity and closet full of matching cardigans, dancing to "Uptown Funk." There are a lot of squares in my family, but everyone loves Katie enough to do just about anything for her.

"Well, chop-chop. Marta's going to read us the riot act if we don't get down there soon," Mom says, beckoning with her whole arm. "You too, Marcus. We need an understudy."

I check my pocket for the key card, then look back to make sure Marcus is coming. He follows, that sweet, close-lipped smile lighting up his face. Sam leads the way, nearly tripping over his Crocs a couple of times as he explains the proper order in which to solve a Rubik's Cube.

When I glance back over my shoulder, I see that my mother has rested a hand in the crook of Marcus's elbow and is chuckling, probably at one of her own jokes. Marcus is now smiling with teeth. Seriously, there must be alien spawn growing inside me, because my chest is about to explode.

Sam clears his throat when he notices my attention wandering, and I focus back on him, trying not to get too anxious about my mom interviewing my fake boyfriend.

The downstairs ballroom is half decorated; a few staff in their neat button-ups unfurl bright white table-cloths for large, round tables. Marta's nieces are chasing one another in the gaps between them, threatening to knock over every passing adult. One of the bridesmaids hollers at them in Spanish, and they smother laughter as they scurry to a line of chairs at the back of the room.

"Sam, sweetie, why don't you go sit down over there." Mom points over to where the girls are now hanging upside-down on the chair cushions, occasionally oozing onto the floor like sea lion pups sliding into the water. She doesn't wait for an answer as she releases Marcus's arm and marches toward where people are gathering.

Before Sam can follow directions, I hear an especially beloathed voice.

"Well, if it isn't Big Gay Zack." As my cousin Robbie approaches, Marcus's smile disappears so thoroughly that you'd think it was never there in the first place. Clearly, his and Jackie's internet stalking had been thorough.

"Stunningly creative," Marcus mutters.

"Oh, don't worry. He's got a million of them."

This nickname was especially lazy. Robbie had probably been watching *South Park* on the hotel TV. But if he's still the same old dickwad I know, he'll try out a few more before the weekend is over.

Robbie is colored like an Easter egg in an oversized purple, blue, and yellow shirt, badly matched with khaki shorts that make his legs look like toothpicks with high-top sneakers at the ends. I'd feel sorry for him if I didn't know from my students that this mess is fashionable again.

His arms and legs are splotched with tattoos at different stages of fading. There's a yellow dog pissing on a fire hydrant; a bulbous green alien's head; a poorly drawn skull that is only a breath away from looking like a neo-Nazi symbol.

His eyes slide over Sam like he's an empty paper plate on a picnic table, flick to my face, then land maliciously on Marcus.

"This your new fuck buddy?"

"My boyfriend." I'm not even giving up Marcus's name if I can help it, and if anyone told him before, I doubt he has the capacity to remember.

All the same, the comment makes me a little sick to my stomach. Because, he kind of is my fuck buddy, isn't he? And he deserves better than that.

Dammit, I can't let this jerk get to me.

Proving he's smarter than all of us, Sam turns tail and wanders away toward the row of chairs across the back of the room. He stalwartly ignores the girls, who are now crawling back and forth beneath the row of chairs growling and hissing at each other.

For Marta's sisters' sake, as well as my own, I hope we all have plenty of time to change before dinner.

Robbie takes a vape pen out of his pocket, sucks on it, and blows an obscene cloud of smoke in our direction.

"What the hell, Robbie, you can't do that here. Outside!" Candace's voice sails from the other side of the room, and I bite back a chuckle. Her claws only came out like that occasionally with me, a couple of times when I was drunk and about to accidentally break something. I send up a prayer that Robbie has brought out every ounce of venom in her blood.

Robbie doesn't respond to her, just jams the hand holding the pen into his pocket and rolls his eyes.

"Fine. Boyfriend." He looks at Marcus and jerks his head toward the courtyard. "So, boyfriend, you smoke?"

Marcus sneers and shakes his head. "I do not."

Robbie throws up ironic jazz hands. "Welp. I know where I'm not wanted. Bye-eeee!"

Then, without another word, he stalks off and shoulders open one of the glass-paned doors into the courtyard (probably another no-smoking area). I can't help but feel like I got off easy. But I also know it's only temporary, especially with how agitated he seems to be. He's probably still doing coke. Maybe Candace is doing it too, and that's why she's gotten so thin.

A protective hand grazes my elbow before I can let anxiety get the better of me. My joints unclench and I release a breath that had been trapped in the back of my throat ever since I heard Robbie's voice.

"Quackers!!" My sister shouts from the center of the glossy wooden dance floor. She's in another pink dress, this one plump with tulle, and more appropriate to wear in front of our more conservative aunts. "Get your ass over here!"

"Language, Miss Carter," my mother scolds.

"Carter-Gonzales, thank you very much."

"Not for another twenty-four hours, missy!"

I smile at Marcus, a little lighter now that one of the moments I was dreading had passed. "I'll make you proud," I tell him, only half kidding.

"You had better." Marcus gives my elbow a squeeze and pats me on the back, dismissing both of us—himself to a few seats away from where Sam is now intently fussing with his cube and me to join Mads and the ladies on the dance floor.

Mads is sporting a Hawaiian shirt and a fresh fade haircut. They stand toward the back of the group, rubbing the short fuzz on the back of their head.

"Thank god you're here," they say as I stop next to them. "I'm super not ready for this."

"Don't worry. I got schooled by Marcus's dancer friends. You can just follow me."

"Sure he can't take my place?" Their nervousness actually gives me a little bump of confidence, now that I might be able to help somebody.

"Uh-uh! Mads, you can't back out now!" Katie shouts, as if we're back with the kids instead of ten feet away. Mads throws their hands up in surrender, which is pretty much the only way to handle her right now.

Then, addressing all of us, Katie holds out her arms like she's emcee-ing an awards show. "And now—my wife!"

"Twenty-four hours!" Mom doesn't miss a beat, and Katie doesn't miss one either as she blows a raspberry at her.

Marta ignores them both, booting up the Bluetooth speaker with a pinched expression. Apparently, she's just now realizing she'd tricked herself into doing schoolteacher work right before her wedding day. With a visible sigh, she starts to direct us to different corners of the floor. Mads casts me a forlorn look as they're sent to the opposite end of the dance floor.

I may have oversold my expertise, because as soon as I'm not in Jackie's backyard, it's like I've never danced a step in my life. But as I glance around the bridal party, it looks like I'm not the only one flubbing it. The only people with flawless moves are Katie, Candace, and Marta. Marta's sisters are practically falling over, they're laughing so hard.

"Maybe we should have had everyone warm up, baby," I hear Katie say to Marta, in her softest, most placating voice.

Marta clenches her jaw, runs a hand over her face, and then takes a visible breath. "So—so, can I have the people who know what they're doing maybe help out the people who...don't?"

Mads all but skips back over to me. Marta says something I can't hear to Katie, and Katie squares her shoulders and strides over to deal with Marta's sisters. The space buzzes with the noise of adults who've been drop-kicked back into a dynamic they haven't dealt with since they were kids. Most people stop doing silly choreographed dances in high school or college at the very latest, but here we are.

My eyes wander toward where Marcus is sitting, half-hoping he'll come over and save us. But his attention is being monopolized by the two little girls, who are busy showing them how good they are at doing cartwheels. That seems like it should take priority for him, or at least that's what the lump in my throat is telling me.

After a few minutes of focused practice, my memory thankfully serves the dance back up to me. Mads is much more confident now, and I'm pretty proud of myself for being able to teach them that damned box step.

"Okay!" The room rings with Marta's soccer-coach shout. "Let's do it again!"

It's better this time. Then it's better the second time. Then it's worse the third time, because we can only handle so much.

But before Marta can start the song over, my mom yells, "Don't you even think about it, Justin Benjamin Carter! Not today!"

Everyone follows her eyeline to where Marcus is coming out of a handstand and the two little girls are shrieking with delight. My father is standing to the side, arms akimbo, watching in jealous fascination. My sixty-five-year-old father is really into doing triathlons. He has apparently also just discovered that handstand push-ups are a thing and clearly wants in.

"I wasn't gonna do it!" Dad insists, sounding every inch like a kid caught standing on the counter to get to his leftover Halloween candy.

"Marcus, don't encourage him! I can't have him break a hip before the wedding!"

"What about after?" I offer. My mom sighs melodramatically.

"Sorry, Mrs. Carter!" I can see the flush in Marcus's cheeks all the way from over here. He looks a little chagrined, but he's glowing with mischief.

My mom softens. "Please. Call me Diane." Then she turns her back on them, satisfied her edict will be followed. "Marta, sweetie, I think we should do the actual wedding rehearsal so the staff can finish setting up and everyone can get changed, hm?" She wiggles her eyebrows. It's her special blend of encouragement and threat, unleashed in all its terrifying glory.

Shoulders sagging, Marta nods. In the end, she is marrying her boss's daughter, after all. "Sure. Sounds good."

As Mom herds us out to the courtyard, Katie smooths a sweaty lock of hair from Marta's forehead and gives her a gentle kiss on the lips. Marta, who'd just had the flustered and indignant look of a wet cat, immediately relaxes. She closes her eyes, smiling as Katie presses their foreheads together.

I glance away and swallow hard against a swell of huge feelings. Something tells me I'm going to be doing a lot of that for the next couple of days.

21

WORKING THE PLAN

The open skylight over the ballroom is fully darkened, but the indoor lights and smog make any sign of stars impossible. It's just as well. There's plenty to look at on the ground level at the rehearsal dinner as it peters out. Katie looks about ready to fall face first into the decimated remains of her dinner, and Marta is hanging onto her lowball glass of whiskey like it's the last load-bearing post in a collapsing building.

"I think your boyfriend is going to steal my wife," my dad whispers in my ear.

I almost spit out a bit of potato croquette as I look up at him, half hunched above me and eyebrows wiggling like caterpillars. Mom is definitely going to make him trim those things before the wedding tomorrow.

We're seated at one of the big round tables at the rehearsal dinner. Marcus's back is to me as he focuses on my mother, and every time I see it, I have to resist the urge to press a kiss above the collar of his dress shirt.

Nobody could really blame my dad for the jab, either. My mom is keeping herself square in the spotlight with a combination of incisive questions, active listening, and pouring more wine into Marcus's glass at regular intervals.

"Guess we better keep our eye on them," I say, much louder than he did, and manage to draw them out of their conversation.

"Don't be jealous. You've been keeping him away from us all this time, and we've got some catching up to do." Mom shifts her gaze from me back to Marcus, who is still turned toward me.

"Your mother was asking me about the design program," he says. Sometimes I forget how she wins people over simply by getting them to talk about themselves, and the fact that she's drawn Marcus out of his shell so quickly is nothing short of a miracle.

There's the slightest flush in his cheeks and he gives me a crooked, tipsy smile that's just asking to be kissed. And fuck it. I take the bait, leaning forward to give him a peck before he turns back toward my mom again.

Dad meanders toward the bar, where a woman in a low ponytail and a bowtie is mixing martinis and old fashioneds. The rehearsal dinner menu is what amounts to heavy appetizers. It all fits with the 1920s theme—stuff that would have been served at one of Jay Gatsby's shindigs, minus the succulent hash. But I'm afraid that everyone is about to find out that the food can't possibly stand up to the amount of alcohol currently in this room.

Nobody asked me to weigh in on the menu, so this is what they get. I'm a little worried about Marcus, despite the fact that he has over a dozen cocktail meatballs on his plate. Mom can be pretty generous with her pours.

"You two are disgustingly cute, you know?" Mads, sitting on the other side of me, shoves half a cucumber sandwich into their mouth.

"Where's that cutie who was all over you at the bachelorette?" I deflect.

Mads swallows their sandwich, but it comes off as a nervous gulp. "Jessie. She'll be here tomorrow."

"Have you asked her out yet?"

They reach for their martini glass instead of answering me.

"Mads, come on," I say. I have no right, but maybe someone else can learn from my mistakes. "Okay, tomorrow she'll be so wowed by your dance moves that you can just sweep her off her feet right afterwards and carry her off into the sunset."

Mads's eyes roll toward the ceiling as they take a long drink, then wipe their mouth as they set the glass down again. "Did you mean to pluck my most embarrassing fantasy out of my head?"

"Oh, and who's disgustingly cute now?"

"Still you," Mads says, but their entire face, everything from their hairline to their chin, is bright pink. Whoever is running the bubble machine in my chest might as well just leave it on.

For a moment, I get this intense urge to commiserate, to admit that things aren't as solid with Marcus and me as they seem. After so many hours in public, I can totally see spilling the whole fake-boyfriend story to Mads if I relax too much. Even though I'm starting to think Marcus wouldn't be super upset, my family definitely would be. Like, I'd probably have to stand in the corner with a bag over my head the entire wedding reception as punishment.

"I'm gonna grab some of that pineapple upside-down cake," I say, before I can get too mopey. "Want some?"

"No thanks," they say. I clap them on the shoulder as I stand up to leave them to their embarrassing romcom fantasies.

When I set down a piece of cake, with its golden ring of pineapple glistening with caramelized brown sugar, in front of Marcus, he looks at it like it's materialized from a beam of heavenly light.

"Thank you," he says reverently, then picks up an unused fork and digs into it.

Mom raises a single eyebrow at me and, surprisingly, doesn't chastise me for not bringing her a piece, too. No. Instead, she launches a different type of assault.

"I was just about to ask Marcus whether he wants kids someday," she says.

"Mom." Maybe it's the gin from the martinis or the exhaustion from masking my anxiety all day, but I feel a twinge of real anger. Even if Marcus and I were exactly what everyone thinks, she'd still be overstepping by a lot.

"Calm down. I'm only asking because of how much Bella's girls took to him." She waves her hand as if to keep billowing smoke out of her eyes. "We were just talking about them before you got here."

I look at Marcus, and he doesn't seem fazed. He raises his head thoughtfully from his plate. "Truth be told, I hadn't even considered it an option for myself until very recently."

Suddenly, I feel like if I don't sit down I might black out and wake up on the floor in time for breakfast. If I don't stop myself from reading into his words, I definitely will.

My mom glances at me with an expression that says, *See?*

"Well, you have plenty of time to think about it." She reaches out to squeeze his shoulder. "Getting that degree first, right? Working the plan?"

"Yes," Marcus nods with conviction. "Working the plan."

The cake disappears quickly (it's pretty good, but I'm already planning how I can improve on it and maybe use it at a future Moveable Feasts potluck—if they let me teach it again). I can't help but notice how ragged Marcus looks. His hair has lost its shape, and there's a sheen of oil and sweat on his forehead and the base of his throat, which dulls his usually vibrant skin.

"Bedtime?" I say it casually, as if it's something I say to him all the time, and he nods.

Once he's on his feet, he sways slightly, and I lean forward just in case I need to catch him. The moment is fortunately covered by Mom standing to give him a firm hug around the shoulders and me a kiss on the cheek.

"Don't stay up too late," she shouts after us. Marcus snickers as I slip an arm around his waist and guide us toward the door.

"You either!" I want to throw another couple jabs in there, about how she's the one on her fourth or fifth glass of wine, but I can't think of anything funny before we're already in the corridor. Really, I'm not ready for any more conversations. I just want to lie down.

Of course, who should be loitering near the elevators but Candace and Robbie, bent toward one another and speaking in hushed voices. Over the course of the evening, Candace's foundation has separated into sweaty clumps, like a split emulsion on her face. If I weren't so tired, I'd be intrigued by how pissed off she looks. As it is, I just want to go to bed and not worry about any of this shit for a few hours.

"Well, well, well, if it isn't *Brokeback Mountain*," Robbie says, squaring his bony shoulders in my direction.

Candace scowls at him, and what I had meant to be an ironic laugh just sounds like a balloon deflating. I reach out with the arm that isn't supporting Marcus and press the brass elevator button that will hopefully take us up to our room as soon as possible.

"You know, I never knew you were *actually* gay back in high school? I was just fucking with you," he says, as if I didn't know that already. His tongue flicks out to run over his oversized front teeth like he's licking blood from them. "But it makes sense. No wonder Candace says you were shit in bed."

Against my side, Marcus's body goes completely rigid. My arm tightens around him, but I don't know if that's more for his or my benefit.

Candace snaps upright from where she'd been leaning against the gold fleur de lis wallpaper. "I never fucking said that, Robbie," she snarls at him, then turns wide, pleading eyes on me. "Zack, I never said that."

I honestly don't know whether she's lying to me or not. I stopped trusting my ability to read her around the time I realized she'd only been pretending to love me.

"This guy looks like he's in charge though," Robbie gestures to Marcus. He's stepped into his usual bit, the one where he acts like he doesn't notice how much he's upsetting people, but still draws power from every cringe and grimace. "What would they call you? A muscle twink?"

If I weren't holding Marcus up, I'd shove Robbie against the fire extinguisher mounted on the wall behind him. I'm about to tell him where to get off when Marcus speaks.

"I would encourage you to explore the world outside your computer," he says, voice like a flat stone. "But then again, I'd rather you not inflict yourself on my community."

The elevator gives a sharp, high-pitched ding, and the shiny brass doors slide open. I corral him inside, trying to suppress the smile twitching at the corners of my mouth.

"Best you remain ignorant," Marcus calls over his shoulder as I lead us inside, "not that you have any choice."

Robbie's mouth gapes, but the doors close on him before he can hurl anything else at us.

As soon as the elevator moves, both of my arms are full of Marcus. The dark wooden handrail pushes into my back as he pushes his wine-soaked tongue into my mouth. For a moment, I let it happen, let my gaze float to the mirrored wall so I can lock the image in my memory forever.

Then my hands drift up to his biceps, and I gently pull him a few inches back. His eyes are bloodshot, lips parted, and everything I can see of the inside of his mouth is purple.

"You're fucking hilarious. You know that, right?" I say.

"He...is a plague sore," Marcus is fully slurring his words, completely unlike when he was roasting Robbie. Sloppy as this is, I'm weirdly touched that he let his guard down just for me. "And she is chicken-livered and lacks gall."

"Wow, deep cuts," I say, trying to balance him on the flats of his feet. "Except I think it's pigeon-livered if you're quoting Hamlet, you giant nerd."

He gives me another wine-soaked grin as my pulse is pounding in my ears and my cute aggression creeps toward critical levels.

With a chime, the doors slide open, and I all but drag Marcus into the hallway. When we finally make it to the room, he spills out of my arms and onto the bed with a huff.

"Your mother got me drunk," he laments.

"She does that sometimes. Sorry I didn't warn you." I chuckle as I kneel and start unlacing his boots, because I know if he tries, he'll just tumble onto the floor. When I glance toward the bed, he's up on his elbows, blinking down at me.

"I was planning to seduce you," he says in a defeated voice. "I seem to have been... cock-blocked."

Pulling off his boots hides my laughter, but only a little. "Well, you did just about the only thing that you could have done that could make me say no to you, Casanova."

He groans and flops back onto the bed again. Standing, I take stock of him, in his dress shirt and black jeans, then decide I can't just let him sleep like this.

"Hey, get up." I grab him by the wrist and tug. "You're brushing your teeth and washing your face. And getting some water in you. It'll make tomorrow just a little less horrible." I've learned that one the hard way more than once.

He groans again, but complies, insisting that I do the same. Somehow brushing my teeth next to him feels like the most intimate thing we've done so far together.

Back in the bedroom, he starts stripping off his clothes. "Oh, god, you're not a naked drunk, are you?"

I can't help but laugh at the way he sneers at me, struggling with the buttons of his shirt. He'd basically dunked his head under the tap, so his hair is hanging around his face like a wet mop that's been used to sop up motor oil.

"So?"

As much as I want to see him naked, this isn't the way I want it to happen the first time. "Just leave your underwear on, please. I don't want you to wake up and think I've taken advantage of you or something."

He makes an indignant noise as I pull back the covers, and he plops into bed beside me. "I would never...you would never."

"True," I say, honored that he trusts me so much. Truly, from what he and Jackie have told me, the bar is on the floor with all the horrible men he's dated.

"I don't often get drunk. I don't like it." He releases a sigh that would knock over a line of school children. "Are we having an earthquake? The overhead light is moving."

The overhead light is mounted flush with the ceiling, actually. In a lot of ways, I'm glad I felt super on guard today. It would have been a shitshow if I'd gotten this drunk, too.

"No, you adorable mess, you have what we in the drinking biz call 'the spins.'"

For a moment, it's so quiet that I can hear the phantom sounds of the day ringing in my ears. One down, two to go. I'm so wrecked that I'm not even having a crisis that the guy I'm in love with is lying half naked in bed next to me.

Well, not until he curls up against me and rests his head on my bare shoulder. He settles in with a soft hum, gripping my side just a little too hard, like he thinks it will keep him from flying off the surface of the earth. I wiggle my arm under him to draw him even closer.

"I love your mother. Do you love your mother?"

"Yeah, of course I do," I say.

"Not many of my friends have families so accepting," he says. "I don't know if my mother ever loved me."

"Marcus..."

"It's all right," he says. It's not all right, but I don't want to upset him right now and have things take a dark turn. I try to murmur a response, but nothing rises to the surface. Instead I kiss the crown of his head, wet strands of hair sticking to my lips.

"And her name's Diane!" His voice is lighter, now that he's talking about my mom again.

"It sure is."

"Like in *Twin Peaks*!"

"I'll need to give that another shot," I offer, happy to steer the subject away from something that would kick any drunk person off a cliff.

He cranes his neck to look up at me, forehead creased with concern. "You don't have to do anything that hurts you."

"Nah, I was having a bad day and it just hit wrong," I say.

He growls, as if he wants to go back in time and punch my bad day in the face. It's like a knife to my heart. I want to tell him how much I love him, but it wouldn't be fair. He's drunk and I'm not.

Things are already uneven enough between us.

"Don't go anywhere," I mutter as I stretch away from him to turn the bedside lamp off.

"Never." He nuzzles my chest as the room goes dark. A strip of cool light shines through a gap in the curtains and cuts the room in half. Remarkably, it doesn't take me long to fall asleep.

22

Don't Censor Yourself

"Not joining us for breakfast?"

Mom is at my side at the buffet table, where I stand in my track pants and a Bruce Springsteen t-shirt, waiting for one of the servers to bring me a couple to-go boxes and coffee cups. We're in one of the anterooms next to where the reception will take place, an extremely typical hotel brunch laid out on a table off to the side.

I sniff, not deigning to look at her. "Someone got my boyfriend extremely drunk last night, and he's currently in bed with a pillow over his face."

Or at least that's how I left him. I was awakened this morning by a somewhat melodramatic groan from beside me. And, no, I didn't laugh, I was extremely sympathetic, thank you. It was partly a relief—a reminder that while Marcus is young, he's not so young that he can't be laid out by a wine hangover.

"Oh, no," Mom puts a rough hand on my upper arm, as if she's keeping herself from tripping. "I didn't think it was that much!"

"Let's just say the Carters hang out at base camp when it comes to alcohol intake, and Marcus just went"—I whistle, lifting a thumb into the air—"right from sea level to the summit with no break."

She nods gravely. "Yes, I remember when your father got altitude sickness in Colorado. I hope it's not that...messy."

"Just a headache so far, thankfully," I say. If Marcus is vomiting, he at least had waited for me to leave the room.

"I hope that doesn't mean he won't sit with me at the ceremony."

My jaw drops into something that should have been a sentence, but all I can manage is "Uh..."

Her hand had been still on my upper arm, but now she shoves it away. "Don't play dumb. I am your mother, and I see the way you look at each other. That one's a keeper."

Sweat seeps from every one of my pores, and suddenly, all I want is a glass of ice water. "Yeah. I...yeah."

Mom looks at me like she used to when I'd skin my knee, like she knew I wasn't really that hurt but I needed a little coddling anyway. She winks. "I know you'll take good care of him."

Any other words I might have had catch in my throat.

"Sir?" The server has returned with to-go containers, and I thank him. I don't know whether Marcus is a dry toast or greasy bacon hangover food guy, so I go about filling them up with an assortment.

"Don't take too long, though," she says. "We've got photos in about an hour and a half, because your sister wants to change before the reception."

Of course she does. This is a theme wedding, and Katie would never pass up the opportunity to wear more than one outfit for it. I promise Mom I'll be there in time as I snap the lid onto the last cup of coffee. Then, I kiss her on the cheek, wave to Dad, Aunt Laura, and Sam (who doesn't look up from his Rubik's Cube), and gather our provisions.

A cloud of steam greets me when I get back to the room; the bathroom fan is running, muffled by a partially closed door. But Marcus is sitting up in bed, wrapped up in one of the fluffy white hotel robes and clutching a glass of water like someone might snatch it away. His hair is damp, including the chest hair peeking out the opening of his robe. I try not to trace the black linework from his mushroom cloud tattoo with my gaze.

But his eyes are on the coffee and food in my hand. "How's your stomach?"

"It's...better now."

"You barfed?" He winces, which is answer enough, and I give him my sunniest grin. "That means you have room for breakfast."

I set a cup of coffee and one of the to-go boxes next to him and return to my side of the bed. He looks a little less clammy, and he doesn't hesitate to release the water glass and replace it with coffee or to use the plastic knife and single-serving cream cheese on a toasted bagel.

He's finished half his bagel before he slows down, eyes drifting from what's directly in front of him to the ceiling—to the light fixture that is obviously very securely attached. "My apologies for last night," he says.

"What are you apologizing for?"

"I was drunk." As if that in itself is going to upset me. "So?"

He stares down at his legs stretched out in front of him, and I realize that he's actually ashamed of himself. There's no other reason he'd be avoiding my eyes. I set down my breakfast and scoot over, inviting him closer with an open arm. Thankfully, he accepts, wiggling closer and resting his head against my shoulder with a frustrated sigh. It makes me squeeze him harder.

"You didn't do anything wrong. You were just having a good time, and that's what I want you to do." It's different now that he's sober. I can self-indulgently bring my free hand to run through his hair. I can press a lingering kiss to the crown of his head.

I can let myself want him.

He stirs, pulling back to finally look at me. "You're..." He trails off, at more of a loss than I've ever seen him. No more words come from his parted lips. Instead he leans in for a timid kiss.

Vulnerability sublimates from the surface of his skin. Never in my life have I wanted to take care of someone so badly. Of course I'm sorry he's hungover, but his softness fills me with a possessiveness I'm not used to. It's an opportunity to show him the same steadiness that he's shown me throughout all of this, and I can't pass it up.

I break the kiss, cupping his jaw in my palm. "Come sit in front of me," I murmur.

Marcus's pupils dilate to wide black discs. "Wait," he says, already short of breath. When I let go, he lunges toward his bedside table, retrieves a bottle of lube from the drawer, and hands it to me.

"Wow, you really were planning to seduce me, weren't you?"

Roses bloom in his cheeks as his eyes linger on the lump in my pants, before they flick to my face. And there's that sly look that always takes me out, dulled just enough that I can still keep the upper hand for once. And if I have an advantage, by god, I'm going to use it.

"Take this off." I tug at the lapel of his robe.

He shrugs out of it and kneels on the bed facing me. He's fucking perfect—every inch of him. Ink that I've never seen before dances over his skin, curling down his sides into places most people never get to see. Agitation burns in my chest at the fact that I don't have the talent to mark his skin so beautifully, along with a little jealousy of the people who did.

But they're not in bed with him. I am.

I follow what must be one of the roots from the tree on his back as it wraps around his side, down, down, until my eyes settle on the thatch of black hair around his cock. He's already hard, which is gratifying enough to make my eyes sting.

His face is beseeching as he inches closer, taking hold of the hem of my shirt. I raise my arms over my head and let him take it. Then, he turns around and leans against me, his back flush against my chest. The skin-on-skin feeling seems to be what he was after, and the shower-fresh smell of him is too intoxicating for this time of morning.

I shift, adjusting myself before I wrap my arms around his front and nuzzle into the crook of his neck. He sighs, melting into me like he's just slipped into a hot bath. Having him so close, with nothing there to divide us, is like finding out for the first time that I have two lungs instead of just one, like I suddenly have capacity for so much more.

My hands linger on his chest, thumb tracing the muscle connecting his pecs to his collarbones, then sliding down to tease at his nipples. The touch draws out a whimper, and my cock twitches against his lower back.

"Are you teasing me?" When he says it, it sounds like a genuine question rather than an accusation.

"Just like touching you," I say, then kiss a spot behind his ear where the curve of his neck meets the base of his skull. "That all right?"

He hums, seemingly content to let me take my time. As my hands smooth over his stomach, the tops of his thighs, his hip bones, I relish the contrast of coarse body hair over soft skin. His head falls back against my shoulder and he lets out another relieved breath as I bask in this vision laid out in front of me.

Marcus's exhale becomes a gasp as I cup his balls, tender as flower petals. When I let them go again, he whines, and I shush him as I go for the lube. He doesn't have to wait too long before I close my fist around the base of his cock. His whine sinks into a groan.

"That good, baby boy?"

He nods against the side of my face. His eyes shut in bliss, eyelashes fluttering against his cheek as his panting breaths grow heavier. The way he trusts me with himself floods every cell in my body with nourishment. Not quite able to reach his lips, I settle for kissing the corner of his mouth. But being able to touch him anywhere doesn't feel like settling at all.

He's mostly quiet, but it's clear how much he's enjoying this from the way he thrusts up into my fist and the way his breath grows more and more ragged. I'm getting a little bit of friction against his back, but it's just a bonus as I coast along in the wake of his pleasure.

Part of me wants to shut my eyes and get lost in the satin texture of his skin and the heat of his cock in my hand, but I don't want to miss a moment of this. I want to commit every follicle and pore, every freckle and drop of ink, to memory. My other hand roams over his abs, his pecs, his quads, all flexing and tightening with escalating intensity as I pull him closer to orgasm.

"You're so fucking gorgeous." I can't hold in the truth, and I'm rewarded by a whine so soft that I probably wouldn't hear if we weren't so close. "Can't believe I get to touch you like this."

"Don't stop," he whispers. My hand slips back up toward his chest, and I press a forefinger onto the tip of one of his nipples, letting my thumb rest on one end of the barbell. This time his moan is full-throated. In fact, they might have even heard it in the next room.

I can't help but chuckle. "You really like that, don't you?"

"Why do you think I—" he moans again as I tweak the piercing. "Why do you think I got them in the first place?"

I turn to kiss his cheek again, but this time he shifts in my arms, so he can turn and catch my lips. The kiss is suffused with gratitude, nudging us into a feedback loop of contentment. We're both exactly where we want to be.

"Faster," he whispers. I oblige, and I feel his back muscles and triceps tense and release, then see his toes start to curl. "Yes. Perfect."

I tighten my grip on him and continue to toy with his nipples—first one, then the other, then back again—until the scant space between our bodies is a mess of sweat and he's writhing against me.

"That's it. Let go for me, beautiful," I say. He doesn't really need my encouragement; he shivers as he comes all over my hand and his own belly. It's all I can do not to put him on his back and lick all of it off him.

But he's already turning around, fixing wild, starving eyes on me. I don't even have time to suggest grabbing a towel before he gets an arm under each of my knees and yanks all two-hundred-and-change pounds of me down the bed. It's only now that I become keenly aware of my own desperate need for him, and thank god he's making such short work of my pants.

Finally completely naked in front of him for the first time, self-consciousness niggles at the back of my mind. After all, his body is legitimately a work of art, and I'm just some guy with a chest rug and a little extra body fat that's not going anywhere no matter how many burpees I do. But all that self-consciousness disappears under the spotlight of his awe.

He sits back on his heels for a moment, blinking, either in thought or against the red wine headache. Then he reaches for the lube, flicks the cap open, and pours a little bit onto his index and middle finger. He smolders at me, and I draw my knees up until my feet are flat on the bed, like my body can tell what he wants to do to it and is one thousand percent on board.

Marcus raises an eyebrow at me, waiting for me to nod before he leans forward and slips his index finger inside of me. I gasp, just from the shock of having someone do this to me for the first time. I've had some really good times with the plug I bought a few weeks back, so this isn't completely unexpected. But it's Marcus's fingers moving inside me, Marcus attentive to every microexpression and shift in my breath.

Then the pad of his finger rubs against my prostate and rips an unholy sound from my core. Reflexively, I clap a hand over my mouth. But when I look him in the face, he looks even more feral, like he might sink his teeth into my neck.

"Don't censor yourself," he says. "I want to hear how good I make you feel."

He straddles my thigh, forcing my leg straight again so he can move up my body and kiss me hard. Then he makes space for the sounds he's demanded of me as his fingers pulse again, then again. He shudders with every cry I release, like they're electric shocks.

"If you hadn't just made me come so hard I'd fuck you right now. Like this."

"Marcus," I sob, and he dives toward me, his tongue plunging into my mouth as he works another finger into me. I'm already so worked up from touching him, from seeing his body, and watching him come that this can't last much longer.

"Touch yourself," he commands, breath hot against my lips. "I don't want to stop kissing you."

And then I'm whining into his mouth again. I barely register it when he puts a third finger inside me. I just know that I feel so full and hot enough that I may vaporize. For a moment, I think about going for the lube, and then I realize just how much precum I'm leaking, and I take myself in hand. I mean to go slowly, to draw this out, but I'm too close, too frantic with sensation.

And loud. So, so loud. But he wants that from me, so I don't hold back, even with his demanding tongue in my mouth. As I draw closer to my peak, he curses desperately under his breath.

"Look at me. Look into my eyes when you come."

I do. I let his stare cut me so deep, I don't know if I'll ever recover. And when it's done, when every drop of pleasure is wrung out of me, I finally let my eyes shut, all thoughts evaporating into the humid air around the bed.

When I come back to myself, Marcus is cleaning me up with a washcloth, looking at me with a lethal dose of affection. I put on a lighthearted tone to try to stabilize my emotions.

"That help with your hangover?"

Mercifully, he doesn't call me out on the tremor in my voice. "I am not fully cured, but I believe that it did." He sets the cloth aside, and I make a mental note to leave out the housekeeping door hanger (and leave a generous tip).

Then, he settles against my bare chest, hooking his leg over mine. His cock is soft against my thigh as he draws a careful finger down my sternum. When I glance down at his face, he looks thoughtful.

"You've never bottomed before, have you?"

"How could you tell?"

He huffs. "Your discomfort with the sounds you made. It's the sort of thing a majority of tops would encourage—at least the ones I know."

A blush burns over my neck and face. I wish I could say I've had a lot of frank talks about sex in my past relationships, but I definitely haven't. My tongue is heavy when I answer.

"Yeah. I guess I was worried I'd be... off-putting."

He comes up on his elbow and frowns. "Quite the opposite, I promise you." He leans down and kisses me once. "Later tonight, if you're interested..."

"Yes." I clasp the back of his head to keep him from moving away. "Abso-fucking-lutely."

He grins, teeth and all, and dives back down for another, harder kiss. We stay like that for a while

The only thing that keeps him from making good on his offer right now is the sudden blare of the phone from the bedside table. Duty calls. We've got a big day ahead of us, and I already can't wait to be back here.

23

MAKE ME PROUD

Everyone is in the courtyard already when I rush downstairs, still adjusting my tie as I pass through the ballroom and through the French doors. My mom looks over her shoulder at the sound of the latch clicking, giving me a mischievous look. It makes me look myself over in a brief panic that my fly is down or my shirt is buttoned crooked or something.

It's all fine. As usual, she's just being embarrassing in a way that's a smidge too endearing to really upset me.

Unfortunately, I've just missed Katie and Mara's "first look" picture, where they see each other in their wedding dresses for the first time. At least they're both still brimming with excitement from it, eyes locked on one another, faces painted with painfully wide grins. Katie is wearing a long, backless, lace dress, her hair twisted in an artful knot at the base of her neck and adorned with pink peony blossoms. While her dress is creamy and textured, Marta's is bright white with sharp creases, and looks more like a Katharine Hepburn-inspired jumpsuit than a dress.

Photos somehow take both forever and no time at all. Before I know it, Mom has shuttled us back into a small side room as people begin to trickle into the rows of white wooden chairs. I spot Sam in the second row, wearing slacks and a plaid dress shirt that he undoubtedly has to wear to his mom's church at least once a month, hunched over his Rubik's Cube. At this point, each face has two rows of fully matched colors, while just the top row is still jumbled up. Sam's mouth moves as he whispers what I assume are algorithms and methodically twists the cube.

"How are you holding up, son?" My dad, a fiddlehead fern boutonniere on his lapel, peeks out the window next to me.

"Fantastic. How about you, old man?"

He elbows me with an offended sound, but his eyes are misty. He smiles and nods toward where Katie and Marta stand behind us, Katie smiling as she fusses with a silver pin that's come loose from Marta's hair. Both brides are glowing bright enough to make up for the afternoon shade falling over the terra-cotta tiled courtyard. I'm already at about a five-alarm level of glow myself, so it just makes my heart overflow all the more. My eyes have got to be as glassy as both Katie's and my dad's.

Lots of criers in the Carter family. But at least we're happy criers.

"I am feeling a little old, now that you mention it," Dad says.

We watch as an elderly Hispanic couple enter the courtyard and one of Marta's sisters rushes over to guide them to their seats in the front row. They're trailed by a middle-aged couple, a preteen girl looking dour in a poofy dress she obviously didn't want to wear, and a little boy hopping along behind them in black cowboy boots.

"I'm just so proud of both of you," Dad says.

My stomach clenches. "I'm not the one getting married today," I say. Even though my dad isn't really the type to say the wrong thing, there's this demon whispering in my ear that it should have been me by now. One of the biggest things I've been dreading about today is the thought of other people saying that out loud.

"Really? Then I take it all back." Dad snorts and squeezes my shoulder a little harder. "That's why I'm proud of you. Just means that if or when you do, it'll be to the right person."

Naturally, that's the moment Marcus walks into the courtyard, still looking like a rock star, black sunglasses the only clue that he's hungover. A frisson sweeps up my spine and into my brain stem until it forms a vibrating ball of knowing. For as much as I've yearned for and daydreamed about dozens of people in my lifetime, this feeling of certainty seems to come from outside myself, something trustworthy and inevitable. I feel grounded and, at the same time, like my spirit is trying to float away from my body.

It's fucking terrifying.

I swallow a lump in my throat and focus back on Dad. "Ya old softie." I clap him on the back and try not to lose myself in a fantasy that, no matter how I feel, might never come to anything.

A familiar waft of wildflowers and red berries is followed by the weight of my mother's hand on my other shoulder. "Are the hordes arriving?"

"In droves," I say, tracking Marcus as he settles into a chair in the back row.

"Oh—absolutely not," Mom mutters to herself. She pulls the door open, barely giving Dad and me time to get out of her way. As she strides over to Marcus, she waves at guests like a mayoral candidate in a parade.

He looks up at her like a school child caught with contraband, and she all but drags him out of his seat and up the aisle to the front row. I groan when I see that she's plopped him down two seats from the center aisle—right next to where she and Dad will be sitting. Dad snorts, gives me one last pat, then mumbles something about going to check on his daughter as he wanders away.

The wedding is flawless, not that I expected anything less. In the back of the courtyard is a clear pool with a cascading water fountain at its center. Sprays of greenery, interspersed with white and blue blossoms, stand like an honor guard as Aunt Laura guides my sister and sister-in-law through their vows, the ring exchange, and the big pronouncement at the end of it all.

With enormous effort, I manage to not look at Marcus until after they kiss. My knees almost buckle when I see he's looking right back.

Compressed big band jazz plays tastefully from the PA system as we file into the ballroom. It's an Art Deco dream come true inside, with bronze and gold accents on every surface and flower arrangements.

The sun won't set for a while, but the light is warmer. Luckily, it isn't shining onto the monumental swan-shaped ice sculpture by the open bar. Most of the wedding party has landed there, and then some. Marcus stands quietly nearby with Mads and Jessie, clearly a heavy third wheel.

(I wonder if Mads notices how Jessie looks at them, how deep her dimples are when she smiles at them. I hope so, or I hope they'll figure it out by the end of the night.)

But standing in my way, looking at me expectantly, is my Aunt Linda. Her platinum hair is so flat and blunt that it looks like she's wearing a wig, her forehead unsettlingly smooth and lips stretched out and plumped into an uncanny pout. She looks like she's taken a couple too many Xanax and washed them down with the glass of white wine in her hand.

"Zack." Both arms rise slowly, like a dry sponge expanding in water.

I bite my tongue and give her a polite hug. She smells like acetone—a little muskier than a nail salon. More like a hospital wing, maybe.

"Good to see you, Aunt Linda."

"Don't tell anyone about this," she whispers, and a sense of foreboding for whatever weird shit she churns up tightens my jaw.

"About what?"

She gestures to her wine glass. "This."

I have no idea what she's talking about, so I just give her the well-practiced fake chuckle I save for family and interdepartmental mixers. "Hey, it's a special day."

If her face could move, she would probably be looking dubious.

"You're not supposed to drink wine on the carnivore diet, but I gave in just this once," she says. "You saw I'm doing that? I wrote about it on Facebook."

Undoubtedly, Robbie has told her more than once that nobody under fifty goes on Facebook anymore. Based on the out-there politics and conspiracy theories she's gathered over the years, it's her favorite place online other than YouTube. If what she's wearing actually is a wig, there's probably some kind of foil lining it to protect her mind from the cultural Marxists trying to turn her gay with telepathy.

"I've already lost three pounds," she says. I can't tell. She looks just as skinny as she always does. "Your body doesn't need carbs, you know. That's what that nice Canadian doctor says, anyway."

I bite my lip before I can tell her that the "nice Canadian doctor" I think she's talking about is actually a psychologist with no background in nutrition or human biology. But I'm sure the conversation will lead to something about culture wars or, god forbid, the fact that her son is dating my ex. Either way, I don't want to have it today, especially since Marcus still hasn't taken his eyes off me.

"You look great. Just enjoy your cheat day and I won't say anything to the good doctor." I say it from a half turn as I walk away. She's too slow a talker to trap me, and I care more about my destination than being polite.

Marcus hands me a negroni, one of the evening's specialty cocktails (because my sister loves me). He hesitates, lips parting as if he's about to say something. Instead he gives me a kiss on the cheek, and I'm left to wonder again what he's thinking.

I gesture to his highball glass. "Hair of the dog?"

He scowls and shakes his head. "Tonic and lime."

"Aaaah, yes. A healing tonic," I say, taking a sip and letting the ice cool gin temper the heat that started bubbling up inside me at the sight of him. Fortunately, my mom shows up and smothers that same fire.

"We've got a problem, boys," she says, gesturing from the afternoon light beaming through the high-set windows, down to where they land on Katie and Marta's multi-layered wedding cake. It glistens with melting frosting. God help me if I let a perfectly good cake get damaged in that way.

"We could definitely use the help of a couple strong men with good coordination," she says. She winks at Marcus, who looks fully taken in by the flattery. Chump.

"Are you sure that includes me?" I joke.

"Don't wuss out." She smacks me in the shoulder and a bit of martini sloshes out of my glass. I could argue that it disproves her theory about me being coordinated, but her attention has already shifted, and she calls, "Robbie, you come help too."

My stomach drops as my eyes follow her pointing finger. From the way he's twitching and swaying, Robbie is on at least his third drink and has taken a couple bumps of something else. He's the type of guy who would topple a wedding cake just for fun, and my mom should really know that by now.

"Come on, Mom," I mutter.

"He's on his best behavior today," she insists. For as smart and no-nonsense as she is, this is an area where she's always been ignorant. But then again, I'd never told her all the things he'd done to me over the years. It felt too pathetic to tell on him after about age five.

Robbie barely acknowledges her, lurking in the corner with a couple of our other cousins from Minnesota. They're ones who would side with him when it came to giving me shit at family reunions, of course. But today, both of them are dressed like adults rather than fifteen-year-olds, and their body language tells me that the conversation with Robbie isn't quite hitting the way it used to.

In fact, one of them, Ted, turns around at the sound of my mom's voice. He's a typical beefy Midwesterner, and if I recall, the lesser shithead. He also seems super relieved to break away from Robbie.

"I've got it, Aunt Diane," he says, smiling at Marcus and me in turn.

The cake is covered in a vanilla buttercream with gold, geometrical trim, classic cylindrical tiers, and a blessedly solid base. As we circle the table, with both Mom and one of the servers spotting us, I catch Robbie glaring at us like a toddler in timeout. I ignore him as we gently coax the table out of range of the death ray.

I'm determined not to let him ruin my day, and I seem to have enough grownups on my side here to keep him from doing it.

Then, I spot Katie in her pearlescent, knee-length flapper dress, peeking through the doorway like a poorly trained secret agent. She locks eyes with me, nodding toward the DJ table. I catch their eye and signal, and the song that we'd agreed on to warn the wedding party that it's almost dance-o-clock begins to play.

I hand my martini glass to Marcus, happy to have one dose of liquid courage in my veins.

"It won't make you sick to hold this, right?" I joke.

He rolls his eyes, sets the glass on the nearest table, and puts his hand out, palm up. When I realize he's asking for my phone, I hesitate.

"Amber would be furious if she didn't see the fruits of her labor," he says, beckoning with his open hand. I hand him the phone anyway, and because I know he's still practically living in the analog era, I first swipe at the screen until the camera is set to record.

"Oh, god, now I'm nervous."

He gives me his most gremlin-ish grin. "Don't be. Just remember your training"—he leans in to give me another peck on the cheek—"and make me proud."

I blush and nod because I can't get any words out. As always, he knows exactly what to say to motivate me. The certainty in my marrow tells me that, at least in this silly little way, I won't disappoint him

24

CRITICAL MASS

As the warning music winds down and the other wedding party members not-so-casually take their places, I'm hit by a bolt of inspiration.

"Marcus, give me your sunglasses," I stage-whisper.

Understanding flashes across his face. He reaches into his breast pocket and passes them to me as the room sinks into the awkward silence between songs. I catch Mads's eyes across the dance floor; their face brightens when they figure out what I'm up to, and they withdraw their own pair of shades from their pocket. Our minds connect in the way that only two war buddies' can, and as soon as the first notes sound from the PA, we theatrically put our glasses on.

Groans of recognition rippling across the room tell me that we've been figured out. What we're about to do is the kind of "surprise" that everyone, including the over-sixty crowd, has seen on YouTube or daytime TV. But as cheesy as it is, I'm already having more fun than I expected.

If introversion and extroversion are on a spectrum, the Carter kids are about as far to the right as you can get. Katie, strutting out in her fringe dress to funky guitar licks and applause, beats me out by a huge margin. Hoots fly in from all corners of the room, and Marta is smiling big enough that I'm sure the only thing that could ruin this for her is a broken ankle (if that).

I don't notice whether we nail the dance steps or not. I know there's one moment where I completely forget what comes next, but I don't stop moving. Either my body knows what's up or I'm just good at faking it. The only person who cares what I'm doing is holding my phone, amused crinkles surrounding his eyes as he films me.

Like any game or performance, I feel like I was just getting into it by the time we reach the end. The guests are riled up and almost everyone is smiling by the time we make it to the front table and dinner service begins.

"Soooo...how do you rate my performance?" I ask as Marcus slides gracefully into the slatted chair next to me.

He presses his lips together and flicks his eyes from my head to my feet. "I'd say 7/10. You fumbled the first box step and improvised in an inappropriate place, but you recovered well."

On the other side of me, Mads sucks air through their teeth. "Ouch. Do I even want to know what you'd say about me?"

"A 10/10," Marcus says. It's generous to Mads and definitely meant to needle me. Mads rolls their eyes, clearly not buying it, and I shake my head.

"You're brutal," I say. "And you enjoy it."

"Keep it in your pants, guys," Mads says.

Marcus snickers and winks at me. Suddenly, I'm flooded with memories of the way he'd felt in my arms and hands, the way he'd taken me to pieces, and the promise he'd given me of more at the end of the night. You could fry an egg on my cheeks with the way they're burning right now.

Dusk falls in orange and pink bands across the walls and floor. Dinner happens, but I barely remember anything beyond the number of times I start the entire room banging spoons against our water glasses to make the brides kiss. And if that's weird because Katie's my sister, I couldn't give less of a shit. It's just so good to see her happy, that we've all finally made it to this point.

It's dark by the time the music shifts again from quiet, dinner-appropriate jazz to dance music. Marta's nieces glom back onto Marcus, and by extension me, as soon as the dancing begins.

After a couple songs, and enough throwing kids into the air to make up for last week's skipped gym sessions, I spot a couple men from Marta's family dragging chairs to the middle of the floor. Katie and Marta pull off their shoes, climb up onto the chairs, and toss their veils at one another to form a bridge. When the little girls see what's going on, they start hopping up and down in excitement.

"What are they up to?" I ask them, and they both start chattering over one another. But my attention is drawn away to an elderly Mexican woman coming toward me, clearly on a mission. She puts her hand out for me to take and says something I don't quite catch.

"Grandma says you have to go make sure Katie doesn't fall down offa the chair," one of the girls shouts up at me, clearly used to playing translator. Grandma nods, beckoning sharply like I'm a lollygagging puppy. She definitely doesn't seem like the kind of person to be kept waiting.

I look at each of the girls in turn. "You two will take care of Marcus, right?"

They shout their approval, latching onto each of Marcus's arms with their sweaty little hands. One of them collapses toward the floor as dead weight, squealing as he lifts her halfway to his waist with one arm. Heart fluttering, I go to join one of Marta's cousins in bride-spotting duties.

The dance is a more chaotic version of a conga line. About fifty people join hands and form a fast-moving chain that snakes underneath the bridge and between tables. I'm only worried about Katie falling off the chair because of how hard she's laughing. She's been alternating laughing and crying all night. But then, I've been doing the same thing.

The feelings hit critical mass, of all times, during Marta's champagne toast.

She recounts the story of how they met—the boss's daughter tagging along to a championship game.

"Which we lost, like bad. Real bad." Marta says. "And maybe it makes me a bad coach, but I was too distracted by this beautiful girl and her ridiculous laugh to be as upset about it as I should have been."

She thanks everyone's parents, her sisters, and then she turns to me.

"And you all know I hate getting emotional, but, Zack, I wanted to finally—" her nose twitches as she cuts herself off, then takes a deep breath. Katie's hand flails toward her wife before realizing she's a little too far away to touch.

"There's never really been a chance for me to say this before, but I've just got to thank you for saving her for me."

It's like I've just missed the last step on a staircase, the way my stomach drops. I put my fork down, half the red velvet cake sitting uneaten on my plate.

"As many of you know, Katie was hit by a car when she was a little kid and spent a long time in the hospital after. And, Zack, she always tells me that if you hadn't been there, she—things could have gone a lot different."

The room seems to shift ninety degrees. The thing I've seen as my fault for years is suddenly lit with a completely different color than before. This is how she remembers it? That I saved her? Not that it's all my fault?

"You've been such a good, protective brother to her over the years," Marta continues, recovering her composure just enough to get the words out. "So thank you so, so much, and I want you to know that she's in good hands. I'm going to work real hard to take as amazing care of her as you have."

"Course you will," I choke out, forcing myself to my feet to give her a hug through my shock. There's a chorus of "aws" and a swell of applause even as I feel like everyone can see what a raw nerve I've become.

I sit down, reeling, and take another sip of champagne. A hand drifts to cover mine where it rests on the table as we sit through the rest of the toasts, as people finish their cake and start wandering around the room once again.

Marcus's breath warms my ear. "Would you like to get some air?"

His attentiveness doesn't do much to make me less emotional, but I still appreciate it. I nod and follow him out into the courtyard. The kiss of ocean air brings into focus how warm the room, and my skin, had become.

"Are you all right?" Marcus's grip on my elbow keeps me standing solidly on the tile.

"Yeah. Just wasn't expecting that. I didn't know she...Katie, I mean. I didn't know she felt that way about it until now," I say. "I thought she blamed me for the accident. I always blamed myself."

"Would you like to talk about it?" Marcus rubs my upper arm. His attention is a brand on my face even in the dim light.

I suck in a deep breath, then release it, the tremor in my chest evening out. "Maybe later?"

He nods, then leans in to kiss me on the cheek. The only thing that stops me from melting into him is a distressed squeal from across the courtyard. It's followed by a sob that's soon covered with a taunting laugh. The voices aren't tough to identify. Sure enough, I spot Robbie standing over Sam, waving something in the air out of his reach.

"Robbie, stop it!" Candace scrabbles at his arm, and he switches what he's holding to the other one.

"Look at him! Look at the little fatty trying to jump!" Robbie cackles as he easily keeps Sam's Rubik's Cube out of both their reaches at the end of his bony arms.

All my vulnerability ices over with jagged rage. I pace over to them.

"What's going on?"

"He messed it up! I almost had it, and he took it away!" My little cousin's face is streaked with hot, humiliated tears. He swipes at them with the back of his wrist, then pointlessly tries to grab the Rubik's Cube again.

My fingers tingle with the urge to smash Robbie's head against the terra cotta. But I'd rather not go to prison, so I snatch him by the wrist and wrench the cube out of his hand.

"Ow! Watch it—" he calls me the same slur he's called me a million times before, but this time I can tell he really means it. His bug-eyes are wild and dilated from the darkness and whatever he's on.

"Robbie, what the fuck is wrong with you?!" Candace's face is flushed, and I wouldn't be surprised if she hits him before I do. But Sam is sniffling behind me, and she gives Robbie one more deadly look before leaving us to console him.

"It was just a joke! None of you fuckers could ever take a joke. Especially you, sad sack," he snarls, zeroing in on me.

"Sad? That's rich coming from an unemployed thirty-five-year-old who dresses like he still smokes weed under the bleachers. If you're allowed within a hundred feet of a school, that is."

He seethes, and suddenly I'm like an unplugged drain. I can't stop the vitriol coming out of my mouth. It feels better than a good cry.

"You're so stunted, you're literally bullying a child. Why? Too scared to try your luck with the big boys? Too scared to fuck with me now that you know you can't win? Not that you're sober enough to land a punch anyway."

From all my years of knowing him, from being the bigger person and holding my tongue, I know he would never refuse that bait. He winds up and throws his fist with all his might toward my face. All I have to do is lean back, and the momentum carries him straight over the lip of the fountain. The air in the courtyard rings with a yelp and a splash as he stumbles into the water.

For a split second, I'm seized with horror that he may have hit his head and the night will end with me in jail after all. But then he pops up, soaking wet and spitting mad. He scrabbles to one knee, but his foot slips and he crashes face first into the water again.

Sam's sniffles turn into full-bellied guffaws.

"I'm going to fucking get you, asshole," Robbie growls at me, crawling out of the fountain and clambering to his feet.

"You're not getting shit," Candace says. Giddy with victory, I step out of her way until she's a few inches from him. "Get a Lyft with your mother, because you're not staying with me."

"Oh, yeah? What are you going to do about it? I have a keycard."

That's when I notice Marcus standing at his flank. "You can give that to me," he says, voice smooth as black enamel. Robbie starts, ducking as if Marcus has already hit him. Marcus's stance is light and prepared, his shoulders squared and pushed back. He looks as dangerous as I've ever seen him without having to raise a fist.

Despite Marcus's calm, the threat is not lost on Robbie. After a useless moment squirming under Marcus's serrated glare, he pulls out his wallet and slaps the keycard into his hand.

"Fucking white knight bullshit. Watch out, boytoy, he's just using you to get her back." With that last pitiful barb he turns and flips off me and Candace. Then he stalks, still dripping with water, toward the ballroom.

"Wrong way," I shout after him. Without looking back, he switches directions, and pushes through an alternate exit door.

We stand in silence, and I wonder if I should go with him to make sure he gets all the way gone. Then I decide against it; probably better not to give him a second chance to land a punch. If I see him try to sneak back in, I'll cross that bridge.

Candace's hair, which had been parted down the side and pulled into a low ponytail, is a frizzy mess. The bags under her eyes would be too big for the overhead compartment on an airplane, and the straps on her soft pink bridesmaid dress sag. She looks from me to Marcus.

"Thanks. I owe you guys," she says. Then she bites her lip, the way she always did when she was about to tell me she was working late again. My muscles brace with the memory of disappointment. How she could disappoint me any further is tough to imagine, but she's sure surprised me before.

"Zack, can I talk to you?"

I look at Marcus, with the facial equivalent of a shrug. His expression is suddenly unreadable, neutral, but with just enough strain to tighten my muscles even further. The uncertainty of it settles in my stomach like bad meat. Finally, he gives me, then Candace, a grim nod.

"I'll take Sam to his mother," Marcus says. Then he does exactly that, leaving me in the courtyard with my ex.

25

A REVELATION

There's something uncanny about standing in front of Candace tonight. It's like a dream where you're the same age you are now, but are, for some reason, struggling to remember the combination to open your high-school locker. At this moment, as the Zack who I am right now, it feels like she has no business being here.

Candace's hands are on her hips, shoulders hunched. She stares down at her shoes, whose shine is dormant in the dim light of the courtyard. This is a different person than the one I knew, a person who unquestionably does not belong to me.

After she doesn't speak for several seconds, I finally bite. "What can I do for you?"

"I wanted to apologize," she says.

My arms cross, almost on their own, like they want to protect my squishiest organs. "Go on," I say.

She tosses a clump of hair back and meets my eyes. She spits out her words like she took a bite of something disgusting and had to wait until no one was looking to get rid of it.

"It was fucked up of me to start dating Robbie. I knew it would hurt you, but I did it anyway. I'm sorry."

"Was that why you did it? To hurt me?" It was never something I would've expected from her in the past. After all, she claimed the entire point of her living a lie with me for all those years was so she wouldn't hurt me.

"No," she says. "But I guess, in a way, I didn't care if I did or not."

"Which is sort of just as bad."

She nods and lets out a strangled, "Yeah."

"Then why? You knew how bad he sucks," I say.

"I guess..." She bites her lip, suddenly interested in her shoes again. "I guess I just wasn't ready to give up on being part of your family."

Adrenaline surges painfully under my skin, then coils in my stomach. I barely know what to say; the words are trapped, half-formed, somewhere at the base of my skull.

Finally, I force them out. "Candace, that's not how that works."

"I know," she mutters.

"You don't get to break up with me and pick and choose which of my family to keep. They're not fucking glass-ware."

"I know." She says it louder, then winces. "I didn't even realize that's what I was doing until last night. I just looked at him and asked myself why the fuck I was with him and then"—she makes a gesture like she's throwing glitter in the air, looking as nonplussed as you'd expect someone with a face full of glitter to be— "the answer was just right there."

Both of us stand silently, eyes on the ground. Billy Joel's peppy vocals are underscored by the quiet trickle of the fountain next to us, its waters finally starting to calm after Robbie tumbled into it earlier. When I finally look at her again, her lips are pressed together so hard they quiver.

"Should I be worried about you?" I ask.

Somewhere in Sweden, Ellie Berglund has bolted awake, enraged that I haven't told Candace to fuck off. And really, what I want is to walk away right now and not hear her out. But, I am who I am. She was too important to me for too long.

Thankfully, she shakes her head.

"This has all been so much harder than I thought, but I think I'm coming out of it." Her nose wrinkles, like she's smelling the residual odor of Robbie even after he's gone, and then relaxes again. "Glad you're doing so well, though. Really, I am. And I'm sorry I was shitty about Marcus. I guess I just didn't expect you to find 'the one' so fast."

That heaviness in the pit of my stomach perks up again. The surprise must show on my face, because Candace rolls her eyes. "Oh, please. Even you aren't that oblivious."

"I..." But there's no ending to that thought. My entire body has become gelatin, except my brain, which was actually gelatin but is now probably melting out of my ears.

"You were a really good boyfriend. But you never looked at me like you look at him, and I don't think I did either."

My gaze drifts toward the glass doors, lit up with the ongoing reception. I can't see Marcus through them, and I'm shot through with urgency. Suddenly, seeing him is the only thing that matters.

"There it is," she says. "That's the one I'm talking about." Her strained laugh brings my attention back to her winsome expression, the one someone makes when they're going to start crying as soon as you turn your back.

But it's not my job to clean up that damage. Not anymore.

"Staying in the family isn't worth dating that fuckhead," I say. "And sorry if I sound like a dick, but you're gonna have to find your own family."

There's a grimace plastered on her face that threatens to break apart at any moment. "Yep," she croaks.

I take some pity on her and give her shoulder a squeeze. There have been a lot of winners today, but she definitely isn't one of them. No point in rubbing it in.

"Everyone in there still considers you a friend," I offer. "That good enough for now?"

She nods, then lets me guide both of us back to the party. I don't give her a hug (I doubt I ever will again), and I don't look back. Instead, I take off in search of Marcus.

I spot my mother, who is sitting at a table and downing a big glass of water. She's obviously taking a break from dancing her ass off.

"Have you seen Marcus?" I shout over a Franz Ferdinand song that, under different circumstances, I'd be scream-singing with the rest of the crew.

"He already said good night to me," my mom says. Her face pinches with annoyance as she looks from me, over my shoulder to where I assume Candace must be, and then back to me. "Zack Carter, you dope, don't tell me you let him go up there by himself."

A bubble of dread forms in my esophagus.

I swoop in and give her a peck on the cheek, racing for the door as I shout over my shoulder, "Tell everyone I said goodnight!" Maybe people will be mad at me later, but that's far from my biggest worry right now.

I stumble a couple of steps into our room with the momentum from running all the way here. Marcus sits on the end of the bed in his suit pants and undershirt, gripping the comforter on either side of him. His jaw drops as I swing into the room, like a wrecking ball is passing inches from his face. I send up a quick prayer that that's not a perfect analogy, and I haven't totally fucked him up for the night.

"You're back," he says.

"You sound surprised," I say.

He stares up at me; his wide eyes make him look so young that I feel like someone's stuck a pin through my heart. It suddenly hits me how bad that must have looked to him. Me, after a dramatic confrontation with her now-ex boyfriend, being taken aside by Candace. Me asking Marcus to leave us alone and telling him I'd catch up later just so I could talk to her.

Stupid, stupid, stupid.

"Shit. Marcus, did you think I was—"

"Not completely," he cuts me off. "But I suppose I was...bracing myself."

Of course he would be primed for me to disappoint him, after all he's been through. Before I can stop myself, I'm kneeling on the floor in front of him, tux and all. I'm ready to beg for my life, to spill all of my feelings into his lap and bare my neck for the ax.

"I'm so sorry I made you feel that way. There's nothing there. It's over," I say. I feel like I'm about to throw up from dread but when I look up, he's smiling and shaking his head.

"It's all right, really. If nothing else, I'd fulfilled my purpose in being here this weekend. It isn't as if I even—" he bites off the end of the sentence. And sure, I could push him to finish what he was going to say. We could have that talk, right here and now. But I could also follow my instinct to kiss him senseless.

Fuck it. I choose the second option.

The kisses are slow, indulgent, like mouthfuls of a rich dessert that will make you sick unless you savor it. He makes a soft, comforted sound as one of my hand cups his face and the other rests on the small of his back. It's a relief that the shaky ground we thought we were standing on is solid after all.

After a decadent stretch of time, I pull back enough to rub my nose against his.

"Does that offer from earlier still stand?"

His laugh sounds as giddy as I feel, which is a full-on fucking delight. Before I can dive back in, he does the work for me, fingers threading through my hair firmly enough to make my scalp tingle. His tongue traces my lower lip, and I think that even if he tells me he's too tired, I won't mind in the slightest.

But things seem to be going my way tonight.

"If you are still interested, the answer is a resounding yes," he says.

I rock back onto my feet and pull him up with me, and he lunges in for one more hard kiss, his hands drifting up to undo my bow tie and the top buttons of my collar. I gasp as his snakebite piercings graze my collarbones and he trails kisses up my throat. There's no way I can wait for him to fully undress me, as mind-blowingly sexy as the idea is, so I shrug out of my jacket and toss it onto the bed.

He doesn't stop, undoing one button after the other as he explores my neck and the stubble on my jaw with his lips and tongue. The whine of a prey-animal slips through my teeth, and he sucks in air. As embarrassing as the sound is to me, it clearly awoke his hunger.

"Would you like to shower with me first?" His voice is low enough to rattle the windowpanes. I tremble at it too.

"Uh-huh." All my words have flowed away from my brain along with all the blood that's rushing to my dick.

A gentle palm on my sternum pushes me a couple steps back. Marcus sheds the rest of his clothes as he makes his way to the bedside table to retrieve supplies, and I fumble with my belt and zipper as I try to do the same. I pray he's not looking as I nearly tumble over trying to take my shoes off. Judging by the way the bathroom fan switches on and the water starts running, the odds are still in my favor. With a steadying breath, I follow him inside.

Marcus is testing the water temperature with his hand when I get there. Maybe I'm reading too much into it, maybe I'm just that far gone, but the thoughtfulness of the act tenderizes my heart. As if he can sense my simpy thoughts, he turns around with a devilish grin before stepping under the water. He picks up a cloth, lathers it up, and beckons to me. I'd follow him into the sea at this point.

In the shower, he's gentle, letting me luxuriate under the stream as he cleans himself up, then switching places and turning me slowly toward the wall. It's not long before I feel firm, soothing circles on my back. I sigh as his other hand grips my naked waist a little harder than he needs to. There's no reason to hide how it makes my cock twitch—we're both so hard I'm surprised he hasn't just jumped me already.

He knows it's your first time, my last remaining brain cell tells me. *He wants it to be nice for you.*

"You don't have to do all this, you know," I chuckle, trying to push down the lump in my throat as he washes me from behind my ears down to my ankles.

"I am aware," he says. His soft lips graze the top of my vertebrae. "Turn around."

Then I'm face to face with him. His eyes are dark but hold none of the danger I'm used to. They're less like blades and more like still, dark pools. If I fall in, I know I'll float. He's just as reverent with the front of me as the back, even as he drags his palm slowly over my cock on his way down and again on the way back up.

"Are we...doing it here?" I ask as I rinse off. Shower sex has always been a little disappointing, but I'd let him fuck me basically anywhere and it would still feel like a gift.

He licks a trickle of water from his lips. "I'd like you to watch," he says, voice gravelly. His line of sight drags me beyond the shower curtain to the bathroom mirror. "I want you to see how gorgeous you are in pleasure."

Even covered in water, my mouth goes dry. If anyone else had suggested that, I would have balked, but it sounds like a Nobel prize-winning idea right now. I switch off the water.

"Then what are we waiting for?"

He gives me that closed-mouth smirk that still manages to be sweet even as his eyes flicker with intent, and I follow him out of the shower. The fan has kept the mirror from completely fogging up, though it's still cloudy enough to make this all seem like a dream. His confidence is contagious, but I'm still kind of happy to have a filter as I stare at my own reflection.

"See?" he says softly, toweling off my flushed skin.

In spite of myself, a nervous laugh escapes my lips. "I'm trying," I say.

He drops the towel and spins me back around. Then our bodies are flush together, chest to chest. I shudder as he reaches behind me and his piercings graze my nipples, hard metal teasing supple skin. There's a click, a wet, squelching sound, and then he's teasing my rim. Half my groan is caught up in his open-mouthed kiss as he works a finger inside of me. It's slow and so good I can't keep my mouth shut. With every twitch of my cock or whimper against his ear, his breath catches.

Another finger, then another. A thorough seeing-to that's completely unnecessary. I've been relaxed under his hands and against his body, like wet clay, since I followed him into the shower. He's already proven he can make me into any shape he wants.

"Are you ready?"

"So ready," I whine. With a huff of fond laughter, he pats my hip. I turn around to face myself in the mirror as I hear the crinkle of a condom wrapper.

I don't have to look at my blown pupils for very long, because my eyes are on Marcus's face. His mouth is slack with something like wonder, eyes half closed as he looks down between us. The head of his cock presses against my hole, and I take a deep, steadying breath.

I watch him as he watches himself press the tip inside of me. A grunt gets caught in my throat. This feels different than his fingers or the plug. It's a more insistent stretch with how big he is. His gaze flicks up to briefly meet mine in the mirror, checking to make sure he's not hurting me.

Nodding, I do my best to smile through the overwhelming sensation. "Keep going," I say, gripping the stone countertop.

He looks down again, eyes a little wider, shoulders tense as he continues to fill me inch by inch. His chest rises and falls with labored breath, and he looks half-wild. Still, he catches my eye with every micro-movement—like he's asking permission, like he's mystified that I haven't stopped him yet. I never thought having another man's cock inside me would make me feel so powerful.

"Oh," he moans once he's fully inside me, his forehead falling against my shoulder. It isn't water from the shower—that's definitely sweat beaded on his forehead. This mirror thing was a fantastic idea after all, though maybe not for the reason he thought.

"You can move now," I say, soothing him. "Please?"

He raises his head, teeth dug into his bottom lip as he stares down his own reflection from under his eyebrows, like he's giving himself a silent pep talk. Then, he does what I asked. At first he's nearly as slow as he was when he entered, and I think about telling him he doesn't need to be so precious with me. But judging from the deep crease between his eyebrows, the glacial pace might not just be for my benefit.

"How does it feel?" His voice is breathy, on the edge of overwhelm.

"Incredible," I say.

"Good," he manages. His hand comes up to my chest, and he watches his blunt nails raking through my chest hair. I may or may not arch up a little to give him a better show.

He's right. I do look pretty damn good like this.

But I'm not really looking at myself as he finally starts to speed up. I'm looking at the way his hands claw at my chest and hip, the determined set of his jaw, his dazzled expression every time we lock eyes in the mirror. With every sound I can't suppress, he pounds harder until I'm clutching the edge of orgasm.

"Close," I gasp.

I'm shocked when, instead of taking my dick in his hand, he hauls me up against his chest. I whimper as I take in the red marks from his fingers, the hot water, and my own body heat; the way my own muscles flex as his cock presses relentlessly against my prostate; the way my cock has leaked precum all over my stomach and thighs. There's no point in scrabbling for the counter; all I can do is hang onto his wrists as he rolls his hips into me in obscene waves.

"I've wanted you like this since I first saw you in the cafe," he hisses into my ear.

"M-me too. So much."

He moans outright at that, holding me tight as he speeds up again. Before long, teeth dig into my shoulder, and I close my eyes as the heat building in my pelvis finally hits its boiling point. The bathroom rings with my shout as I come, and by the way he's lost his rhythm, I can tell Marcus is following. We both nearly topple to the floor as he grinds his hips into me with a groan, and I grab onto the lip of the counter to rebalance us.

The wake of it isn't quiet. We're both panting like we've just finished a really grueling workout, and my legs and upper arms definitely feel that way from bracing against the counter.

"Fuck," I say, although I'm almost sure the pounding in my chest drowns it out.

"Was that satisfactory?" Marcus twinkles at me from the mirror.

I almost snort-laugh. "Was that a joke? Yeah, it was satisfactory. It was a goddamn revelation."

When I turn around to face Marcus, he draws me in for a hard kiss before I can get a good look at him. I feel him smiling against my lips after we part. Before tonight, I don't think I've ever seen him smile so much.

A man could get used to this kind of thing. Maybe I'll even get the privilege.

26

PART OF THE FAMILY

I'm not exactly known for being a downer. The opposite, in fact.

But as I wake up and feel the shape of Marcus's naked body in my arms, I am shocked at how blindingly happy I am. Every inch of me buzzes, so much that I'm having a very hard time keeping all this joy contained. No level of morning wood can stop me from pulling Marcus closer. After last night, I can't be embarrassed about it.

Marcus stirs in my arms and smiles blearily over his shoulder at me. He fell asleep with wet hair; half of it is plastered against his head and the rest is a chaotic cloud rising from the pillow.

"Good morning," he rasps as he grinds back against my erection.

"Well, hello there." I'm trying to play it cool, but I've never been great at that. Plus, how could I, with all his gorgeous skin pressed up against me, with my cock rubbing against the curve of his ass? When he rolls his hips again, I shiver.

With a rumbling laugh, he rolls out of my grasp so he can slip down the bed. As he licks up my shaft, flicks his tongue over the head, hope swells with the same intensity as my arousal. I want to keep this. I want this to keep going after we get home. Long after. Forever if I get my way.

(I can't say something like that out loud, though. Not yet. Not if I don't want to scare him off.)

We barely make it out of the room before checkout. Part of me wishes I'd paid for an extra night so we could just stay in bed all day. But Marcus has to work tomorrow, and when I reserved the room, I didn't want to do anything that made him feel pressured. The very idea of that being a problem seems like a joke after the last twenty-four hours.

Katie and Marta have already left for their honeymoon, but we get a chance to say goodbye to a few other guests in the lobby. I hug my Aunt Laura and Sam (who triumphantly waves his completed Rubik's Cube at us). Marta's nieces both throw themselves at Marcus before their mother lures them away with chocolate donuts.

When it comes time to say goodbye to my parents, my mom gives us both suffocating hugs.

"You two, come visit us soon," she says. "And, Marcus, you better tell me when tickets go up for sale for that play of yours."

Marcus dips his head and mumbles something incoherent, and my mom lets him get away with it this time. Invisible fingers dance down my spine at the suggestion of a future where that would be possible—where she's visiting us, visiting my boyfriend and me. I give into the urge to rest my hand in the center of his back. He glances at me, features soft and glowing.

The weekend dissipates, and we all drift into the parking lot to make our various ways home.

It's a quiet drive—early enough on Sunday that traffic isn't too terrible. As soon as we're out of the parking lot, Marcus puts my grungiest playlist on. Then he leaves his hand resting on the center console. It's just begging for me to take it in mine, so I do.

We hold hands as we follow the coastline and let salty air seep through the cracked windows. His thumb sweeps idly over my knuckles as we cut across strawberry fields outside Camarillo to the 101, the sky a rare and perfect turquoise. Part of me longs to feel his soft grip on the back of my neck, but as I follow the sweeping sea-level curve at La Conchita, I figure that it would be much too distracting. It's bad enough that I can still feel where he'd been inside me last night every time I shift in my seat.

For the first time in a while, I mostly keep my mouth shut (other than to point out the odd silly bumper sticker or road sign). The only things I really want to talk with him about would better be discussed face to face, preferably over a dinner that I make for him myself.

But about twenty minutes from home, he breaks the silence. "May I ask what Candace had to say last night?"

"Oh!" Honestly, I'd almost forgotten the conversation had happened. Getting fucked over the bathroom sink had kind of wiped all other information from my head. "She wanted to apologize. By the way, real stand-up move on your part to get the key from that asshole."

"Thank you," he says. His sunglasses fully hide his eyes from me, and his flat tone is kind of hard to parse. "For what part was she apologizing?"

I try not to laugh at his refusal to put a preposition at the end of his sentence. "Dating Robbie, for one thing," I say, as the memory of our conversation starts to come back together. "And this was the weird part—she told me that she 'wasn't ready to give up being part of my family.' Kind of fucked up, right?"

"Hm," he grunts.

"So fucking entitled," I say. Now that I'm trying to digest it again, the exchange sits like rancid oil in my stomach. "I sort of felt like an asshole, but I just told her she couldn't do that anymore and needed to work on finding her own family. I mean, I get that we're pretty great, but she can't just insert herself like that after what she did."

"Right. Of course not," he says, his affect still flat as a plywood board. The sick feeling lingers inside me. I know he doesn't like hearing about her, but then again, he asked. Either way, the response he's giving me makes me feel like he's still upset about me staying to talk to her.

He squeezes my hand again before finally releasing it and taking his phone out of his pocket. Even though our hands were sweaty and driving with one hand was sort of a pain in the ass, there's still a pang in my chest at the loss of contact. He taps on his phone as familiar palm trees and Spanish-style buildings thicken on either side of the highway.

"Would you be willing to drop me off at Jackie's house?" he asks after a minute or two.

Another pang. My impatient ass had already been thinking through what ingredients I had at home to cook with. And even if he declined dinner, dropping him at Jackie's still cut about ten minutes off our time together.

But I'm an adult. I can handle a little disappointment, especially after how well everything else has gone over the past couple days.

"Yeah, I remember how to get there." My voice climbs in pitch. Again, I've never been great at playing it cool.

The remaining drive is quiet, other than the sound of traffic and some moody early '90s rock. Marcus doesn't speak again until we park in front of Jackie's bungalow and we get his luggage out of the trunk. As we stand facing each other, his eyes are still hidden from me.

"Thank you for this weekend. And, well, for everything you did before that," I say. For all that I deal in words, I'm having an impossible time trying to find the right ones to express how much this has all meant to me. I settle for, "You made everything so much better."

Understatement of the fucking century, honestly, but I don't feel like this gutter is the right place to declare my love.

"I'm glad," he says. His jaw tightens, as if he's also casting around for something to say. Instead, he leans in, cupping my jaw and giving me a chaste kiss. Then it's over, and he's stepped back from me before I can even raise my hands. He doesn't invite me in, so I watch Jackie welcome him as I sit behind the wheel.

When I get home, it's much, much too quiet.

I have to white-knuckle all of Sunday night and most of Monday, trying not to text Marcus with every little thought that pops into my head—dirty or otherwise. The way he was acting yesterday made me think he might need some space, and the last thing I want to do is be the "oh-we-fucked-now-I'm-never-going-to-leave-you-alone" guy. Marcus is reserved, an introvert, mostly analog. He just needs a little break.

Or at least that's what I'm telling myself.

I finally give in around three on Monday afternoon. It hits me that, before we left the hotel Sunday morning, I'd emailed him the bridal party dance video—the perfect opener.

Did I make Amber proud with my dance moves?

A few minutes pass without him answering, which could mean nothing. He has clients and classes to teach, unlike me, who is wasting my vacation by lying on the couch with my laptop balanced on my chest, fucking off on Reddit and watching *Kitchen Nightmares*.

Hours pass. After two microwave burritos (only god can judge me), I go back through my luggage to make sure I hadn't accidentally stolen his phone charger. Then I dig around under the front seat of my car, but all I find are some stale French fries, a broken pencil, and a flier for one of Ellie's concerts from last fall semester.

The thought that I've been ghosted, or that this truly had never been more than a temporary thing for Marcus, seeps in through every crack in my thoughts. After all, it's not like we'd ever talked about a different arrangement. We hadn't really talked about anything that might happen after the wedding.

Had I missed my chance?

On Tuesday, I pull up in front of CLITS, feeling so tight in the chest I'm worried I'll pass out during warm-ups. I assure myself that once I see Marcus, everything will feel right again. There must still be some rejection sensitivity from the Candace ordeal, despite the closure I'd gotten over the weekend.

But when I walk in, there's nobody at the front desk. Marcus's bike is nowhere to be seen either. The only people there are Dylan and Bea, the latter of whom is in the middle of a set of front squats. After three reps, she re-racks the bar, and the two of them look at me like I'd forgotten to put on pants today.

"Whoa, whoa, what are you doing here?" Dylan says, taking a step back even though he's all the way across the room. "I thought you were sick."

"Huh?"

"Marcus called and said he caught some kind of bug. Figured you both got sick at the wedding."

I seriously doubt Marcus would ever say he'd "caught a bug," but that's not the point. The point is he didn't tell me, and apparently his phone still works.

"Oh, I, uh..." So much for my nerves. And my dignity.

Bea's mouth hangs open, shoulders rising and falling as she recovers from the heavy set. Pity mingles with the sheen of sweat on her face.

"He didn't...tell you? Did you two fight or something?"

We didn't fight. Did we? I shake my head, but I am all too aware of what a tool I must look like right now. I rally as best I can.

"Must have just gotten our wires crossed somewhere." I back away, feeling for the door. Bea waves at me with a sad half-smile, but Dylan has already turned his back and is sliding a fifteen-pound plate onto the bar.

I toss my gym bag across the front seat and plop down. For a few moments, I sit staring at my phone, willing it to light up. I have no idea how I'm going to handle this—whether I should leave him alone or try calling him again or just pack it up and not come back to the gym on Thursday at all. Maybe he did get sick, and my immune system is just so good that I didn't.

But my gut tells me that's not it. Not that my gut has been very helpful over the last couple days.

As if my prayers are being answered, my phone pings with a message, but as if they're being answered by a trickster god, the message is from my mother.

Just wanted to check in and say how nice it was to see you this weekend. Everyone just loves Marcus. Make sure he knows he's part of the family now!

A sense of unease creeps over me, and then it's as if someone's dumped a bucket of ice water over my head.

Oh.

Oh, shit.

I think back to the way he'd shut down when I told him what Candace had said to me. There'd been so much scorn in my voice when I talked about her inserting herself into my family. Then I think about Marcus on Friday night, drunk and adorable in bed next to me, telling me how much he loved my mom.

Shit. Shit. Shit.

I flap my hands around like a 1950s housewife who is not ready for the guests who have just rung the doorbell. My phone clunks against the floor of the car and bounces under my seat, and I curse as I fold myself in half trying to get it. There's no use in flailing around like this. I need to take a deep breath and think.

He's not answering my texts, so he definitely wouldn't answer my call. And I've never been to his place, so I can't go. Would I just have to wait until Thursday or try to catch him at Silverskins? This is my fault, and I need to be the one to fix it. If he thinks I've rejected him, I can't wait two more days to set things right.

As I'm thinking this, staring down at my phone menu, a hot pink app catches my eye. I flash back to standing outside Snappers after the bachelorette, watching him get into a Lyft and wishing he were getting into one with me. Holding my breath, I poke around until I spot what I'm looking for.

Then I start my car and try not to peel out of the parking lot.

27

SPEAKING IN RIDDLES

Cars are packed bumper to bumper in Marcus's neighborhood, like grocery store produce you're afraid to disturb for fear of the entire bin tumbling onto the floor. I have to park three blocks away from the address in my app, and even then, I'm nearly beaten out by a very cranky frat boy in a Jeep.

When I finally reach Marcus's building, acid wells up in my throat. The street number is on the screen in my hand. The building is two stories and U-shaped with more than eight units, each door opening to the central courtyard. But Marcus hadn't included the unit number when he punched his address into the app.

Fuck it. I'll knock on every door if I need to, no matter how many of my students I might accidentally catch smoking weed or drinking some Fanta and spiced rum atrocity. If I end up bombing this, I'll go home and drink a few liters of it myself.

Sucking a breath through my nose, I rap on the door closest to the street. Sophie, one of the TAs from my Shakespeare class, opens the door, and the scent of coconut sunscreen and mildew wafts over me. She's wearing a '70s-style crochet bikini top, baggy pants covered in elephant prints, and flip-flops. Other women's disembodied voices murmur deeper in the apartment.

"Dr. Carter! What, uh..." Her eyes are wide, and I try to keep from wincing. The voices go quiet, their owners curious about what the fuck I'm doing at her door.

"Sophie! Sorry, I had no idea this was your place—I'm looking for someone else," I say. "I got the street number but not the unit number, but...maybe you can help me?"

Her shoulders sink an inch or so and her forehead relaxes. I know why I'm here, and I know who I am, but a part of me still feels like a dirty old man just for standing here. Then again, at least she knows me and isn't some random, terrified freshman.

"Sure," she says. "I don't really know everyone here, but maybe if you describe him?"

"His name's Marcus Berens, and—"

There's a chorus of "oohs" from the girls in the apartment. Sophie casts an annoyed look over her shoulder, then faces me again.

"The hot alternative guy, right?"

"Uh, yeah," I say. It feels like my face has suddenly taken massive solar damage. From her smirk, I can only guess that I'm transparent as hell.

She leans closer, then points next door. "He's been listening to The Cure for, like, two days," she whispers. "Is that your fault?"

Even now, I can hear synthesizers from the cracks in his door jamb. There's also a shadow moving behind the curtain, and my heart tries to leap out through my mouth as if it thinks it can get to him faster than I can.

"Afraid so. But I'm going to try to fix it, now."

"Yikes. Good luck," she says.

Sophie and Bea must have a common ancestor or something, because pity looks exactly the same on both their faces. As she shuts the door, I hear someone stage-whisper, "Seriously? He's gay, too?" If I weren't so nervous, it would crack me up, but at the moment I'm a little busy trying to keep all my internal organs from abandoning my body.

The latch clicks, and I move toward Marcus's door and knock before my nerves totally take over. A second later, the music stops. Two seconds later, the door opens.

If it were possible, Marcus would look like shit, but I refuse to ever think that about him. However, I can admit that he looks completely wrecked. His nose is bright pink, and there are purple bags under his eyes. He's dressed in black sweats splashed in bleach stains and an oversized black sweatshirt, which is just as ratty.

All the things I'd planned to say escape me, so what comes out is, "Are you cold?"

Marcus's mouth is hanging open as he stares at me with swollen eyes. "Am I...?"

"Shit, sorry, I mean..." I glance over toward Sophie's apartment, as if I'd be able to tell if they're eavesdropping or not just from the way their door looks. "All right if I come in? I think we should talk."

He looks over his shoulder at the inside of his apartment reluctantly. Then, slowly, he steps back to let me inside.

It's so small there isn't even a table—just a counter with a stovetop, a twin bed, and a single flakeboard bookshelf squeezed next to it. An old boombox with one slot for CDs sits on top, his sketchbook and pencil case neatly stacked next to it. There's also a half-empty tissue box and a full wastebasket on the floor.

I push down a flash of indignation. He deserves better than this, and I want to give it to him. But there are some hurdles to overcome first.

"When I got to the gym, Dylan said you'd gotten sick at the wedding," I say.

"He was supposed to call you." Marcus's voice is thick and raspy. He could easily fool someone else, or even fool me on a different day, into thinking he'd gotten a virus. But even though I feel like an enormous buffoon right now, he and I both know I'm wise to that.

"I want to know why you didn't think you could call me," I say, clearing my throat when I realize it sounds like I'm on the verge of tears. I'm not, I'm just nervous, but I can tell Marcus fell over that particular ledge way before I got here. And it's not just all the tissues. "Do you want to tell me what's up, or should I tell you what I think?"

He doesn't answer, just stares down at his bare feet like he's a kid who's in trouble with his dad. The giant sweatshirt, which, no shit, has thumbholes cut into the sleeves, doesn't help. It makes him look tiny and vulnerable and so very emo that I don't know whether to cuddle him or take away his flip phone.

"I think I said something that you took in a way I didn't mean, and then it made you spiral," I say. "Does that sound right?"

His head snaps back up, and his eyes are so glassy that it almost sends me into a panic. This is clearly a feelings-management emergency that I've stumbled straight into with no prep, like coming around a bend in the road and then seeing the entire hillside is on fire. I'm about to keep talking, but a voice inside me tells me that it might be time to listen instead—either Ellie or my mom, or some combination of both of them.

"Can I sit?" I ask, glancing back at his unmade bed.

Cheeks flaring red, Marcus pulls the blue plaid bedspread up over his rumpled sheets and gestures toward it. When I accept the invitation, he backs up against the kitchenette counter, still facing me as he grips the lip of it with his fingers. I fold my hands in my lap, cock my head, and hope it makes me look attentive.

"What you said about Candace..." he starts, then stops, then tries to clear the huskiness from his throat. "I became concerned there was a secondary meaning. That you were cautioning me against pushing the same boundary."

My hand rises and falls uselessly; he's too far away to comfort with touch. But the sympathy on my face must give him a little confidence.

"This weekend I felt so welcome, and I felt like I had bonded with"—my mom, I know he means—"members of your family. But when you told me what she had said, it caused me to view my feelings as inappropriate. Presumptuous. I worried it may seem as if I was trying to manipulate you or use you in some way."

I curse under my breath, and he squeezes his eyes shut as if he'd taken that personally too. My thoughts race as he dips his head again, biting his already red lower lip raw. I swallow back exasperation—with myself mostly, but a little with him too. I know that's not totally fair of me, but it's hard to reconcile how I actually feel about him with what he's just said.

"Respectfully, do I seem like the kind of guy who speaks in riddles?"

That punches a breathy laugh out of him. Now I feel like I'm getting somewhere, even though his gaze is still fixed on the chipped bronze paint of his bathroom doorknob. All this time I've been under the impression that he was in control of everything that happened between us, but now it's like someone's polished the glass I'm looking through.

It's so clear that he desperately needs me to take the wheel right now. I can't disappoint him.

"Come here," I say. He hesitates, then pushes himself off the counter and sits a couple feet away from me on the bed. "First of all, you can basically take anything I say at face value. But more than that, I think the biggest problem here is the stuff I haven't said."

That gets his full attention. His eyes bore into me like drill bits, which is good. I need to bleed in front of him right now.

"I wanted you to take the lead as much as possible, because I know you've been with some really shitty men. And especially since, well...I'm...I know the power dynamic stuff with age and money is a sore spot."

He rolls his eyes, as if he's forgotten that he cried in the bathroom the first time I took him to a nice restaurant. I don't remind him of it; I just press on.

"Also, this whole thing started as a ruse,' and I didn't want to bait and switch you into a relationship. But"—I take a steadying breath—"my feelings for you have gotten too intense to ignore, and I was kind of gearing up to ask..."

Now he looks like he's reading the last page of a really intense book as he waits for me to finish my sentence. I hadn't really wanted to do it this way, but if that's what he needs, so be it.

"Ask me what?" he says.

"If you want to be with me. Like, in a real relationship."

Life flickers back into his eyes, and his lips part. Within a second, he's crossed the mile of space between us and is in my arms. The impact and the hard kiss he gives me nearly topples us over the side of the bed. Once I regain my balance, I force myself to break away.

"So that's a yes?"

He lets loose one of those horrendous, honking laughs, then pulls back and covers his face with his hands to muffle it.

"That's the sexiest thing I've ever heard," I say. It kicks him into another round of laughter. This time I join in, wrapping my arms around his shoulders and whispering in his ear. "That's it—you've bewitched me with your laughter. I can't resist anymore. I must have you."

He gives one last snort and nuzzles the side of my neck. "In that case, I'm all yours," he says. "And this never felt like a ruse to me. Not for a single moment."

Now, I'm the one with a hand wrapped around the back of his neck, the one who's licking into his mouth because I can't help but want every inch of us to touch. But as his hand strays up my thigh to my swiftly hardening cock, I grip his wrist to stop him.

"As much as I'd love to fuck in your bed, I think you should come home with me," I tell him. "There's a nonzero chance that my Shakespeare TA and her friends have a glass up to the wall, and I'm not really in the mood to give them more of a show than we have already."

From the other side of the wall, someone hisses, "Shit!" and is violently shushed. Marcus pulls away from me and covers his mouth again, eyes glittering.

"Come home with me," I say again, interlacing his long, gorgeous fingers with mine.

"All right." He says it softly, but not because he's trying not to be heard. I think he's just as overcome as I am.

"And, uh...how long did you tell Dylan you'd be gone?" I ask as he stands up.

He half-turns toward me, and the corner of his mouth twitches. Mischief radiates from his skin. "Through Thursday at least."

My stomach flips, and I start to vibrate with the promise of the next few days. "Then I think you should pack a bag, because I have nothing to do either."

Turning around fully, he lays his palm against the side of my neck, running his thumb along my jawline. "Oh, I think you have plenty to do."

Blood rushes out of my head, leaving me dizzy. "Fuck," I say. "Hurry up before I embarrass myself, all right?"

As he packs up, I try not to stare at him and instead focus on anything that will make my erection go away before we walk to my car. Mercifully, he changes into something less mopey in his bathroom with the door shut. When he finally locks the front door and follows me out of the courtyard, I see a curtain flutter in the front window of Sophie's apartment.

Once we're back in my car, I give him a sheepish smile. "So, my plan had been to cook you a really nice dinner and ask you to be my boyfriend. Sorry what actually happened was so unromantic."

He smiles back—the one that reminds me of what an enormous dork I am. "Showing up on my doorstep during my dark night of the soul and confessing your feelings for me is exceedingly romantic."

Honestly, as an English professor who is also a gigantic sap, I can't argue with that. "Maybe I can whip up something tonight to make up for it."

"Tomorrow," Marcus says. The familiar dark edge that forms around his voice makes me shiver. "I already told you that I have no intention of leaving you with enough energy to cook."

I gulp, pulling out of the tight parking space and hitting the accelerator a little too enthusiastically. "Tomorrow then," I agree.

It's only about a ten-minute drive, but once we're out of the maze of Marcus's neighborhood, I set my hand in the space between us. He takes it right away, placing a much-too-gentle kiss on the back of my hand.

There's no way I'll make it through the end of the week without telling him I love him. Hell, I might not even make it through the night. But even now, there's no question in my mind that he'll be glad to hear it, and that someday—and maybe even someday soon—he'll say it back.

Epilogue: Four Years Later

"Don't be shy, Zacky-Boy! Just—really get in there," Jackie says, phone raised high as she snaps a picture.

"When have I ever once been shy?" I scoff, but I pull Marcus closer so abruptly that he gives a little "oof" at the impact. The tassel hanging from his cap tickles the end of my nose and I try to stifle a sneeze, my face contorting to the point that I can barely see.

Jackie lowers her phone, stares at it for a moment, and bursts out laughing. "Oh my god, I'm framing this one."

"Wait, wait, wait! Don't move yet!" My mom is standing at Jackie's shoulder, taking photos of her own. "Darling, give your man a little kiss on the cheek."

"Mom," I say before I realize I sound like I'm fourteen again. Marcus giggles against my shoulder, then covers his mouth before it can get out of hand.

Naturally, I end up doing what she says. But only because I want to anyway.

We got lucky that the English department graduation ceremony was a full day before the theater department's. That meant I could give Marcus all the attention he deserves, then throw this little party having had plenty of time to cook. It's a relatively small group—just us, my parents, along with Katie and Marta, Ellie, Jackie, and a few of the friends that Marcus made through his classes.

When the amateur photo session finishes up, my mom wanders over to the picnic table, which is filled with the freshest seasonal stuff I could get my hands on. Vegetable trays and sweet potato fries, sliders for both meat-eaters and vegans, a half flat of strawberries with a side of hand-whipped vanilla cream, and a pasta salad with homemade dressing (I bought the pasta pre-made though, because I don't hate myself).

Marcus rips the mortarboard off his head, letting the sun glare down into his eyes. He makes a face like he's stuck his nose in a carton of expired yogurt, running his fingers through his flattened hair.

"If I don't get out of this hideous robe immediately and fix my hair, I'm going to rip it out."

"You better not!" I playfully shove him toward the house, and he squints at me before heading inside.

I wander over next to where my family hovers over the food.

"You've had enough," Marta says, batting Katie's hand away from the bowl of strawberries. "You know strawberries give you rashes now."

"You're not the boss of me!" Katie says, dipping another strawberry in cream, popping the whole thing into her mouth, and booping her wife on the nose with her finger. With a smudge of cream lingering on the tip of her nose, Marta looks about ready to turn the bowl into a frisbee.

For some reason that no one can figure out, my sister and sister-in-law decided they wanted to be pregnant at the same time. The fact that their marriage has lasted through month six is nothing short of a miracle. Mom has made no secret of how absolutely batshit a choice she thinks it is, but there's no way she won't be fawning all over those babies once they show up.

As the girls bicker, Mom stands next to me and shows me the photo she took of the two of us together. I look like an enormous dork and Marcus makes his cap and gown look like haute couture, but together, both of us look uncontainably happy.

"Does he know how proud of him I am?" Mom says, voice restrained.

Mom had come to every one of Marcus's plays, regularly checked in with him about his assignments, and talked him down from several ledges during late-night phone calls. It filled me with more love for both of them than I ever thought a person could manage.

I give her a one-armed hug around the shoulders. "You've definitely told him so, but I'm sure he won't get tired of hearing it. And he may not have made it without you."

Her grin leaves no doubt that she knows the difference she's made. As irritating as her smugness can be sometimes, today I'll let her have it.

Other than an occasional breeze that stirs up the edges of the tablecloth, the afternoon is idyllic, and the spread looks amazing. My homemaker streak came back with a vengeance when Marcus moved in. I got the backyard fixed up with a flagstone patio and a drought-tolerant garden for company. I even finally bought new glassware.

As much as Marcus says he felt at home here from the beginning, he kept his awful apartment for his entire first year of school. And he made good use of it too, insisting on staying there during the week when classes started up.

When I say I was pining for him every Monday through Thursday night, I mean that I nearly cried myself to sleep a couple times during the first week of that fall quarter.

But of course I didn't tell him that. As much as I wanted to, I didn't complain. Marcus needed to be secure in our relationship first, and in the idea that, should it not work out, he could make it on his own. Apparently we both passed the test. He moved in the following summer.

Now, Marcus's calendar is full for the next several months with theater and film work, a big chunk of which he can do from his home office. Well, our home office, which he happens to use a lot more than I do. Even before graduating, he started getting more work, enough that he could quit his job at the gym and demand to start helping out with bills.

I told him not until we officially put his name on them. But that might be on the horizon sooner than he thinks.

My hand strays to my pocket, where I feel the rounded corners of a small velveteen box. I wander around to the side of the house, where no one else can see me, and pull it out of my pocket for a peek.

Inside is a platinum band, inlaid with four pinprick rubies spaced evenly around the ring; dividing it into quarters. It reminds me of the earring he wore on our first "fake" date, and, of course, of his eyes.

Right on cue, Ellie shows up at my side. "You still gonna..." She sticks her thumb in her mouth, and pulls it out with a pop.

"I assume that was supposed to mean 'popping the question'? And you wonder why your students say you're cringe." I shut the box and slip it back into my pocket.

"Look who's talking," she says. "Although, I guess if I had an ass as famous as yours, I could get away with being even more embarrassing."

"Ellie..."

"Juuuust kidding," she says, bumping her shoulder against mine. Then she sizes me up. "Look, there's nothing to be afraid of, okay? He's gonna say yes."

"You can understand why I might be a little freaked out about this, though, right?" I say. I haven't thought about Candace in ages, but the memory of the last time I proposed to someone has been haunting me ever since I started ring shopping.

Ellie blows a raspberry. "Oh, boo. This isn't the same at all. You love him, right?"

My heart feels like it's got a fist around it, squeezing. "More than anything."

"And he loves you back, right?"

When I don't reply, she frowns.

"How mad would he be at you if he saw you hesitate right there?"

Well, when she puts it that way...ever since we made it official, Marcus has been beyond demonstrative about how much he loves me. The affectionate touches have only increased since we moved in together. He shows up for me whenever I need him, brings coffee to my office when I'm in an afternoon slump, and puts me to bed when I'm overtired. He leaves notes and sketches in my school bag every so often that always make me laugh or tear up or both. And he still listens to all my stories and laughs at my stupid jokes.

I love going to sleep with him next to me. I love waking up with him in my arms. And never for a second has he given me reason to doubt that he feels the same way.

And that's not even mentioning our sex life, which is...well, healthy is an understatement. It'd be better to say that sex with Marcus changed my relationship with my own body and reversed the poles for how I think about pleasure and intimacy.

"Dude," Ellie says, snapping her fingers a couple times near my face. "Get back here before you get a frickin' boner in front of your family."

"Sorry, sorry." I blink a couple times. "You're right. I know he loves me."

"And even Jackie told you she thinks he'd be into it?"

"Uh-huh."

"Then let's fuckin' go," she says. She beckons me with one arm to follow her back around the side of the house.

When I spot him by the sliding door, my stomach flip-flops. His hair is perfect, and now that he has regular work, he's replaced his high-school edgelord wardrobe with properly cut button-ups and slacks. Taking a slight departure from his usual black, he's wearing a gunmetal gray shirt with white pinstripes, the sleeves rolled up to show off muscular forearms.

No matter how many times I see him, and no matter what he's wearing (or not wearing), I'm never going to be normal about him. And no matter how confident I am that he's going to say yes today, I still feel like I'm going to hurl.

I give it a little while—wait until everyone's eaten and until after we've cut the cake (which I bought from my favorite bakery because, again, I don't hate myself). Ellie throws me a few impatient looks. Even Jackie wiggles her eyebrows meaningfully once or twice. Around the time I've poured a third glass of wine, there's a lull in the conversation that tells me it's time. I edge closer to where Marcus is standing with Jackie, then tap on my glass with a fingernail to call for everyone's attention.

"Couple things! First, thanks to everyone for coming over to celebrate Marcus. I'm ridiculously proud of all he's done," I say.

"Same," Jackie says, elbowing Marcus in the ribs.

"Hear! Hear!" My mom raises her glass.

"Don't drink yet, Mom," I say. Then I mug a little. "And it's certainly not the first time that sentence has come out of my mouth."

"Oooooooh," Katie hoots. My dad laughs, my mother boos me, and the people who don't know my parents chuckle nervously.

"But since I'm talking already, and since we're all here together, I wanted to say how grateful I am that Marcus is in my life. This may come as a shock to some of you, but when I first met Marcus, I said some really dumb stuff to him."

"No way!" Katie says, putting her hand to her chest.

"Yes way! And, this also may surprise some of you, but he was, understandably, extremely bitchy to me about it." Jackie laughs out loud, and Marcus gives me a playful scowl that looks more like a wink. "But eventually, I charmed him with my perfect deadlifts and excellent cooking, and managed to trick the hottest, most multi-talented man I've ever laid eyes on into dating me."

Marcus shakes his head. "Self-deprecation doesn't suit you, my love."

"Maybe not," I shrug, then turn fully toward him, trying to keep my voice steady and keep my eyes on him as I speak. "But I didn't realize it was possible to feel so completely accepted just for being my blundering, nerdy self. Like...like, you put the Hall & Oates playlist on for me when I get home, even though I know you hate them."

"They're...fine," Marcus says, lying, and Ellie gives a single, "Ha!" from across the yard.

"And I didn't know how intensely I could love someone else. I didn't know it was possible to pine for someone just because they went to bed an hour earlier than you. But I hate going to sleep without you next to me, and I don't want to do it ever again."

He's smiling broadly at me, unreservedly, in a way I consider a personal success every time I see it. Static buzzes at the tips of my fingers as I take the box out of my pocket and go to one knee. There are scattered gasps; Katie suppresses a squeal.

"Marcus Berens, will you marry me?"

The smile on his face has turned into something completely different—something that I can't read but looks a lot like annoyance. My ears start to ring. No. There's no way this is happening again, not with him. I'd been so sure...

But the panic only lasts a second. Before the whirlwind can go full cyclone, Marcus reaches into his own pocket and pulls out another small box.

"Only if you'll marry me as well." The annoyance slips from his face. Underneath it, he's beaming.

Something hot and wet trickles over my cheekbone, and I'm confused about where the rain is coming from until I realize that it's my own tears. "Pretty sure that's the only way it'll work," I say, voice strained. Marcus takes my hand and pulls me to my feet, opening the box with my ring inside. It looks almost exactly like his, but with emeralds instead of rubies.

Beside him, Jackie starts laughing like a supervillain. No wonder she'd been so fucking delighted by the idea of me proposing today—she knew this was going to happen. My theory is confirmed when Marcus sees the ring I'd chosen for him and narrows his eyes at her.

"Did she help you pick that out?" I ask, slipping his ring onto his finger.

"Yes," he says, with just a smidge of reproach.

"You're welcome, bitches!" Jackie says. "They would've been all mismatched otherwise!"

I shrug, completely unable to answer with anything but a tearful grin as he slips my ring onto my finger. The rest of the party bursts into applause. Across the patio, there's the sound of a cork popping.

"Well, kiss each other, already!" Ellie shouts, one hand cupped around her mouth and the other gripping the neck of one of the champagne bottles I'd hidden in the garage refrigerator.

And really, how could I not?

For the rest of the afternoon and into the evening, Marcus is glued to my side. Even after everyone else has gone home, after we've quietly cleaned up the dishes together, he tucks himself against my side. No music, no TV, just the two of us looking down at the rings on our fingers.

"So. Should we do the hyphenation thing?"

"Hm." I can't see his face, but I can tell his wheels are turning.

"Carter-Berens? Berens-Carter?" I prompt.

He's still quiet, but it's not uncomfortable. I give him a kiss on top of his head, breathing in the familiar blend of his hair product and natural scent. His finger lazily ghosts over my ring, up my metacarpals to my wrist.

"Not a single member of the Berens family was there for me today, but all of the Carters were." He's cautious, like he's walking into a cramped room full of glass objects. "I wouldn't be unhappy doing away with the name altogether."

A lump rises in my throat, and I swallow it before saying, "Zack and Marcus Carter?"

He sits up and meets my eyes, and I can see the plea in them. "Would that be objectionable?"

It does feel right, that he would be a Carter. Not because it shows off some kind of claim—I don't really think I'm that possessive. Not even just because the rest of the family considered him one of our own since the moment we made that Instagram post. More like, for all our differences, we make up something that's much more than just two individuals smooshed together. Not everyone wants that, sure. And even lots of people who do never get it. We just got lucky.

"Oh, sweetheart, no. That would be perfect." I squeeze his hand. "And if you change your mind, that's—"

Suddenly, I have a lap full of fiancé. His arms are slung around my shoulders; his lips are on my forehead, my cheeks, the corners of my mouth. It takes me a second to get my bearings enough to kiss him back.

"I won't," he insists between kisses. "I won't change my mind."

"Okay, okay," I say, breathless again. Breathless every time he kisses me, still. "Come to bed with me?"

He smiles, sliding out of my lap. He holds out his hand for me to take, and I let him pull me to my feet.

"Every night," he says.

"Every night."

For the rest of our lives.

ACKNOWLEDGEMENTS

None of this ever would have happened without the love of my favorite flock of geese (you know who you are). I'm so glad I met all of you. Thank you for being so supportive of Zack and Marcus's story and of me and my writing. Also—shout out to everyone who followed the first draft of this story on Vella and Patreon. Seeing you enjoy this story gave me the strength to finish it.

Finally, much love and gratitude to my spouse, who keeps my faith in love alive.

ABOUT M.L. NOLAN

M.L. Nolan lives in the Pacific Northwest with their spouse. They love cookie dough ice cream, lifting heavy things, and (of course) cozying up with a good book. To stay up to date, join M.L.'s mailing list or visit their website at mlnolan.com.